Alice's Notions

By

Tamera Lynn Kraft

M ✦ Zion Ridge Press LLC

Mt Zion Ridge Press

http://www.mtzionridgepress.com

Copyright © 2017 by Tamera Lynn Kraft
ISBN 13: 978-1-949564-39-6

Published in the United States of America
Publication Date: May 2019

Editor-In-Chief: Michelle L. Levigne
Cover Artist: Gwen Phifer

Cover Art Copyright © 2017

Other Books By Tamera Lynn Kraft

From the Lake to the River: Soldier's Heart
Red Sky Over America: Ladies of Oberlin Book 1
Resurrection of Hope

Dedication and Acknowledgment

I would like to acknowledge author Lisa J. Lickel for all the help she gave me in writing this novel. Without her plot ideas, input, and knowledge of quilting and sewing, I couldn't have written this.

I dedicate ALICE'S NOTIONS to my grandmother, Goldie Cooper Warden "Nanny", who raised a family in Kimberly, a small coal-mining town in West Virginia, and who inspired my love of reading by reading novels to me when I was young.

Burning Bush is based on Kimberly, West Virginia where my grandmother and grandfather raised their family during the Great Depression and World War Two. They lived there until my grandfather died in 1958. Much of the setting and atmosphere comes from stories told by my mother, uncles, and aunt who grew up there.

Chapter One

January 1945
Fifty miles outside Berlin

OSS Sergeant Joe Brighton wished he were fighting Nazis in Belgium instead of hiding in the shadows waiting to meet a double agent. He paced the length of the small barn, illuminated by a partially shaded lantern. The man should have been here an hour ago.

An owl hooted, but nothing indicated anyone was around. Soldiers could be hiding in the woods during this cloudy, moonless night; after all, they were in the heart of Germany. Most likely he would hear them coming. Their Russian informant knew how to be invisible until he gave the code word and stepped inside, or he wouldn't have survived this long.

The Soviets, of course, were considered allies fighting to defeat the Nazi war machine, but after the intelligence he'd gathered, Joe had a hard time believing they were on the same side. The war in Europe would be over soon, and he couldn't seem to shake that nudging in his gut they were as much of a threat to the free world as Hitler had been.

"Will you light somewhere?" Bear leaned against the wall with his arms crossed. Joe's lieutenant hated the nickname, but since he'd growled his first order at the men, it stuck. "What's got you so jumpy? You know Krysov is on the up and up. He'll be here."

"I know."

Joe sat on a nearby hay bale and blew in his hands to warm them. The information the Soviet agent had given them made him edgy. It was hard to swallow Burning Bush, the small town in West Virginia where he'd grown up, had been infiltrated by Soviet spies. He had considered dismissing it at first, until his commanding officer reminded him Burning Bush was only an hour's drive from at least five important military targets.

Colonel Myers had ordered Bear and Joe to find out as much as they could. The colonel had chomped on his cigar, spouting out orders. "Find out who the Soviet agent in Burning Bush is. Who are his associates? What is his target? How does he plan to communicate with his fellow agents? General Command needs answers before they risk relations with the Russians by letting Krysov defect."

If the report checked out, Joe's orders were to take charge of this operation in Burning Bush. He'd make up some story about being discharged early. His past relationship with the town would alleviate any suspicion about why he was there.

Alice wouldn't be happy about moving back home. Even though they'd been born and raised in Burning Bush, she'd fallen in love with big city life. They'd moved to New York City after he'd been recruited by COI, Coordinator of Information. He pictured her turning up her nose and giving him that look. His chest tightened. It would be good to see her again. He missed her so much.

"What's that?" Bear stepped away from the barn wall and tilted his ear toward the door.

Joe started toward the crackling sound.

"Wait for the signal."

The barn door burst open, and three Soviet soldiers surged through with SVT-40 rifles. Two Russian sergeants moved behind to encircle them. Joe took a step toward the door, but the captain stood in front of the opening, rendering it impossible for them to make a run for it.

"Drop your veapons," the soldier to his right said in a thick Russian accent.

Joe set his Colt .38 Army special on the ground, not daring a side glance to see if Bear would try to make them heroes. The Soviet captain lowered his rifle, closed the barn door, and smiled under his big bushy mustache as if Joe had just told him a joke. "Commander Krysov won't be coming." He said it in Russian, but both Joe and Bear had been trained in Russian, German, and a number of other languages. "We executed the traitor this morning."

Joe swallowed the lump in his throat and tried to remember Russian verb tenses. "Who is this Krysov you speak of? Why do I care what you do with your men?"

"Come now, Sergeant." The captain patted him on the shoulder as if they were best friends. "What did Krysov tell you? Give us what we want to know, and you and your friend can live to fight another day."

Images of Alice and their lives together flashed through his mind. He wouldn't betray his country no matter how persuasive their techniques, but as he pictured his wife getting a telegram from the war department and considered the future they would never have, a profound sadness came over him.

Chapter Two

Wrapping her arms around herself and swaying to the music, Alice Brighton remembered her husband singing romantic ballads, rivaling howling dogs, as they danced around their miniscule New York apartment. He would call her his Judy Garland. Her dark hair and brown eyes might have looked something like the movie star's, but Joe exaggerated the resemblance.

The song ended, and Frank Sinatra's crooning of "Full Moon, Empty Arms" blared from her new Crosley radio. A gun clicked, fired. She trembled. Joe was gone. Her arms were empty. After a long swipe with a tissue, she tied a blue chiffon scarf around her hair. Enough daydreaming about the life the Germans stole from her. She needed to get to work.

In three days, she'd have the grand opening for her fabric shop, Alice's Notions. Dozens of boxes waited to be unpacked, threads and fabric had to be sorted, and she still needed to set up the quilting frame near the front.

Alice had designated a corner of the store for quilting and set up shelves with lap hoops, materials, fat big-eyed needles, and threads. From the time she'd been a little girl playing underneath the tent-like quilting frame until she could help tie or stitch, she had quilt block patterns swirling at the edge of her consciousness.

One thing she loved about the big city was the fabric and quilting shops in every neighborhood. She'd helped many women in New York City learn to piece together victory quilts for the war effort. Opening a fabric store here would help her contribute to the economy of Burning Bush.

She let out a sigh. This wasn't the life she had wanted, but she would make the best of it. She perused the room determining what still needed to be done. Shelving would go against the back wall, where she could lay out the new rose-patterned cotton and the everyday linens.

The needles and scissors though could be a problem. How to display them without resorting to an expensive glass case, yet keep them away from curious children? Perhaps someone in town could help her build one. Mr. Toliver was a good carpenter. At church last Sunday, Mrs. Toliver said to call on them if she needed help. So many old friends offered help. Alice even arranged a sewing circle at the shop next Friday.

Blinking back a tear, she remembered her Mamie's quilting bees where women would gather for companionship. Mamie helped her put together patches for a log cabin quilt for her marriage bed, but when Joe got the job in New York City as an interpreter, they'd rushed to get married so she could go with him. A few months later, the war started and Joe enlisted and shipped out. The quilt remained in Alice's hope chest, unfinished like their lives together.

"Well Joe, do you think I can make the place ready in time for opening day?" Alice sniffed. He wouldn't answer. He was buried in Belgium with so many other brave men who died during the Battle of the Bulge. Somehow that didn't matter. She'd talked to him about everything since they were children, and it didn't stop after the telegram from the U.S. War Department.

Talking out her problems with her dead husband helped her decide to leave the city where they started their lives together. She had thrived on big city life, every day being an adventure, every city block a new area to explore, and with her job at the Brooklyn Navy Yard, she did her part contributing to the home front.

After Joe died, it wasn't the same. She wasn't the same. The final stitch in the quilt came when soldiers were shipped home and they laid her off to provide jobs for the men. The money she'd saved went to open a fabric shop where she could pursue her love of quilting. She ached to come home to Burning Bush, a place where life was predictable and safe.

Grabbing a soft cloth, she hummed along with Perry Como as she dusted the shelves where the material would set. "If only the immigrant girl from Europe would get here. She could help me finish."

After reading an article in *The New York Times*, Alice had decided to sponsor a displaced refugee from war-torn Europe. As a sponsor, she was only required to provide room and board and a small salary. It was a perfect arrangement since the upstairs apartment had two bedrooms, and she needed the help. The woman was due to arrive any day now.

The song ended, and the radio broadcaster announced Bing Crosby crooning one of his classics. When he started singing "I'll Be Seeing You," a lump formed in her throat. She dropped the rag and ran toward the radio determined to turn it off before Bing got through the first line.

Visions of the last night before Joe shipped out.

She tripped over the box of threads and landed on the floor as pain shot through her foot.

They'd danced to that same song as he hummed it in her ear.

A howl erupted from her lips.

She remembered the scent of his Colgate shave as he'd promised he'd see her again. Told her not to worry.

She scooted across the floor toward the counter.

He'd promised.

The cord dangled over the edge. Alice grabbed it, ripped it from the socket, and grasped her ankle. Tears rolled down her face. An unfortunate wooden spool of cotton thread was close at hand, and she threw it, letting frustration get the better of her. It banged against the wall and unraveled as her life had. "I could use some help here, Joe."

Her husband must have heard her request. The bell over the door tinkled and a tall girl walked in. She was a little younger than Alice, maybe early twenties, with long curly blond hair, round blue eyes, and a square chin.

The girl's cotton dress and wool jacket had the look of being retrieved from a church clothing drive, and her simple wool hat, frayed around the edges, had a bent feather leaning precariously over the brim. She carried an old carpetbag.

"Help, I'm over here," Alice called from where she sprawled on the floor.

The girl ran over to her. "What happened?" Her accent was thick with guttural vowels and swallowed w's.

"I tripped over a box. Could you help me up?"

The girl helped her to a chair and removed her shoe to inspect the damage. Her whole foot and ankle had already started to swell. "So, are you the refugee who's come to help at the shop?"

The girl nodded. "My name is Greta Engel. Thank you for your kindness."

"I'm Alice Brighton." She winced as pain shot through her foot. "You speak English very well."

"*Ja*, I learned in school. Do you have icebox? I could get ice for your foot?"

"Upstairs in the apartment. It's a Frigidaire. The stairs are in the back."

Greta bounded down the steps a few minutes later with a towel filled with ice. She helped Alice into a chair, propped her foot on the box of thread she had tripped over, then placed the towel on her ankle.

"Thank you," Alice said.

"You are welcome."

"Greta Engel sounds like a German name. Where are you from?"

Greta twisted her mouth. "My family and I lived in a small village eighty-five kilometers outside of Berlin."

Heat rose to the back of Alice's neck. "Then you're German?"

"*Ja*, when we escaped Soviet occupation, only I could get a visa to the United States of America."

"A mistake was made." Alice clenched her jaw. "I don't need your help after all."

"I don't understand. I brung mein -- ach -- scissors. It say 'Singer.' Aunt Winifred, she was a seamstress." Greta knelt and emptied the pockets of her dress. "Und the tape measure. It's small, merely three zentimeters, inches. I can carry it in my pockets. Winifred, she taught me mending, hemming, buttonhole making. I will help you. I am ready."

"I'm sorry you've come all this way for nothing, but I won't have a German working in this shop."

"Without work, my visa will be revoked." Greta's voice cracked. "They will send me back. The man at the immigration office, he say it all worked out."

Alice stood, placed weight on her foot, and collapsed to the floor.

Chapter Three

The cold tile floor matched the clamminess of the sweat on Alice's forehead. She struggled not to clutch her throbbing ankle and moan, vowing not to show this German weakness.

Greta pressed her lips together, then let out a noisy sigh. "I will get you help. Where should I go?"

"Next door," Alice said. "There's a brick office building. Ask for Rick Morrison."

Greta ran to the door. "I will be back. Do not move." The door slammed behind her.

Don't move -- like she had a choice. "I'm really in a fix now, Joe. How can I open the store in time if my ankle's broken?"

She removed the ice to look at her foot, now the size of a cantaloupe. Closing her eyes, she took some deep breaths. Maybe it wasn't broken. Probably just twisted. She'd be fine. She had to be.

Rick Morrison, Alice's landlord, followed Greta into the store. "What happened?"

Alice lifted onto her elbows. "I'm all right. I tripped over a box and hurt my ankle. It'll be fine in a couple of hours."

Rick knelt near her, and raised an eyebrow. His wavy brown hair and permanent smirk reminded her of Cary Grant. "Greta, help me get her to my car."

"No!" Alice narrowed her eyes at his usual uniform -- single-breasted, black, tailored suit with a white shirt and a narrow black tie. "You shouldn't ruin your only suit by kneeling on the floor. I'll be fine." She clenched her jaw as shocking pains thrummed along her whole leg. "I just need to lay here for a couple of minutes."

He swept her up into his arms. "Greta, the door."

"You have no right." Alice pushed against his chest. "Put me down."

Taut lips were the only sign he gave of her pitiful assault.

Greta grabbed Alice's purse, stuffed it into her lap, and opened the door. "Would you like me to go to hospital?"

"I can't leave now!" Alice drew in another breath, glad to lose some of her shock and frustration in a shout. "I have deliveries coming. I'm expecting patterns from Advance and Simplicity, and the Happy Home Company is sending a representative from Beckley with a selection of sewing needles. The store's nowhere near ready for opening day." She tried to wriggle out of Rick's firm grasp. "I don't have time for this."

"I will stay," Greta said as Rick carried Alice through the door. "I will do what I can to help."

Alice let out a sigh and submitted to being stuffed into the front seat of Rick's light blue Fleetmaster. Despite her woe, she breathed in the scent of new leather. One whiff was all she'd allow herself. She folded her arms and turned her cheek away from the soft, luxurious padding. With the rent she paid, how could he afford a Town Sedan?

Rick headed toward the river. "Who's the girl? You didn't tell me about Greta when you rented the building."

Apparently he expected her to unclench her jaw as they jostled between ruts. "I signed up to give a displaced European immigrant a job and a place to live. They sent her."

He turned left onto Mockingbird Road toward Montgomery and the only hospital for miles. "She sounds German."

"She is, but she's not staying. I didn't expect..." She rubbed the palm of her hand on her leg. "It won't work out."

"Because she's a Kraut?"

"You got it." She clutched her purse tighter as the automobile started around the curves between the railroad tracks at the base of the mountain and the river.

He checked his rearview mirror. "How are you going to run your little fabric shop without help if your foot's broken?"

Alice stared out the window and counted to twenty. A deer darted out of the woods onto the road.

Rick swerved and barely missed it. "This is why dames shouldn't have businesses."

The surge of fury masked her immediate pain of almost being tossed to the floor of the sedan. "It was an accident." Her stomach roiled. She bit back a groan and chewed on the inside of her cheek, trying not to draw blood. "Even men have accidents."

"If you hadn't set a box in the middle of the floor, you wouldn't have taken a tumble over it." He swerved around the bend following along the Kanawha River. "I'm just saying you should watch it."

The brakes squealed as Rick drove around a sharp curve. The unsafe speed made her hold her breath. Since her parents' old Model T had barreled down the side of the mountain only one month after she'd received word about Joe, she'd been leery enough to give up driving, though she'd kept his car. At least Montgomery Hospital was in the opposite direction from the mountain where it happened.

"You don't have to work like some war widows do." He increased his speed. "Your brother would take you in. From what I understand, his city wife could use your help."

She grasped the handle on her door. "Why would you think that?"

"Folks around town are saying she can't even plant a garden, and Pete had to show her how to feed the chickens and milk a cow. The typical Burning Bush housewife, she ain't."

"You're not being fair. Lois grew up in the city. She's never done farm work before. She'll catch on. Besides, since she lost the baby, she has to take it easy. Doc Brenner said so."

"Maybe, but it would help if you'd live with them, and it would free up my building for a man to start a business and support his family. There are a lot of vets who need jobs right now."

"I've already been freed of my job at the navy yard for a returning vet. You can't tell me a big strong marine wants to run a fabric shop?"

"No, but Burning Bush needs practical businesses and factories. Housewives have been buying their fabric and threads and whatnot from the department store in Montgomery for years. They don't need a special shop for it. Now, some GI wanting to open a department store would be a boon for the town."

"I'm not changing my mind," she said through gritted teeth.

"All right, but if you do, I'll let you out of your lease. You've taken on more than you can chew. I'm okay with gals working when they have to, like spinsters and war widows who don't have families to support them, but like I said, your brother needs you."

"You don't understand. I used my savings for this business." Alice grimaced at how pathetic she sounded.

Rick's forehead wrinkled.

She decided to try another tactic. "It will help the housewives in Burning Bush. They won't have to drive clear to Montgomery every time they need a spool of thread or a skein of yarn."

"Yarn doesn't put food on the table."

"You're wrong!" Alice sat up and accidentally jostled her leg. Beads of sweat rose in her hairline. "Stop!" Her stomach churned. "Stop the car." She put her hand over her mouth.

"I'm not going to stop just because you don't like hearing the truth."

She threw up all over his new interior.

Rick stopped the car.

*****

Rick didn't say anything as he drove home.

"I'm sorry about the upholstery," Alice said.

"You've already apologized five times." The muscle in his jaw throbbed. "It wasn't your fault."

"You're right," she muttered. "It was yours."

He took his eyes off the road to direct a hazel glower toward her. "My fault? You threw up all over my new upholstery. How's that my fault?"

"I told you to stop."

He focused on the road and clutched the steering wheel. "Why did you come back to Burning Bush? If you wanted to be a career girl, I would think there would be plenty of chances in New York."

"This is where I grew up and where I married my husband. I have family here. Why wouldn't I come back?"

"That's not a reason."

"It's the only one I have." No way was she going to admit the truth to him. Without Joe, New York had gotten scary. The crowds walking down the avenue and pushing into the subways startled her. Danger lurked in every corner. She needed to get away. "Besides, the store will do a lot for the economy."

Rick chuckled. "How?"

"The department store in Montgomery doesn't have a large selection of sewing notions. This store will bring customers in from surrounding towns and villages."

"Give up this malarkey, and go live with your brother. You can't get the store ready to open with a badly sprained ankle."

Alice twirled her hair around her finger. "At least it's not broken." Like her heart. The doctor's diagnosis might force her to stay on crutches for a couple of weeks, maybe more, but not having to wear a heavy cast almost made her want to dance the East Coast Swing. He'd bandaged her ankle and told her to stay off of it as much as she could, but she had too much work to do to follow those instructions.

Rick was right about one thing. She only had three days until the store opened, and there was nobody to help, except Greta. How could she let the enemy work in her store?

Without a job, Greta might be carted back to Germany on the next ship, but she deserved it. They all did. If the Germans hadn't placed Hitler in power, none of this would have happened. Joe would still be alive.

Alice wiped a tear from her face.

"Don't snap your cap," Rick said. "I'll get the upholstery cleaned. The car will be as good as new."

"I wasn't crying about that."

He handed her a handkerchief. "Then what's wrong?"

She wiped her eyes and blew her nose. "Nothing."

"Women," he mumbled under his breath.

Deciding to ignore the comment, she leaned her head back to watch the scenery. Purple flowers blossomed from redbud trees, and the white ash started to display their buds. The train tracks curved around the Kanawha River between the mountains where purple and white wildflowers dotted the mountainside. How could anyone not be entranced by this beauty where life was peaceful. Here, she was safe from the turmoil going on in the world?

The automobile raced around a curve.

Alice only had two choices, and she didn't like either one.

One bend twisted after another as they made their way around the river.

After Joe and her parents died, she wanted to run home to Burning Bush and stay in the house where she'd grown up, never poking her head out or letting herself be wounded again, but she couldn't do it.

It wasn't only because the idea of Pete taking care of his widowed sister for the rest of her life made her feel like some kind of pathetic charity case. She needed to take charge so she could start living again.

The vacant rental property in the center of town was the answer to her prayers. She'd make a living for herself doing the things she loved. Being an independent business owner was nerve-wracking, sure, but like the man said, she had options. She owed it to herself and Joe to at least give the store a chance. If it didn't work out -- well, she'd cross that bridge later.

The road turned into one lane as Rick slowed.

She wasn't crazy about keeping a German girl on until her ankle healed though. Allowing Greta to stay in her apartment made Alice's head throb as much as her ankle.

Those people killed Joe. Greta may not have fired the gun, but she was a part of it. They all were. Before Alice would welcome a Nazi into her home, she would give up her plan to become a self-sufficient business woman. She'd never admit it to the know-it-all sitting next to her, but it would be better to play it safe, surrender to her fears quietly, and move in with Pete.

Alice hobbled to the door on crutches with the handle of her black clutch purse hanging around her neck. Her landlord tried to help her, but she shooed him away. She'd had enough of Rick Morrison and his sarcasm for one day.

She cautiously placed the crutches on the door step and hopped up with one foot, and reached for the handle. It was locked.

"You sure you don't need some help?"

She glared back at him leaning against his car with his arms crossed and blew a stray hair out of her face. "No thanks. I'll manage." Reaching for the clasp on her handbag with one hand while balancing on a crutch with the other, she fumbled for her keys.

"What made you think I only have one suit?" Rick asked.

"Suit? What?" She slid the key in the hole. "Oh. It's just every time I see you, you're wearing the same thing."

Before she could turn the key, Greta opened the door and wrapped her arm around Alice's waist. Alice hopped through the doorway.

"Tch," Greta said. "You have much pain. Was it broken?"

Alice glanced back at Rick who waved a sardonic salute and sauntered away. "No." She slid into the chair and gave Greta the crutches. "Only badly sprained, but it looks like I'll be on crutches for a couple of weeks. I'm going to have to--"

"Tis bad. It is good you have me here to help you. *Ja*?"

Alice wiped a hand across her forehead. "About that..." She scanned the store.

The boxes stacked against the wall were gone. All the wooden spools of cotton and silk marched on stepped rows near the fabric. Magic Match instant winders made a kaleidoscope of jewels in a basket. Another basket by the checkout contained those little mending kits, Dritz's.

Shelves of blue and brown gingham bolts stood in side-by-side regiments while the silk, peacock, and rose cloths were posed with the black crepe. They looked like they belonged together. Black meant mourning, and Alice had determined never wear it again, but the display almost changed her mind.

The floral voile, daisy cotton, and striped linen created a bouquet. Netting and brocade hung provocatively close by, begging to be sewn onto a matching hat or collar.

She grinned. "Did you do all this?"

"*Ja*." Greta shrugged. "We had deliveries while you were at hospital. I want to help so I started putting things in their place. If you do not like where I put them, I can move. Is all right?"

"Is very all right." Maybe Alice been too hasty. Since everything was coming together, it would be a shame to give up and send the girl away. "You can stay."

"Thank you. I am so happy."

"Only until I get on my feet again."

Greta nodded. "I will help you get upstairs. I have bratwurst cooking, and I made some knodels. You must be hungry."

"Knodels?"

"Potato dumplings."

"I am hungry and tired. I don't know how I'm going to get up the stairs. I'm still trying to figure out these crutches."

"My mutter once broke her foot. She scooted up and down the stairs on her... how do you say it? Her bottom."

Alice took the crutches from Greta. "Then let's go eat." She would let Greta help her for now.

She hadn't forgotten Greta was German.

Chapter Four

Alice spent the next morning sitting in a chair with her leg propped up on a stool. She felt like she was directing a movie set instead of setting up her own store. "Over there," she pointed. "One in the window."

She had splurged on two Singer Featherweight model 221 sewing machines. One she'd keep and use in the shop. The other... well, maybe someone would buy it. Most folks around here probably wouldn't bother with the newer model portable electric sewing machines.

Greta handled the precious machines with ease. Despite their name, they weren't at all light. The girl must be stronger than she looked. She held up a handful of candy bars.

"They go in front of the counter," Alice said. "We have Baby Ruth, Hershey's, Paydays, and Whiz bars, everything the children like."

"Why do you sell to children?" Greta placed boxes of candy behind the sales counter. "I would think the store would be for their mutters."

"Yes, but they come into the store with their mothers. Any child will behave if he or she is promised a candy bar on the way out."

"Ah, I understand." Greta picked up a yardstick from the counter. "Where do you want this?"

"It will go on the table by the fabric bolts. We can cut lengths of fabric there."

"*Ja*, is good idea."

Someone pounded on the door, and Greta answered.

Pete charged in, still in his overalls and plaid shirt, and dashed to Alice's side. "Are you all right? Rick Morrison said you were hurt." The fragrance of her brother's morning chores settled around them.

Greta's wrinkled her nose.

"Smells like you got the hogs fed early." Alice didn't know how Rick had time to run his business, whatever it was, when he was so busy butting into everyone else's. "It's just a sprain."

"Oh, Sis, with the grand opening in two days?" Pete rubbed his chin the way Pappy used to. Joe used to call it a sort of Farmer Pete meets John Garfield look. "This is a bad time of year, getting ready for planting season you know, but Lois could maybe come by for a couple of days to help out." He shrugged. "She's better, after the--" His expression took on a bewildered expression. "She's not much good planting crops anyway."

"I'll be fine." Alice grabbed the crutches and pulled herself upright to show her brother she could get along without him. "Greta's helping me."

"Greta?" Pete tilted his head toward the refugee. "Is she the immigrant you sent for?"

"Yes," Alice said.

"I'm surprised you took her in."

Heat bloomed on the back of Alice's neck. With all the excitement and preparation of getting ready for the opening, her accident, and the delicious dinner last night, she'd almost forgotten Greta was a German.

"I'm glad you're finally put aside your anger," Pete said. "The war is over."

"She was supposed to be a displaced European. How did I know they'd send me a Nazi?"

Greta's eyes watered. "I will go so you can talk to your brother." She ran upstairs.

Alice's face grew warm. "Now see what you made me do."

Pete brushed his hand across her cheek. "Are you sure you know what you're doing? You're welcome to come live with Lois and me."

"Did Rick put you up to this?"

"Ah, honey. He's concerned about you. We all are, but it's a good idea. Lois would love the help. Especially now."

"I'm doing all right."

"At least let me ask the Tolivers to lend a hand," Pete said. "They seem to always show up when somebody has a need. Mr. Toliver helped me repair the floor on my pig pen, and Mrs. Toliver stops by at least once a week to try to teach Lois how to cook. Besides, Mrs. Toliver quilts. She must know something about what quilters need."

"It might work." Alice bit the inside of her cheek. Her foot throbbed, but she didn't want her brother to know how much. "If you figure they have time."

"Sure they do. Mr. Toliver gets bored since he sold his farm so they could travel together, but they hardly go anywhere except on Sunday drives to Charleston."

"Would you mind asking them to stop by?" A pain shot through her leg, and she winced. Giving up on proving her foot didn't hurt, she slid into her chair.

He kissed her on the forehead, "I'll do it right now," and started to the door.

"Pete..."

He paused with his hand on the doorknob.

"If you could spare Lois for a few hours, I would enjoy a visit."

"Will do," Pete said and walked out.

Now she had to figure out a way to smooth things over with Greta. She still didn't want the girl around, but she needed her, at least for a week or two. Hobbling to the bottom of the steps to the apartment, she shouted. "Greta!"

The girl appeared at the top of the stairs. "*Ja.*"

"Could you come down here?"

"Not yet," Greta said before disappearing back into the apartment.

Alice's stomach knotted as she hobbled back to the chair. If Greta took a powder, there was no way she could manage even if the Tolivers did agree to lend a hand.

Greta's footsteps pounded on the stairway. She bounded down like a herd of elephants.

"She's going to break her neck." Alice let out a sigh. "Or maybe she'll just sprain her ankle like her sponsor."

If Greta did decide to leave, maybe she could ask the immigration board to send someone else, but this time she'd make sure she knew what country the refugee was from. How did Greta get on the sponsorship list anyway? Germans weren't supposed to be included.

Greta carried a tray with two plates of sandwiches and two bottles of Coca-Cola. "I made lunch. Are you hungry?"

"I could eat a horse."

A puzzled look crossed Greta's features. "Why would you want to eat a horse? They are very tough."

Alice placed a hand over her mouth so Greta wouldn't see her grin. "It's an expression. It means I'm very hungry."

"Ah." Greta set the tray on a nearby table and handed her a plate. "While we are eating, we can talk, *ja*?"

"We do need to come to an understanding."

"I am not a Nazi." Greta pressed her lips together. "Not every German supported Herr Hitler. I assure you, I and my family did not."

"I'm sorry for what I called you." Alice took a sip of pop. "You have to understand where I'm coming from. Hitler started this war trying to take over the world, and when the Nazis saw they were going to lose, instead of surrendering, they had to launch one last battle, the Battle of the Bulge, the battle that killed my husband." She took a bite of her sandwich to stuff down her emotions.

"I am so sorry for your husband, but things like this happen in wartime. No?"

"If your countrymen would have laid down their weapons and refused to fight, it wouldn't have."

"I did not fight in the war. I am not to blame." Greta bit into her sandwich.

"Do you have brothers?"

"*Ja*," Greta wiped her mouth with a napkin. "Four brothers. They are all dead along with my fadder."

If Alice's ankle wasn't sprained, she would have kicked herself.

*****

The Tolivers arrived later in the afternoon. Mrs. Toliver, a thin elegant lady, always reminded Alice of Joan Crawford.

She and Joe used to make a game of comparing their friends and neighbors to their movie star look-a-likes, and she never broke the habit after he went to war.

Mrs. Toliver bustled to Alice's side. "You poor dear. Tsk, tsk. I broke my leg once. I was on crutches for months."

Alice tucked her hair behind her ear. "It's not broken, just sprained. Besides, Greta's helping."

Mrs. Toliver glared at the girl. "Yes, I heard about your servant."

Greta's jaw jutted as she darted toward the staircase. "I will make coffee." She tromped up the stairs.

Mr. Toliver moved to his wife's side and took Alice's hand. "Do you think it wise allowing a German to stay here?"

Alice bit her lip. "I have no choice at the moment."

"We'll see," Mrs. Toliver said. "Now, what can we do for you?"

"I hate to bother you, but I need help, and most of the folks around here are getting ready for planting season."

"Nonsense." Mr. Toliver said. "Just tell us what you need, and we're at your service."

"Oh, thank you." Alice pulled herself up on her crutches and hobbled to the counter where the threads were displayed. "I need a case to hold about ten pairs of scissors and various needles. I want to keep sharp objects out of little hands."

"I'll get right on it," Mr. Toliver said. "It'll be ready by opening day."

"You're a life saver," Alice said. "I really didn't know what I was going to do, and you swoop in and save the day like... like Spencer Tracy in *Northwest Passage*."

Mr. Toliver blushed. "I don't know about that, but I'm happy to help. Your folks were our closest friends. It's a tragedy what happened to them. They ought to close that road before somebody else gets hurt."

Mrs. Toliver looped her arm around her husband's. "Your quilting corner is charming, absolutely charming. What can I do?"

"You could help Greta set up the quilting rack. I've already got two rows of Goose Tracks started—"

"Greta?" Mrs. Toliver glanced at Mr. Toliver. "I still don't think it's a good idea for you to allow her to stay, dear. She might even be one of those war criminals they're looking for. You never know."

A muscle in Mr. Toliver's cheek twitched.

Alice slumped her shoulders. "I'm not happy about having a German in the shop either, but what can I do now. She says she didn't support the Nazis."

"Haven't you been watching the Nuremberg trials on the news reels?" Mr. Toliver glanced toward the stairs. "That's what they all say."

"Well, we'll do everything we can to make sure this shop succeeds." Mrs. Toliver's brow furrowed. "If only there was a way to bring more money into town. With returning vets moving to Powellton to work in the mines or Akron, Ohio to work at the rubber factories, this village is dying. We need something to revitalize Burning Bush or it will end up a ghost town."

Alice leaned against the counter. Propping herself up on her crutches was wearing her out. "I have an idea. If it works, it might get our town back on its feet. Have you ever thought of a barn quilt tour?"

"A barn quilt tour?" Mrs. Toliver nodded. "Hmm."

"What's that?" Mr. Toliver asked.

"We had one once when I was a little girl in Pennsylvania," Mrs. Toliver said. "Thirty years ago..."

Mr. Toliver rolled his eyes, and Alice stifled a giggle.

"It brought in folks from all over. We painted different quilt block patterns on the barns, and had a festival where tourists could see the pleasures of country life."

Alice picked up the thread of the idea. "The New York lifestyle made me think of tourism. People come from all over just to see the Big Apple. Of course, once they've come for the shows and the sights, they stay, they eat, they spend money."

"We don't have any shows in Burning Bush," Mr. Toliver said. "Unless you count the town meetings."

"The barn quilt tour is like a show."

"I love the idea, dear," Mrs. Toliver said. "Henry, what about the Fourth of July as the opening? Women could sell their quilts and crafts in Alice's little shop for a fee, and the bakery could display homemade baked goods. The diner could show city slickers what good home cooking really is. Later in the summer, farmers could set up stands to sell their vegetables. It would be a great excuse for outsiders to come here. I mean... it would give them a reason to come to a small village like Burning Bush."

Alice's mind raced through ideas. "It would sure boost the town's economy." She shook her head just thinking about the amount of work. "It's only a little over two months away. I could never get it ready in time."

"You don't have to do it alone, my dear." Mr. Toliver said. "If Gwynnie thinks it's a good thing then we'll do our part to convince the right people to join in."

Mrs. Toliver rubbed her hands together. "The whole town will help. It's our patriotic duty to get the economy moving again, just like back when... uh, after the first..."

Mr. Toliver laughed. "We know what you mean. This is just what we need to save the town. Say, why don't you put one of your famous committees together and meet here so you could coordinate?"

"Sure!" Mrs. Toliver rubbed her hands together. "We can plan it during the sewing circle next Friday. I know we could make it happen."

"I can be in charge of arranging which pattern is painted on which barn," Alice said as anticipation stirred her stomach. "We can put a map together." She twirled a loose thread from a spool around her finger. "Do you really think people would come from all over to see it?"

"Yes, I do," Mrs. Toliver said.

Alice had hoped her business would boost the economy, but she never dreamed opening a fabric shop in Burning Bush would generate an idea to save the town. "Let's do it."

"I'll take care of the advertising." Mr. Toliver raised an eyebrow as a satisfying grin crossed his face. "By the time I spread the word, you'll be amazed at the people who will come to Burning Bush to see your barn quilts. This will work out perfectly."

Chapter Five

Six ladies attended the first Friday sewing circle at Alice's Notions. They'd agreed to help with a barn quilt tour and unanimously elected Gwendolyn Toliver as chairwoman.

They met in the quilting area of the store where Alice had put some of her artistic quilts on display. Nobody would buy them since every girl in Burning Bush was taught to quilt at an early age. Storm at Sea, in blue triangles and little gray paisley diamonds pieced to resemble a jumble of waves, was a favorite of hers. The frame was set up and waiting for their first project.

Alice's sister-in-law Lois sat on one of the slatted wooden folding chairs borrowed from church, completely overdressed for the occasion. She wore her blond hair up in a Lana Turner style coiffeur and a powder blue suit, making her look more like a movie star than one of the Burning Bush housewives in their cotton day dresses. She pinched her freshly painted red lips, staring in wounded fascination as an exceedingly expectant Janice Felton hemmed the bottom of a soft white baby gown.

Janice had tried to show Lois how to sew a button on one of Pete's shirts, but she'd pricked her finger twice and refused to thread the needle again after the last blood blossom stained the white cloth. Bernice Gorman tried to start Lois on some simple knitting. The hopeless tangle Lois produced a half hour later resulted in a few angry tears. Only Greta's coffee and *krumkaka* kept her from slipping out of the shop.

Alice set some stitches in the quilt she was currently working on, "Goose Tracks," with Joe's saucy peacock blue Sunday shirt and an old flowered chintz apron of hers. She'd managed two rows so far. Hmm... maybe she could put out a basket with a sign: used clothes or linens, old blankets for store credit.

Grateful for Greta keeping a surreptitious eye on their only customer, Alice wondered why he was more intent of memorizing her inventory than making any purchase. Rick Morrison's flimsy excuse of needing a patch for his work shirt didn't ring true. He never wore anything other than his white dress shirt, not even when he hung the Alice's Notions sign above the door of the shop. What work did he do?

Of course, as her landlord, he could come in any time. At least he had on a different suit today although charcoal gray with a thin black and white striped tie wasn't much different from the standard black.

Alice watched him out of the corner of her eye while Gwendolyn Toliver nailed down the last committee positions.

"Mrs. Round, you're in charge of entertainment."

After having just taken a sip of coffee, Mrs. Round spewed it in a coughing fit. Bernice Gorman rushed to her side and patted her on the back.

Poor woman. Pastor Round and his wife had been here less than a year. How could she possibly know who the local musicians were?

Alice made a mental note to give her a list. A few of the men in town, including Pete and Deputy Eddie Tyler, had started a barbershop quartet. Turned out they were pretty good. Pete was a great tenor, and the deputy's low voice provided them with a good bass.

Rick stopped at the window display where the dress dummy stood modeling a red and white polka-dot outfit. Greta had fashioned a sort of head for the ancient form shaped from straw and wrapped in cheesecloth, and hid the facelessness with a hat tilted just so.

Resuming her sewing, Alice fit another triangle of blue to the piece of calico she held in her hands and made a stitch.

Mrs. Toliver's voice droned on. "So, who will attend Tuesday's town meeting with me? Mrs. Gorman? Good. Alice, I have you down already, of course. I need a volunteer..."

Alice couldn't help but let her attention wander. Rick's hands were in his pockets, and he gawked at the dummy like it was Public Enemy Number One. Was he planning an interrogation?

"Huh? Oh, sorry, Lois. What did you ask me? I'm afraid I was--"

"I said." Lois's voice was just short of hysterical. "Why do pigs have to be so filthy all the time! They...they have such a peculiar, horrid, awful, disgusting odor--"

"They can't sweat," Janice said. She snipped her thread and pursed her mouth. "They have to wallow so they can stay cool. Mud helps." She snapped the gown straight and folded it with sharp creases.

Mrs. Round made a dismissive grunt. "Of course, dear," she trilled, making Alice grit her teeth at the off-key sound. "How many of God's dear creatures does your husband have now?"

Janice had been trying to convince her husband to attend church with her since a baby was on the way. Jeff wasn't having anything to do with it, and the tension swum around them. Sounded like the pigs got most of Janice's sympathy nowadays. She pressed her hands to the small of her back.

"Are you all right?" Alice asked.

"Yes, the little one is just learning to tap dance in there."

Alice glanced once more at Rick, then at the antique clock hanging above the counter. Rick must have got the hint because he frowned and trudged out the door.

Greta flipped the sign to closed. "Lunch time," she announced.

A couple of cheers erupted, but they were cut off when Mrs. Toliver cleared her throat. "Afterward I will begin the selection process of the individual stops and designs. You girls can divvy up the neighborhood to present the designated barns and blocks."

"I don't know anyone," Lois moaned. "I can't talk to anyone."

"Sure you can." Bernice Gorman scoffed as she stuck a loose bobby pin in her auburn hair.

The impact of Mrs. Toliver's words sunk in. Alice had planned to organize the design of the blocks. She tried to catch Mrs. Toliver's attention, but the woman was talking animatedly to Janice about the coming baby.

Alice shook off her ill will. She'd explain things to Mrs. Toliver in private later. The main thing was the tour would go on.

"Come, now, please," Greta said. "We haf a nice food table all prepared."

The last to hobble behind a curtain at the back of the store, Alice glanced at the mannequin in the window. What was so fascinating about it, and what was the real purpose behind her landlord's visit?

*****

Rick Morrison had been blatantly eavesdropping on the Ladies Sewing Circle. If Alice had any doubts, they were erased as he spoke at the town meeting held at the Burning Bush Community Church at the mouth of the holler.

"Gentlemen," Rick said to the assembled townsfolk, "it is not without a certain irony I address you now."

"How did he even get on the agenda so fast?" Pete muttered. He sat between Alice and Mrs. Toliver, fists clenched.

Alice sat on the end of the aisle, her bandaged foot and crutch sticking out like a flashing Times Square sign reading, "Clumsy oaf here." Well, the crutches would be gone soon enough. She was already limping around the apartment gingerly without them.

"Obvious," Mrs. Toliver said to Pete, not bothering to be quiet. "He's got some kind of hold on Mayor Wilson."

Rick frowned but continued his spiel. "We don't need busloads of strangers bringing their trash and disrupting Burning Bush."

"But--"

Mayor Wilson rapped the gavel like Judge Hardy in one of the Andy Hardy movies Alice loved to watch before the war. "You'll get your chance, Gwendolyn, but right now, you need to let Mr. Morrison have his say. We are a democracy here."

Mrs. Toliver snorted under her breath.

On her far side, Mrs. Jenner's knuckles were white as she kept a death-grip on her handbag. Alice couldn't help but feel sorry for the woman, what with her husband sitting at the head table staring daggers at her.

Sheriff Jenner's wife confided she had stooped to using her feminine wiles on her husband to influence his support for the tour's cause. Alice could only offer her one of Greta's cinnamon cookies and pat her back as she hiccupped and cried her chagrin earlier in the afternoon. "H-he told me he'd ar-rest me for attempting to bribe an o-officer of the law!"

What was the matter with all of them? Couldn't they see a tour would be good for Burning Bush? Alice scowled at Rick while the man continued to make her look like a fool. How could she have ever compared him to Cary Grant? Must have been the smirk.

He swept a hand in their direction. "We need legitimate businesses to supply jobs for men to provide for their families. Goods which have a purpose."

"You can't honestly think clothing has no purpose!" Mrs. Toliver stood up, marched to the platform, and shook her finger at him.

"Like those sold in a hardware store, or a pharmacy, or even one of those department stores."

"You got that right!" Frank Summers stood up. "Taking jobs from us men! We need work so we can care for the wimmen folk."

"He's been fired twice for drinking since he got back from service," Pete whispered. "Morrison probably hired him to spout off."

Alice swallowed a giggle.

The mayor rapped. "If I have to warn the audience again, you'll all find yourselves on the sidewalk!"

"Huh!" Mrs. Toliver narrowed her eyes at Frank.

Alice was glad she wasn't the one receiving her displeasure.

"This tour being proposed by my tenant will create chaos for the rest of the summer and would cause all kinds of havoc and expense for this community. Who's going to clean up?"

"We will!" Alice raised her crutch.

Rick turned and studied her, one brow raised in that infuriating way of his. "That's all." He glared in her direction and left the podium.

A cold chill went through Alice. She'd come to Burning Bush to get away from all the politics and intrigue. Now a full blown war was brewing. But why?

"Thank you, Mr. Morrison," the mayor said. "I'm sure the whole town is interested in your opinions and will take them into consideration when we vote." He let out a gusty sigh. "Next we need to hear from Sheriff Jenner about whether Burning Bush can handle the extra traffic and crime a scheme like this will cause."

A knot formed in Alice's stomach. Maybe she should withdraw her request for the quilt tour. She could retreat to her shop and let the dust settle. Anything to feel safe again.

*****

Alice would have danced back to her store like Ginger Rogers if only her partner was Joe instead of the crutch. She had every intention when it was her turn to speak to call off the whole thing. Then she remembered Joe's favorite motto, seize the day. Boy, did she ever.

"Did you hear me, Joe? I sure told them, didn't I? You would have been so proud." The sound of the train chugging by was the only answer she received. She turned the key in door.

"There you are." Greta met her. "You smile. Means gut news, *ja.*"

Alice accepted Greta's arm around her waist as they hobbled up to the apartment.

"Swell news, Greta." She tossed her hat and gloves on one of the matching blue and green flowered chairs in the living room. "Not only did they vote to allow the tour, but the mayor gave us a hundred dollars from the town treasury to help."

Greta sat on the low-back, fern green sofa with her hands folded, composed to listen. Alice relayed the meeting, the discussion, and Mrs. Toliver's antics. "The best part was..."

"*Ja?*"

"Rick Morrison was shot down." At the alarmed look on Greta's face, Alice laughed. "It's just an expression. I mean, they didn't listen to him."

"Oh." Greta bunched her eyebrows. "So, you are pleased Herr Morrison did not stop your plans."

"You got that right, sister." She sank into the couch beside Greta.

"He won't be angry?"

"So what if he is?" Alice blinked, thinking more about getting ready for bed than concentrating on her blond roommate.

"Angry men sometimes commit angry acts."

Alice mulled it over. "You think he might retaliate by canceling my lease?"

Greta shook her head and rose. "We can't know for sure. I've seen worse. Is never good to anger others."

"Certainly not your landlord."

"*Ja.*"

"*Ja.*"

They spoke in tandem, then laughed.

Alice gathered her gloves, gripped her crutch, and took a step toward her bedroom. "Well, even if Mr. Morrison tries anything to hurt us, we'll have the support of Mayor Wilson and most of the town. At least they understood I'm not trying to hurt anyone, and I only want to do what's best for Burning Bush, and I have the Tolivers to back me up."

Even as she said it, her knees grew weak.

Chapter Six

Much to everyone's relief, Lois had found her calling as part of the Friday Ladies Sewing Circle. She still didn't sew, but she charted the work going on and the supplies being used, and when Alice suggested selling their crafts on commission, she made up the descriptions and paperwork. When the Circle turned into the Burning Bush Quilt Tour Committee for the summer, she was the natural choice as clerk.

Alice watched fondly out of the corner of her eye as Lois shook her fountain pen and paid avid attention to the chairwoman.

Gwendolyn Toliver flaunted to everyone a small gavel Henry had made for her. "Based on Mayor Wilson's, of course." She gave a sharp rap on the cutting table.

Alice winced, hoping she hadn't left a dent.

"The first meeting of the Burning Bush, Lafayette County, West Virginia, proud United States of this great country America Quilt Tour Committee is called to order!" *Rap, rap.* She pointed toward Lois with the gavel. "See here, Mrs. Morgan. Make sure you note the time, one-oh-one p.m., exactly, the tenth of May, in the year of our Lord, 1946. Thank Mrs. Round for the ginger snaps, and Mrs. Felton for the lemonade."

Lois bobbed her head, writing busily. She stopped to pull the lever to refill her fountain pen then paused, gazing at Mrs. Toliver again.

"Roll call!" the chairwoman sang out.

Bernice Gorman sat next to Alice placidly knitting a pair of socks. Her stitches were fine, so tiny. Alice drooled in envy. Bernice winked and went back to counting stitches silently. Janice Felton, on Alice's other side, shifted in her chair. The poor dear's ankles were swollen. Hopefully Doc Brunner would have an easy trip up Mockingbird Road to deliver the baby when the time came.

Alice heard her name and jumped. "Ye-yes?"

Mrs. Toliver leaned toward her over the cutting table. "Mrs. Brighton, I asked whether or not you had brought your list of possible designs."

"Oh! Oh, right. Yes, I did. Just a minute."

When Alice had reminded the other women she had originally offered to work out the designs, Mrs. Toliver looked deeply hurt over the slight. "Of course dear Alice must work on the patterns."

Now she hopped up, using one bothersome crutch to limp over to a shelf near the steps to the apartment and pick up her manila folder. She waved it. "Here."

Lois set her pen down and started toward Alice.

"No, no, Mrs. Morgan, you go on writing. Mrs. Jenner, if you would be so kind," Mrs. Toliver said. "Please give our Mrs. Brighton a hand."

The sheriff's wife had joined the sewing circle today, though she had brought nothing with her to work on, nor had she purchased anything in the shop. Alice got the point. She was here only for the meeting. Well, not everyone sewed.

Alice handed her folder to Mrs. Jenner. Even though the sheriff's wife looked unassuming, long mousy brown hair worn in a bun, a plain cotton housedress which had seen better days, her wide Betty Davis eyes revealed a spark she kept hidden. Maybe the sheriff hadn't completely browbeaten her.

When Alice was a teenager, Sheriff Jenner went to a lawman convention in Cleveland, Ohio and came back with a new wife. He was in his forties at the time, and everyone was surprised he'd found someone, let alone a woman he'd known for a week. Nobody knew much about her except her parents immigrated from a small European country, Estonia. At the time, all the girls in the high school chattered about how romantic it was. It was a shame he didn't have the same affection for her he used to show.

No matter how annoying Mrs. Jenner was, Alice was glad Mrs. Toliver managed to get her away from her garden and cooking for the couple of regular weekend prisoners her husband rounded up on Friday nights. Maybe the quilt tour would bring Mrs. Jenner out of her shell.

After shuffling back to her seat, Alice passed the tray of ginger cookies the pastor's wife had baked. She decided she'd had about enough with the crutches and would get rid of them as soon as she could. The two weeks the doctor had ordered her off the foot were nearly up.

She bit into the ginger cookie with a loud crunch. Four heads swiveled her way. Alice held up the cookie with a sheepish grin.

Mrs. Toliver paged through the folder, frowning. She flipped it closed with a bang almost as loud as her gavel. "Yes, well, we'll discuss this later. I have some ideas I'm sure will work. Moving on. Mrs. Round, how are you coming on the entertainment list I gave you?"

Alice struggled to her feet. "Mrs. Toliver! What's the matter with my ideas?"

Mrs. Toliver frowned at her. Lois continued to record every living second of the meeting. "Mrs. Morgan, no need to write down everything. Mrs. Brighton, as chair of the route and security, it's my duty to come up with suitable stops. Each stop has a particular character. Each character cries out for a particular type of block."

"Yes, well, these are all favorite, traditional designs, with colors--"

Mrs. Toliver rapped the gavel. "We'll discuss this at another time, Mrs. Brighton. I have an appointment I cannot miss."

Alice longed to grab the piece of wood and rap something else.

Bernice tugged her sleeve. "Shh, sit down, dear. We'll handle this later."

"She's trying to take over everything."

Bernice looked at her over the top of her wire rims, compassion in her faded eyes. "Things aren't always what they seem." She nodded toward the staircase.

Greta sat there, three steps up in the shadows, with her hands wrapped around her knees, the most peculiar look of longing and disgust on her face.

*****

On Sunday, Alice arrived early at Burning Bush Community Church with two goals in mind. First she would talk to Rick Morrison as soon as he set foot through the door. What Greta said about Rick being angry gnawed at her. As much as the man annoyed her, she would try playing nice.

She wore her navy blue skirt and jacket with matching felt hat. The outfit was conservative like Rick Morrison's suit, but the A-line skirt up to her knees showed off her legs. Mamie wouldn't have approved, but Alice was sure any able-bodied veteran would. Joe would have loved it.

Next, a conversation with Mrs. Toliver about designing the squares for the barns was long overdue. On Friday, Mrs. Toliver had left the meeting in such a rush, Alice hadn't been able to set her straight. Mrs. Toliver just couldn't waltz in and take over Alice's favorite part of the whole shebang.

Greta took her seat in an unpadded wooden pew near the front. She wore the same cotton dress and worn-out hat as the day she showed up in Alice's shop, but she held her head high like she was arrayed in the latest fashion from New York City. Alice lent Greta a pair of gloves to replace her old stained ones. It had only been a week and a half since the she'd arrived, but Greta had started worming herself into Alice's heart.

A wave of heat swept over Alice. She missed Joe, and considering the Germans killed him, was she betraying him by giving Greta a chance?

Sheriff and Mrs. Jenner strode to the front and sat in the pew next to Mayor and Mrs. Wilson. Mrs. Jenner's eyes were swollen and puffy, and the sheriff's taut lips and jutted jaw caused a pang of guilt. Alice knew it wasn't a good idea when Mrs. Toliver deployed the sheriff's wife to influence his vote, but she didn't do anything to stop it.

Deputy Eddie Tyler sauntered in and sat in the pew behind the sheriff. It came as no surprise Sheriff Jenner hired him as his deputy when he came home. A fighter pilot, Eddie had received at least three medals for shooting down enemy planes during the war. He was still a kid in high school when Alice left Burning Bush, and now he'd become a war hero. The deputy kept staring at Greta, but if she noticed, she didn't let on. She didn't even look in his direction.

Eddie stood and marched to Greta like a man on a mission. "Could we talk?" He tilted his head toward the back of the church. "Alone."

Greta blushed, nodded her head, and followed him before Alice could protest, but she did stand and lean on her crutches watching them in case Greta needed help.

The deputy said something in an animated way. Greta shook her head and placed her hand on his chest. Obviously, a heated discussion. Alice started toward them.

She was halfway down the aisle when Mr. and Mrs. Toliver marched through the door. She bit her lip. Church was about to start, and she needed to talk to the Tolivers. Greta could take care of herself.

Mrs. Toliver wore her Sunday best, a dark green dress with a full skirt. Her wide-brimmed hat with green and yellow flowers had been chic a decade ago. The brown leather purse she toted on her sturdy arm bested the size of Alice's lap quilting frame. In her regal manner, Mrs. Toliver greeted everyone with a smile and a wave like Queen Elizabeth did in the news reels at the movie theater.

Mrs. Toliver sat beside her husband and six well-dressed but obnoxious nieces, ranging in age from about ten to eighteen. The nieces lived with their mother in Beckley. They had an older brother, but she had never met him. Their father passed away a few years back, and they visited their Uncle Henry and Aunt Gwynnie every summer for as long as Alice could remember. When they swarmed into Burning Bush, a pestilence worse than one of Moses' plagues visited the town. It looked like locust season had come early this year.

Alice approached Mrs. Toliver and cleared her throat.

Mrs. Toliver was too busy checking her lipstick in her compact mirror to notice. Or maybe she couldn't hear over the cackling of her nieces commenting on the quaint decorations in this small country church and on how big their church was, and how their church had stained glass windows and cathedral ceilings, and how their pastor wore a robe. The same spiel they clucked every year.

Alice tried a second time. No reaction.

She placed her hand on Mrs. Toliver's shoulder. "Excuse me."

Mrs. Toliver startled and set her hand on her heart. "My dear, I didn't see you there. You should have cleared your throat or made a noise or something."

Alice rubbed her temples.

"Do you have a headache coming on? I have aspirin in my purse. It never hurts to be prepared."

"True," Mr. Toliver said. "By the size of her purse, I'd say she's prepared for anything short of an atomic bomb."

Mrs. Toliver laughed. "Oh, Henry, you say the funniest things."

Alice looked at the clock. Five minutes until service began. "I'd like to invite you and Mr. Toliver for Sunday dinner. Around five o'clock."

Mr. Toliver looked like he'd swallowed a pin. "We couldn't possibly. Gwynnie and I always drive to Charleston every Sunday."

"Henry's right, dear." Mrs. Toliver's lips tightened. "We'd never be home in time."

Alice bit her bottom lip. "Charleston's only an hour and a half away, and you were planning to go there to place an ad in the Charleston Gazette tomorrow anyway. Surely you could make it to dinner."

"I said no."

Alice took a step back. The stern tone didn't go with Mr. Toliver's normally easy-going manner.

Mrs. Toliver flashed Mr. Toliver an angry look.

Mr. Toliver's face turned red. "I'm sorry, Alice. Gwynnie and I never miss our Sunday drives. I didn't mean to bark at you."

"I understand," Alice said. Why were they making such a fuss about it? "We'll make it another time."

She excused herself and made her way to the front where Greta had returned to her seat. "Was the deputy bothering you?"

A quizzical look crossed the girl's doll-like features. "The deputy?"

"Eddie Tyler, the man talking to you back there."

Greta pursed her lips. "*Nein*, he was, how you say, welcoming me to Burning Bush."

Alice raised an eyebrow. "It didn't look very welcoming to me."

Bernice scurried over to them. "How's your ankle?"

"It's doing better. I should be off the crutches soon."

"Good. I was supposed to tell you something."

"What?" Alice braced for the news. Bernice, who lived on the farm next to Pete and Lois, usually couldn't wait to tell her sister-in-law's latest disaster.

"I ran into Rick Morrison the other day. He said I should tell you he'd be out of town for a few days."

"Did he tell you where he was going?"

"He didn't say much. He'll be back Wednesday. If you need anything, you should tell us or Pete and we'll take care of it."

The youngest of Bernice's five sons, the six-year-old with freckles, tugged her sleeve. "When are we sitting down? My feet are tired."

"Excuse me, I need to get this one settled," Bernice said as the child tugged her toward the middle pews.

Need anything? Alice didn't have time to finish the thought before Mrs. Round sat at the organ and led the first hymn. She was halfway through *Leaning on the Everlasting Arms* when Pete and Lois scurried into the pew beside Alice.

"If I had running water," Lois whispered to Pete loud enough for Alice to hear, "and an inside toilet, maybe we wouldn't have been late for church."

"It wouldn't matter." Pete said under his breath. "You primp so much you'd be late to your own funeral."

Lois swiped at a tear rolling down her cheek.

As the preacher came to the pulpit, Alice leaned forward excited to hear the message he would deliver. Pastor Round had a way about him in making the Bible easy to understand, but as his message on forgiving our enemies hit too close to home, a knot coiled inside of her. Greta was the enemy, but in every way, she'd shown herself a friend to a sponsor who had called her a Nazi.

Alice didn't know if she could ever put the war behind her or forgive the countrymen who killed her husband, but she would try to get to know Greta a little better. After all, it wasn't Greta's fault Hitler tried to conquer the world.

The service ended, and Alice turned to Pete and Lois. "Would you like to come to dinner tonight around five?"

Pete raised an eyebrow. "Are you cooking?"

"I am cooking," Greta said.

"We'll be there." Pete wrapped his arm around Lois.

"Would you mind if I take a bath there after dinner?" Lois asked.

Alice snickered. "Sure."

Pete scooted out of the pew. "I don't know why you want to take a bath at Alice's. We have a tub at home. All you have to do is heat the water."

Lois stood. "I want real running water for a change and a bathtub long enough for me to stretch out in. You promised to put in running water and an indoor bathroom, months ago. That toilet bucket and outhouse are disgusting."

"It's planting season." Pete said. *Well, that explained everything.*

Lois pulled back and delivered a glare scorching worse than the burn mark near the collar of Pete's freshly ironed shirt.

Pete plastered on his little boy grin. "I'll do it as soon as I get a chance, Sweetie Pie."

Lois, stiff-shouldered, followed Pete as they stepped into line to greet the pastor.

Sheriff Jenner marched over to Alice's pew. "I need to say something to you, Mrs. Brighton."

Alice raised a brow. Judging by his sour expression, this couldn't be good. "Go ahead."

"You stopped being a part of the Burning Bush community when you moved away years ago. You're a New Yorker now, and we men don't need you coming in here riling up our women with all your big city ideas."

Alice held up a hand. "Sheriff Jenner."

"Wait until I have my say. I didn't mind my wife going to your quilting bee, but I didn't think you would put all these foolish notions into her head about tourists coming in here and upsetting the whole town."

Mrs. Jenner blushed. "Please, George. You're embarrassing me."

Sheriff Jenner turned and faced his wife. "Think how I felt when you tried to get me to shirk my duty to the town?" He turned back to Alice. "Mrs. Jenner won't be attending any more of your seditious meetings, and if you know what's good for you, you'll go back to New York City where you belong."

The sheriff grasped his wife's arm and escorted her past the line of people waiting to greet the pastor and out the door.

A shiver went through Alice. Sheriff Jenner had been the sheriff in Burning Bush for twenty years, and he'd always been a by-the-book kind of guy. When she was a young girl, he was larger than life, like John Wayne or Gary Cooper. Now since she'd grown up, married, and left town for a while, she saw the truth. Sheriff Jenner was a bully with a badge.

Maybe Burning Bush wasn't safe after all.

Chapter Seven

Wham!

Alice winced as the reverberation of the slammed door to their bathroom echoed in the upstairs apartment. Lois's sobs rose above the splash of water gushing into the new white bathtub.

Pete stared at the shiny wooden floor in the living room while making circles on his knee with his finger. His face was ruddy, but whether from embarrassment or anger, Alice couldn't tell. Either way, her brother and sister-in-law had just had another monumental argument.

Greta set a tray of lemonade-filled glasses on their coffee table with enough force to rattle them. Her tight lips should have made a grown man tremble.

Alice cleared her throat and picked up a glass. "Thanks, Greta. Your lemonade is the cat's meow." She crossed her legs, thankful silk nylons were once again readily available. They were a luxury she'd foregone during the war.

"I do not..." Greta furrowed her brow. "We do not have a cat."

"Cat's meow is a saying. It means the lemonade is swell." Alice turned to Pete. "So, brother of mine, how are things on the farm?" The acerbity in her voice made Pete glance up for a second.

Catching Greta's frown, he went back to studying his knee. "Aw, not you too."

Alice exchanged looks with Greta. "So what did you do to get Lois so upset?"

Pete sent a disgusted nod heavenward. "Is everything my fault?"

"I don't know, dear brother. Is it?"

"Depends on who you ask."

At the thunderclouds in his eyes, Greta murmured, "I will check on dinner, leave you to talk."

Alice leaned forward from her chair to take Pete's hand. "She loves you. Just give her a little more time and patience. Losing the baby was traumatic."

"It was for me too, you know. She doesn't cut me any slack. I just don't know if love is enough anymore."

The hopelessness in his tone cracked Alice's heart. "Horse feathers. We've all had to make a lot of adjustments. She'll come around. You'll see. Once she gets busy thinking about other things, like learning something new, your ship will right itself. She'll be cooking on a wood stove in no time."

Pete propelled himself to his feet, anxiety in every footfall to the window looking down on Main Street. "All she does is nag. The smell. The pigs. The bathroom. No one to talk to. No place to shop. No shows to see." He pounded his fist on the window frame then bowed his forehead against it. "It's worse since Doc Brenner said we might not be able to have any kids after what happened. I don't know what to do anymore. It's not like I don't try."

"She's just going through a lot of changes all at once."

His voice went so low she could hardly hear. "Her cooking is worse than Aunt Jo's."

Alice let out a whistle. "That bad?" Jo was Dad's spinster sister who'd never learned to use the stove or bothered with recipes. Her bread was flat, her cakes charred under their frosting, and her "stews" flavorless. Come to think of it, "stew," or little pieces of usually unpeeled vegetables and mystery meat in a pan on the back of the stove, was all Jo had ever served with her manna bread, as she referred to it. "If the children of Israel had no yeast, then it must not be necessary," she'd say in her no-nonsense tone.

"Lois doesn't even try," Pete said.

Alice crossed the room to squeeze her brother's shoulder. "We shared a room during those last hard years. She was really carrying a torch for you. All she could talk about was Pete this, Pete that -- getting away from the big city and being your wife when you came home. After we got the news about Joe, in some ways, she took it even harder than I did."

Pete turned and put his arms around Alice. She set her cheek on his shoulder whiffing the faint aroma of hay and manure under the cover of his aftershave. To her, the smell was welcome, natural, home.

"I think maybe Lois turned off a part of herself," Alice said. "Like you expect the worst so you're emotionally prepared when it happens."

"So I'm the worst thing that could happen to my wife?"

"Of course not, Peter Alan Morgan!" Alice raised her head, took a step back, and shook her finger in his face. "Don't you ever think such a thing!"

"Think what?" Lois's soft voice startled them both. Pete's tension vibrated onto Alice.

"How was your bath?" Alice asked.

Lois wore a different dress, this one with pink flowers. It had a small waistline and wide skirt like one of the new Christian Dior fashions. Her eyes were faintly puffed under her pancake makeup, yet she looked pink-cheeked and innocent with both pencil-line brows raised.

"You've been talking about me, haven't you? Everything is my fault? I can't even make a baby."

"Now, hon--"

"He said the same about himself!" Alice interrupted.

"So it's true? You were discussing me behind my back?"

Greta appeared in the doorway to the kitchen wiping her hands on a towel.

Pete strode toward Lois, both hands raised. "Sweetie--"

"Will you stop that! I hate that! I hate everything!" Lois spun on her pink spiked heels and clambered down the steps.

After the jingle of the front door went silent, Pete put his hands on his hips and considered Greta. "Can we eat soon?"

"*Ja*, the food is ready to eat."

Alice shook her head. "What about Lois?"

"She won't get far," Pete said, morose. "Not in those shoes."

*****

Alice broke off another piece of the delicious roll and slathered it with butter. "Wow, Greta, you are amazing. Where did you learn to cook so well?"

"You should give Lois lessons," Pete said.

"I would," Greta said. "*Mein* -- how you say? Aunt? Aunt Bertilde, she was baker in our village. You know? She always say '*Liebe geht durch den Magen.*' The way to man's heart is through stomach. I liked to visit." Greta smiled, a faraway gaze in her round blue eyes. She sipped her coffee. "My visits cost me when I got older."

"Let me guess." Alice chuckled. "Chores."

"*Ja.* She first told me to fetch ingredients, so I learned what goes in. Then I must measure. Finally, I must heat ovens and take food in and out. I never got burned," she stated with some pride.

"Sounds like an idyllic childhood," Alice said.

"Idyl -- idyllicht?" Greta asked. "I do not know word."

"It means perfect," Pete said. He shoveled another forkful of mashed potatoes into his mouth and gestured with the fork. "Like these."

"Oh, like cat's meow," Greta said. "For a while, living was good." Her lips pressed together.

Alice nudged her brother's foot under the table, but ever curious Pete didn't take the hint. "So, what happened?"

The German took a quick breath. "Change. Our friends... gone. School. It was different. We must wear uniform, learn new pledge. Join, join."

"It's all right." Alice patted Greta's hand, rose, and began to clear the table. "You don't have to talk about it." She hesitated at the unused place setting as the train roaring by shook the table.

Pete sighed and got to his feet. "All right, all right, I'll go catch up to her. She's probably having a pop at Daria's and waiting for me to pay." He jingled coins in his pocket.

"It's Sunday." Alice said. "The diner's closed."

Pete smacked his head. "Aw. Right. Sheesh, will she ever be hopping mad if she has to wait in the sun. She might wreck her skin, then I'll be hearing it for the next--"

"Pete! Just go."

Greta pushed a hastily-wrapped plate into his hands. "For your wife."

Pete hesitated only a moment. "Thanks. Thank you for being so gracious. I'm sorry about... ah... your life... um. Sorry." He headed out.

Alice shook her head. "Have you ever met anyone so clueless?"

"Cloo Liss?"

Alice laughed at Greta's puzzled expression. "So unable to understand women."

"*Ja*, but he tries."

"I don't know what to do, Greta. I love them both."

"Love is good," Greta said, "but interfere one should not. They are grown."

"Not mature."

"Like crops. Takes time and nourishment. We welcome Lois to help with tour, *ja*? Put her to work using her skills."

"She's a good organizer, and she does have a gift for arranging things, making them look pretty," Alice said. "You're right. I have to come up with something special for her to do, besides taking notes, to build her confidence. Maybe Mrs. Toliver has an idea."

Greta hmpfed in her German accent. "I do not understand the Tolivers. They want to take over your project. Take blame for it."

"Blame? Oh! You mean, take credit."

"Credit? No, no, not money, but fame."

Alice couldn't stop the giggle. "Credit means profit or gain, but it also means recognition for doing something, but you're right. It seems they want to be famous."

"They want something. I don't know how to say in English. I think they not mean so well."

"What makes you say that?"

"Is look. I've seen it before. At home. Before Goldblatts disappear from our village."

Chapter Eight

Alice turned on the radio and poured some Vel powder into the dishwater for suds. Greta insisted on washing, leaving Alice to dry. The kitchen, decorated in black and white with a checkered linoleum floor, had black countertops, white cabinets, black splash tiles, and the newest appliances.

They cleaned up the kitchen to the beat of Bing Crosby and the Andrews Sisters singing *Don't Fence Me In*. Greta even harmonized as she washed the plates and silverware. The radio station featured the Andrews Sister tonight, and while Alice and Greta tackled the pots and pans, they sang along to *Boogie Woogie Bugle Boy*. At one point, Greta even started tap dancing.

Alice wiped her hands on the dishtowel and clapped. "Where did you learn all these American songs?"

"We had a radio. It was forbidden, but we listened to BBC. They play all kinds of songs. I like American music. Frank Sinatra is my favorite."

"He's dreamy." Alice put away the last pan. She hadn't had this much fun since her husband died. She swallowed the lump in her throat. "Joe had blue eyes like Sinatra."

"Your husband. *Ja*?"

"Yes." Alice wanted to change the subject. It didn't seem right talking about Joe to... well, to a German, but maybe it was time to get things out in the open. "Would you like to talk about what happened?"

"What do you mean?"

She hung her blue apron on the hook behind the door and got two bottles of Coca-Cola out of the Frigidaire. She motioned for Greta to join her as she hobbled to the chrome kitchen table. Greta sat, and Alice grabbed a bottle opener and pried off the caps.

"What happened during the war?" Alice said gently. "I wouldn't ask, but it sounds like you had a hard time. You can talk to me about it if you'd like."

Greta pinched her lips together.

For a moment, Alice was worried she'd gone too far. She shouldn't have meddled.

"Might help," Greta said in a faint voice.

Alice drank a gulp of pop.

"My family did not approve of Herr Hitler's methods. He was not a good man. It made things... how you say... difficult for us. The Jews were ordered to report to the ghettos, and the next day, the Goldblatts vanished. The Nazis used their house as headquarters. Another Jewish family we knew came to us. They begged us to help. What could we do? Mein fadder knew someone from the Underground, and they forged papers saying the Jews were our cousins. It helped we lived in the country."

"Oh, Greta. You must have been terrified."

"Yes, we were frightened." Greta voice cracked, and she took a shaky sip.

"I was only a child when it started. At school, everyone chanted '*Heil Hitler*' and wore uniforms, so I would chant too. My mutter told me I mustn't, but I still did. All my friends wanted to be Hitler's Youth. I didn't want to be left out. I was angry at my fadder when he told me I couldn't miss church on Sundays to attend meetings."

Alice placed her hand on Greta's. "When did you change your mind?"

"My oldest brother was told he must join the party. He was about sixteen. Mutter and Fadder told him he must not, the Nazi party was wrong, but Wilhelm did as he was ordered. He didn't like Nazis, but he told my parents we must get along. If we opposed them, they might find out our cousins were Jews. So he joined the party. By the time he was eighteen, they forced him into the army and ordered two more of my brothers to join."

A loud pounding at the door downstairs interrupted Greta's story.

Alice started down the stairs. "Who could be knocking at this time of night?"

"Wait." Greta ran after her with a cast iron skillet. "I will take this. It might be someone who means harm."

"This is Burning Bush, West Virginia, not Nazi Germany." After scooting down the stairs, Alice limped to the door and unlocked the latch. "Most people here don't even lock their doors."

Greta gripped the skillet like she would a baseball bat, obviously not convinced of their safety. Alice shook her head and opened the door.

Pete burst in and panted to catch his breath. "Did Lois come back here?"

"No." A lump formed in Alice's throat. "You didn't find her?"

Perspiration beaded on her brother's forehead. He swiped at it with a faded red paisley bandana. "I checked everywhere -- the general store, the diner, the church. I even went to the river to see if she took a walk."

"Did you try the house?"

"There's no way she walked there in those heels." Pete's jaw twitched. "Yeah, I checked there. Sis, it's getting dark. She could be lost."

Alice grabbed a sweater and her crutches. "I'll help you look."

"I will come too," Greta said.

"No, wait." Alice said. "If she comes here, we need somebody to let her in."

Greta nodded.

"Did you talk to Sheriff Jenner?" Alice followed Pete to his six-year-old black Ford pickup truck. Nobody had driven it during the war, and it looked like it had just come off the car lot. It even had the new car smell.

"No." His voice cracked. "I wanted to check with you first. You don't think anything--"

"Don't." Alice opened the passenger door of the cab, threw her crutches in the back and scooted in. "She's fine. Let's go see the sheriff."

Pete drove toward the Kanawha River to the sheriff's office in record time. He jumped out as soon as he put on the brake, ran to the office door, and pounded.

She caught up with him when he hit his fist on the door a third time. "He probably wouldn't be here this late on a Sunday. Why don't you check the house?"

Pete didn't take time to answer. He darted toward their front door of the two-story farmhouse next to the sheriff's office. A dog barked in a low ferocious tone, and the porch light came on.

Alice trod to the foot of the steps leading to the front door as Mrs. Jenner answered. She held back her German shepherd by its collar as it growled at them.

Her puffy eyes showed she and Sheriff Jenner hadn't made up yet.

"Who is it?" Sheriff Jenner's voice bellowed from inside the house.

The dog snarled.

"It's Pete and Alice Morgan. Ah, Brighton. I mean."

Sheriff Jenner came to the door still wearing his uniform. "What are you doing here? If this is some kind of ruse to get me to let my wife get involved in your harebrained schemes--"

"It's Lois," Pete said. "My wife. She's missing."

Sheriff Jenner strapped on his gun and stepped outside. "When's the last time you saw her?"

Pete's Adam's apple bulged. "We had a fi... disagreement. She took off."

"Maybe she doesn't want to be found." The sheriff crossed his arms and glanced back at his wife. "The whole town knows the problems you two been having."

"Sheriff." Alice could feel her blood pressure rising and took a slow deep breath. "Lois wouldn't have run off like this."

Jenner ignored her. "You wouldn't be the first GI to marry a dish from the city just to have his war bride take a powder when things get rough. I heard she was getting pretty friendly with Rick Morrison at the diner a few days ago."

Pete's hands fisted. He stepped toward Sheriff Jenner.

Alice dropped her crutches and grabbed his arm. "We need to find Lois. She's what's important right now."

Pete's voice had a hard tone. "Are you going to help me or not?"

"Yeah, leave this to me. Why don't you go on home and wait," Sheriff Jenner said. "I'll bring back your wayward wife."

Pete picked up Alice's crutch, wielding it for a second before he handed it to Alice. He about-faced and marched to his truck. "Sis, you coming," he yelled and climbed in.

Alice grabbed the other crutch and hobbled after him. "Where are you going?"

"To look for my wife."

Most of the residents of Burning Bush lived in the holler, a dead-end road surrounded by mountains on three sides. Pete headed past the church toward the mouth of the holler then drove past the carpentry shop, a mill, and some nicer farms with two-story houses. Close to the mouth, most houses had electricity, and some even had running water. Sometimes he would jump out and check a building or knock on a door. Always the same answer. Nobody had seen her. Then he would hop back in the truck without saying a word.

As they drove further into the holler, the houses were smaller, and the poverty of the area became more apparent. Outhouses were located at every farm. Then the houses became little more than shacks barely capable of keeping out the wind and rain. Some of them didn't even have windows. As they approached the head where the turnaround was, old rusted railroad cars no longer in use found their final resting place. The poorest families and outcasts lived in those cars. A few colored children, dressed in little more than rags, played outside in bare feet even though it was late and there was a chill in the air. Most of them didn't have to go to bed early because they didn't go to school during planting and reaping seasons. They were needed to work the farms to help their folks scrape out a living.

Pete turned the truck around, spinning the tires in the dirt as he did, then raced toward the mouth.

Alice's stomach knotted tighter. She'd never seen him act like this before, and it scared her. "Maybe she headed back home after you checked."

"I doubt it, but I'll check." He drove out of the holler and turned on Mockingbird Road travelling toward his home a half mile up the mountain road.

Her brother was right. Alice couldn't imagine Lois walking this far in high heels or even barefoot, but she didn't mention it.

He stopped in front of the old stone farmhouse built by their grandpa after the Civil War and rushed inside. "Lois." A moment later, he came out of the house and darted toward the barn. "Lois. Lois." He shouted, but there was a catch in his voice making it sound more like a pitiful wail. "Lois!"

He got in the truck, slammed the door, and raced to town.

The sun had gone down hours ago, and only a sliver of the moon shone. Even without clouds, the truck's lights barely penetrated the dark night.

He cut it too close crossing the tracks, barely missing the steam locomotive screeching its brakes and stopping at the water tower in the center of town. He stopped at the store and parked.

"Now what?" Alice asked.

"I'm dropping you off at your apartment. I should have thought of this earlier, but I'm going back to the house to get the dogs. If she got lost on the hill or in the woods by the river..." His voice grew thick. "She might be wandering out there trying to find her way home. I have to find her."

"You can't do it alone at this time of night." She patted his arm. "You need help."

"From who? Sheriff Jenner?" He spit out the words.

"No, but what about Deputy Eddie, Mr. Toliver, Ralph Gorman, Jeff Felton? Frank Summers knows the mountain better than anyone."

"Maybe you're right." Pete pounded his fist on the dashboard. "I'll get the dogs. You call them. Tell them to meet me here."

She grabbed her crutches and slipped out of the truck. "Don't worry. We'll find her."

*****

Alice wasn't surprised when so many of the men in town showed up in front of her shop. One of the things she loved about living in a small town, neighbors helped each other.

Sheriff Jenner drove up in his black and white squad car with red lights flashing and sirens blazing and barked out orders. "Frank, you and Jeff take the mountain path. Eddie, check along the river bank. Mr. Toliver, come with me, and we'll walk the railroad tracks."

It was about time he acted like the sheriff even if he was putting on the show so he wouldn't look bad in front of the men in town.

Pete drove up with his hound dogs.

"I'm glad you thought of them," Sheriff Jenner said. "Ralph, you help Pete."

Pete's lips thinned, but he didn't say anything.

After everyone headed out, Alice leaned on her wooden support and gazed at the stars littering the sky. "Oh, Joe. I wish you were here now." In New York City, you could never see them. Too many buildings and street lights. "Lord, keep Lois safe, and help the men find her."

"Amen," Greta said.

Alice forgot she was standing there and took her hand. Greta squeezed back comfort before letting go.

The soft roar of an automobile engine sounded as headlights illuminated where they were standing. Rick Morrison's Fleetmaster surfed to a stop, and he rolled down the window. "What are you two doing out here this late at night?"

Alice flushed. "I thought you were gone until Wednesday."

"I had important business." It was the only response he offered.

She dashed away the wayward tear on her cheek. "Lois is missing."

His brow furrowed. "What happened? Tell me everything."

Alice, along with Greta, told the whole story and how the men were searching for Lois.

"How long did you and Pete look for Lois while Greta was alone in the store?"

"I don't see how it matters," Alice said.

"They looked for hours," Greta said. "Maybe three or four."

"Ladies, go in the store and lock your doors. I'll find her."

"The men--"

Rick drove off midsentence.

Alice bit her lower lip. Lois might be out there lost or hurt. She couldn't bear to lose anyone else she loved.

Chapter Nine

"I'll get more ice." Greta started up the stairs.

"Stop," Alice said. "No more." If Greta placed another towel of ice on her foot, she'd end up with frostbite. What she wanted was company to keep her from worrying. "Why don't you sit and have another cup of coffee with me."

"You want no more." Greta took away Alice's chipped mug. "You've had three cups."

"I hadn't noticed. I guess nobody's sleeping any tonight."

An engine revved in front of the store and breaks squealed. Doors slammed, footsteps sounded on the walk.

Greta dashed to the door and opened it.

Pete rushed in, carrying Lois. Rick was right behind him.

Hopefully Lois had fared better than her pancake make-up. Mascara streaks lined her face and made her look like she had two black eyes, and her lipstick smeared giving her the resemblance of a clown.

"Greta, go for the doctor." Alice said.

"She's okay. No need," Rick said.

Alice glared before leaning over her sister-in-law. "Pete?"

Pete ignored them all. He set her in a nearby chair and pulled down the Storm at Sea quilt displayed on the wall. He wrapped Lois in it and held her tight. "Are you warm now, sweetie?"

Lois nodded her head. Her hair went every which way. Her face held an expression of mingled fear and awe. She couldn't have looked worse if she'd been in Normandy on D-Day. From the look on the men's faces, she had.

Alice couldn't hold it in any longer. "What happened? Lois?"

Pete delivered a glower to Rick their pappy had used once when a hobo stopped by the house and made rude remarks to Mamie. The tramp never showed up again.

Lois shifted in the chair, its squeak thunderous in the silent war. Alice reached down to pat her shoulder. "There, there. What's going on? We were so worried. Everyone's out--"

"No! No!" Lois put her hands over her eyes and shuddered. "I'm already a laughing stock."

"It's only because we care," Alice said.

Pete stood, fists slightly raised, waiting for a move from Rick before attacking him, and Rick wasn't giving him any chances. Only thing missing was uniforms and a trench.

Alice knitted her brow. What was the matter with everyone?

"You had no right," Pete growled. "She's my wife."

"Please!" Lois begged. "Stop it. I told you already."

"Well, then, somebody tell me!" Alice snapped.

Without taking his eyes off Pete, Rick said, "I found her tied and blindfolded in the old blacksmith shop by the river. I need some answers, Mrs. Morgan, what were you doing there?"

"Tied!" Alice reached for her sister-in-law's arms, too aghast to be angry with Rick's interrogation. Her wrists were slightly chapped, her fingers blue with cold. "Who did it? Some tramp? Did he hurt you?"

"I'm all right!" Lois said, but she slumped further into the quilt. "I just want to go to bed. Can I...can I..." Tears cut off the rest of her request.

"Not until I get an answer!" Rick took a couple of steps toward Lois. "You must have had a reason to go there."

"Look here, now," Pete positioned himself in front of Lois. "She's my wife."

"So you keep saying," Rick said. "Who you trying to convince, one striper?"

"Stop it!" Lois was crying in earnest. "I told you. I would have come back. I was on my way back. I just -- I just stopped for a moment. Those shoes..."

"There, now, Lois," Alice crooned. "What happened?" She sent a side glare to Rick. If he wanted answers, try being gentle.

Lois hiccupped. "I heard a noise. Like rustling paper."

"Leaves!" Pete said, dismissively.

Alice raised her hand in the mock threat she'd tortured him with when they were kids. He had the grace to look abashed.

"Go on, honey," Alice said.

"I'm not stupid, like everybody says."

"We know you're not." Alice patted her hand. "The noise?"

"Well, here's the thing. It came from inside the... the... what did you call it? Oh, never mind. I swear there were people inside, unrolling papers. I knew the sound from when we worked in the office at the navy yard. Anyway, I just thought maybe I could go in and sit down for a minute." She leaned over and rubbed her legs. "Get outta those shoes."

Alice knelt by the chair and removed the stained and tattered pink spiked heels. "How did you get tied up, dear?"

Lois raised her tear-stained face. "I don't know. Everything went black, and when I woke..." She reached up and felt behind her ear. "I think... ouch!"

Alice gently brushed her hair to one side and whistled. "Greta. The doctor."

"No! No, please. They'll just go tsk, tsk, tsk and blame me. I... I'm all right. I just want to lie down. Can I please?"

"Of course you can stay here tonight. It's too late to take you back to the farm now." Alice glared at Pete, daring him to decline.

In the meantime, Greta stood at the door gesturing to the searchers who'd trickled in. Alice heard the word "lost" a few times. Pete looked defeated, devastated even, while Rick appeared plain mad as they stood near the cash register, listening to the conversation outside the shop.

"Let's keep this quiet for now, shall we?" Alice whispered. "No need to spill the beans, as long as you're all right. Are you sure you didn't recognize anyone? Even their voices?"

"I'm not sure," Lois whispered back.

"Can you walk?"

"I think so."

After handing the sheriff a mighty simplistic explanation of their adventures, Greta locked the door and accompanied Lois up the steps. Alice clumped along after.

After getting Lois settled in Greta's bed, Alice tossed aside the crutches before heading back to the shop. The low murmur of voices warned she wouldn't be turning off the lights and locking the door just yet.

"I told you," Rick said with some asperity, "I didn't know."

"You said it was the first place you headed."

Alice stepped hard with her good ankle to make some noise. The men jerked their heads toward her. She took the reins and sat in the abandoned chair. "Lois is asleep, poor girl." She bit her lip at their matching narrowed gazes and amended her question. "So what's the official story?" She watched, annoyed, as Pete and Rick exchanged long faces.

"Hi-de-ho," she called out when neither answered her.

Pete blinked and turned to her, sullen as a mule. "I found the two of 'em at Jonesy's old place."

"Right. The abandoned blacksmith shop," Alice said during the pause.

"They were all hugging--"

"It's not what it looked like!" Rick tugged at his tie to loosen it. He looked exhausted with lines across his forehead and alongside his mouth. His day-old whiskers looked none too comfortable. "Your wife was scared out of her wits with no one to rescue her for most of the evening."

"How dare you!" Pete clenched his fists and crouched.

"Keep it down!" Alice hissed. "I get it. Rick somehow got to Lois before you and the dogs did, and Lois was grateful to her rescuer. Pete, you should be ashamed."

"How did he know she was there?" Her brother insisted.

"Who cares?" Alice said, trying to diffuse the situation, but dying to know.

"Jenner, for one," Pete said.

"What?"

Rick seemed distracted by her display of threads.

"He implied it wasn't the first time your landlord had a -- rendezvous," Pete spit the word, "at the shop. With my wife."

Rick's neck corded, and his gaze shot toward Pete. Much as she barely tolerated her landlord and was madder than a wet hen at her brother, Jenner wasn't going to be the wedge in their uneasy alliance.

She sighed and rose. "Pete, how often has Lois been out of sight of either of us?" She clutched his beefy arm and shook him. "C'mon, be sensible. You can't tell me you're going to start taking Jenner's side. Jenner?"

"I told you." Rick's attention went back to the thread. "Sometimes it takes fresh eyes to scout out the terrain." He picked up a spool of red cotton. "When you live in a place, everything is familiar. You look at the abandoned shop and think, 'no one would go in there.'" He set the thread down and looked at Alice. "When I passed it, I thought, 'wonder who's checked there.'"

If she hadn't known better, she would have sworn Rick's hazel eyes pleaded with her to believe him. Trouble was she did. She crossed her arms and glared at Pete then Rick. "We ought to be more concerned with who was there before Lois."

Pete backed up looking stunned, then rounded on Rick. "You dirty swine! You lured her there! What did you do to her!"

Before Alice could move, Rick had Pete in a headlock on the floor. "Now you listen to me, and listen good. Ain't no war here. We're on the same side, pal." Rick banged Pete's head on the floor gently when Pete refused to stop struggling.

"I want to help catch whoever did this as much as you. Maybe for different reasons. Got it? Something's not on the up and up and we're going to figure it out."

Rick opened his hands, letting Pete go. "I'm going back there at first light, check around." He flexed his hands, got up, and turned away straightening his collar, tightening his tie, and adjusting his sleeves. "We square?"

Pete nodded.

"Okay, then. I'm going home, get some sleep." With that, he was gone.

Alice blinked, feeling more like Alice in Wonderland than Alice Brighton. Pete rocked to his feet, nonchalantly brushing his pants.

She snorted and rolled her eyes.

"What?" he asked.

"The war's over, and you're still playing soldier. Men!"

Chapter Ten

Alice called Rick early to let him know she was going to the abandoned blacksmith shop this morning to look around even if she had to walk there herself. After trying to talk her out of it, he was kind enough to offer a ride.

She bustled around, trying not to put too much pressure on her foot. Her ankle felt good enough to ditch the crutches a couple of days early, but she was still leery to trust it too much.

Thankfully Lois was still sleeping. Alice wrote a note asking Greta to open the shop. She sprinkled brown sugar on her oatmeal and slurped hot coffee, wishing she had let Greta make it. She'd forgotten how bad her coffee was.

She tied the laces of her saddle shoes, slipped down the steps, and ambled to where Rick was waiting. He even wore his standard black suit and tie to investigate a shack.

Rick nodded his greeting. "I see you're no longer on crutches."

"The doctor said I could go without them as soon as I felt up to it, as long as I'm careful not to twist it."

Rick opened the door of his Fleetmaster for her then slid behind the wheel. "How's Lois doing this morning?"

"She's still asleep, poor dear."

"Did she say any more about what happened?" He sounded casual, but there was an edge to his question.

"She's been asleep since last night, so no."

They turned onto the road by the river where Jonesy's shack was located.

All the kids of her generation had avoided the abandoned blacksmithy due to the rumor Jonesy had deliberately burned Reggie Forbes, a boy two years older than her, when Reggie was in there on a childhood dare playing with the billows. At least, that was Reggie's story. Jonesy had died six years earlier, and Alice hadn't put much stock in the story. Reggie more than likely burned himself with his father's matches while sneaking a smoke and told the story as a cover-up.

They approached the dilapidated building with its blackened windows and swayback roof. Jonesy had painted it blue at one time, but now it looked bruised.

"I'll check in the back, make sure nobody's around." Rick closed his door and leaned over the open window. "Wait for me in the car while I check it out."

Alice shook her head.

Rick let out a sigh. "You are the most stubborn--Look, I'll call you in after I look around."

"I'll give you ten minutes." She glanced at her watch.

He delivered a mock scowl before heading toward the building.

Ten minutes later, she scooted out of the car and headed to the front on the dirt covered path. Footprints! Too late, she muttered under her breath and hopped onto grass. Had she already ruined evidence? No, with Lois, Rick, Pete, and the dogs all over the place last night. Still.

She ducked around the outside of the building. What would have made the sound of unrolling papers? She peered into a wide crack between boards. Just the anvil.

A warm hand covered her mouth and another pulled at her shoulder. When she recognized the odor of her brother's clothes, her scream died a foul death. "You would never make it as a Fed. I can smell you coming."

"Good thing my only aspirations are to feed my family. At least I make an honest living. Unlike the mysterious Rick Morrison."

"Pete! What are you implying?"

"You got to admit, he's not the type you'd normally find in Burning Bush."

Rick rounded the corner. "Shall we?" He held up the key. "Got it from Jonesy's daughter."

"How'd you get in yesterday?" Pete asked as he followed Rick to the door.

"Broke through the tarpaper on the west window." Rick glanced at her. "Didn't think Alice would be ready for a climb with her bum ankle." He winked.

Warmth swept through Alice. She tried to be affronted, failed.

Inside the shop, Rick swung a lighted lantern about before setting it on the bulk of the ancient anvil. "I found Lois there." He pointed to the northeast corner. "You came almost right away," he told Pete. "You almost made it before I did."

Alice grinned at the grudging thanks dripping out of her brother's pursed mouth. Good for Rick's attempt at diplomacy, but why extend the effort? She turned away to look for... what?

The building was dusty, empty, and rustling sounds came from the rafters. A pigeon cooed. Maybe Lois was mistaken about what she heard?

Rick picked up a bent feather and studied it.

"There's nothing here," Pete said. "Maybe she just fell and hit her head." He pointed to the fireplace. "There are sharp edges all over."

Rick's angry sigh echoed Alice's desire to smack some sense into her delusional brother's thick skull.

"Then she tied herself up for extra good measure? To make you feel sorry for her?" She stopped just short of grabbing him and shaking him. "She was fine when I checked on her this morning, by the way. Still sleeping--"

"Hey!" He held up his hands in surrender. "Why do you think I was late? I stopped by your place first."

"He gave me a mighty fine wake up call too." Lois's sweet voice sounded from the open door.

Pete rushed to his wife and swung her in a wide embrace.

"Careful, Sweetie, my head."

Although joyful at their apparent reunion, her brother and sister-in-law's delight in each other only made Alice feel left out and lonely. An accidental glance at Rick caught a strange look on his face -- much like the one he wore last night in her shop, all but begging for her trust. He slipped the feather in his pocket.

Trust? Alice cocked her head.

"I was saying," Lois placed a hand on Alice's arm, "don't you agree? This would make the perfect headquarters."

"Headquarters? For what?"

"The quilt tour, goose."

Shocked, Alice could barely voice her concern. "This place? You can't be serious. Didn't you have nightmares about what happened to you?"

"I told you," Lois said, impatient now, and tapping her little foot, clad in low heels this time. "I don't remember anything. Just waking up to..." A sidelong glance at Pete changed the course of her words. "Anyway, in the daylight, it's not scary at all. It won't take much to fix up, and it's out of the way. Even the businessmen can't complain about too much bother downtown. Right?" Her cheeky little grin at Rick's discomfort didn't fool Alice for a minute.

"I won't allow it," Pete said.

Lois just fluttered her lashes. Pete melted in seconds. "Oh, all right. Anything for you, Sweetie Pie."

"Well, I certainly won't allow it," Rick said. His voice and rigid stance flaunted no forge would ever be hot enough to bend his will.

Chapter Eleven

Alice blinked, trying to process what she heard. "You won't allow it?" She pulled herself up and tried to stand as rigid and unmovable as Rick, at least as much as she could manage leaning on her good foot. "Who died and left you president of the world?"

That *trust me* look again. This time, she wasn't buying it. He wasn't going to snatch the only dream she had left away from her.

"It's too dangerous." Rick planted his feet in a wide stance and crossed his arms. "Your sister-in-law was already accosted the last time she wandered in here." He sent a glare in Lois's direction. "If that's the real story."

Pete took a step toward Rick. "Now, hold it right there. Are you accusing my wife of something?"

Rick held his hand out. "Let's not go there again. For the moment, I'm willing to take it at face value."

Pete's jaw clenched, and he locked eyes with Rick. Lois slipped her hand into his, and he relaxed his stance.

Rick unfolded his arms. "I would like to ask Lois a question, with your permission, Pete."

Pete's furrowed brow told Rick what he could do with his question, but he nodded instead.

Placing his hands behind his back, Rick paced back and forth. When he stopped to face Lois, Alice couldn't shake the notion she was in the scene from *Casablanca* where the Nazis were interrogating Rick Blaine. "After you heard the sound of papers rolling, before you were knocked out, did you hear anything else, maybe voices? Or did you see or smell something out of the ordinary?"

"I told you before, I heard paper rolling, walked into the building, and the next thing I knew--"

"Papers?" Alice asked. "Where? This place is filthy."

"Except for the anvil," Rick said and ran his finger along the top of the huge flat iron surface. "Any footprints were messed up last night and this morning."

Alice lifted her foot, but she couldn't erase her part. "Sorry."

"Well, that anvil is big enough for a table," Pete said.

Lois paused, tilted her head. "Hold on. There was something else."

"Yes." Rick took a step closer.

"I smelled perfume. I remember thinking it was strange in an abandoned building, but after that... nothing."

"You were imagining things, Sweetie," Pete said. "Or maybe you caught a whiff of your own perfume."

"No," Lois said. "I wear *Soir de Paris*, the French perfume you bought me in New York City. This fragrance was more flowery." She turned to Rick. "Does that help?"

Rick nodded. "There was at least one woman involved." He fumbled in his pocket. "Alice, could I come over for supper tonight? I hear Greta is a great cook."

All Alice could do was stare. "Who are you?"

Rick tightened his tie and delivered a wide grin. "What's wrong with a lonely bachelor looking for a home cooked meal?"

"I mean, what do you do? You can't earn enough to buy an expensive automobile and wear those tailored suits by renting out one building–not at the rent you charge."

"Been wondering that myself," Pete said. "Morrison, what do you do for a living?"

Rick cleared his throat. "I guess I have been going around here like J. Edgar Hoover. It's my military training during the war. Old habits die hard."

Pete crossed his arms. "You still haven't answered my question."

"Real estate." Rick adjusted his collar. "I have business all over West Virginia: Charleston, Parkersburg, White Sulphur Springs, Beckley, even Elkins." He winked at Alice. "So, how about the invite?"

Alice didn't believe it for a minute. Somebody with property everywhere wouldn't live in Burning Bush, but she'd get to the bottom of this. Later, when Pesky Pete wasn't around to take over her interrogation.

"Around five?"

His adorable smirk didn't fool her a bit. Rick Morrison was up to something.

*****

Alice decided to wear her rose colored dress, the one she bought for special occasions. The first time she wore it was at Pete and Lois' wedding the day before he shipped out. Looking in the mirror, she was pleased with what she saw. The tight waistband showed off her figure kept trim by grief after Joe died and work getting her shop running since moving to Burning Bush. The knee-length hemline and matching rose Mary Jane shoes showed off her legs. Joe always said she had gams as nice as Ginger Rogers.

The doctor told her to stick to flats for a couple more weeks, and the two-inch heels did put some pressure on her sore ankle, but it was worth it. At least, she wasn't on crutches any more.

"Joe, is it wrong to be attracted to another man? I'll never love anyone as much as I do you, but it's been over a year." She hooked pearls around her neck and clipped on pearl earrings. "I don't even know what the appeal is. He's sarcastic and bossy, and he always seems to be implying something. The man infuriates me. Then he'll give me his trust me look and..."

The wedding ring Joe gave her was still on her finger. She twirled it around but couldn't bear to take it off. Not yet. "It's not like it's really a date. He just wants a home cooked meal. Greta will be there."

She hobbled into the kitchen where Greta was cooking a feast. The aroma made her mouth water.

Greta turned toward her and whistled. "You look like a movie star."

"Thanks. It's just something I threw on."

Greta's raised an eyebrow.

Alice's face grew warm. "Is there something I can help you with?"

"*Nein.* You sit at the table. You must not walk in those shoes. I will take care of everything."

A knock on the door caused Alice's pulse to race.

"I will get it. Stay here." Greta bounded down the stairs.

Alice tried standing in heels took a few steps around the kitchen. She could do it, but if she needed to walk, her ankle was too weak to manage any lengthy distance.

Rick followed Greta into the kitchen and gave Alice the once over. "Whoa. You look great." He balanced a box of candy, a bouquet of chrysanthemums and daisies, and a hat box in his arms. "I come bearing gifts. Flowers and candy for my hostess, and a special present for the cook."

Alice giggled.

Greta took the flowers, placed them in a vase of water, and set them in the middle of the table. Rick handed the candy to Alice.

She peeked inside. "Chocolate covered creams. My favorite."

"This is for you, Greta." Rick handed her the box.

"*Danke sehr*. I will open it after supper."

"I insist you open it now."

"I will do as you say." Greta opened the box and pulled out a chic small-brimmed hat with white flowers. "It is so pretty." She rotated the hat in her hands and let out a squeal. "I must put it on. Excuse me." She ran in the direction of her bedroom.

"Bring me your old beat up hat," Rick called out. "I'll take it to the clothing drive for you."

He pulled out a chair for Alice who gratefully sat. Her ankle was starting to throb. "What a nice thing to do."

"She needed a new one," Rick said. "The old one had a bent feather."

An uncomfortable silence hung between them.

Greta swooped back into the room and spun around showing it off as she crunched the old hat in her hand. "How do you like it?"

"It's beautiful," Alice said.

Greta curtsied to Rick. "You are a kind man."

Rick nodded. Greta tossed the old hat on a chair. While she dished up their supper, he picked it up and studied it like it contained military secrets.

"Heir Morrison," Greta said. "Would you like to say the blessing?"

Rick raised a brow but tossed the hat aside and complied. They started eating. Alice had her fork up to her mouth when he spoke. "Where's the feather?"

She put the fork back onto her plate. "What feather?"

Rick pointed his fork in Greta's general direction. "Your old hat used to have a feather in it, a white one, bent about half way down, if I remember right. It's gone now. Where's the feather?"

It sounded more like an interrogation than a question, but then most of Rick's questions did.

Greta lowered her eyes and stared at the dumplings on her plate. "It looked bad. When I went to church, I was embarrassed. Everyone had such pretty hats. I pulled the feather out and threw it away."

"Oh, Greta." Alice placed her hand on Greta's. "It doesn't matter what your hat looks like."

"Is silly, I know," Greta said. "Mein mutter would scold me for being... how you say... vain."

Everyone continued eating and commented on the delicious German food.

Small talk took over the conversation.

Dinner was almost finished when Rick asked, "Where did you throw out the feather?"

Greta finished chewing the bite in her mouth before answering. "I don't know. I think it was at the church. I might have thrown it in the grass."

Rick took a bite of Rouladen and washed it down with a sip of Coca-Cola. "It must have been frightening last night, Greta. All that time alone, wondering what happened to Lois. What did you do with yourself before we arrived?"

The hair on the back of Alice's neck stood up. Rick was accusing Greta of something, but what?

"I prayed for Lois's safe return." Greta ate a bite of dumpling. If she was unsettled about the accusations, she didn't show it.

Rick wiped his mouth with his napkin, leaned back, and patted his stomach.

Alice cocked her head. What was he up to now?

"Greta, you're a good cook. Thank you for taking pity on a bachelor."

"You're welcome," Greta said. "Why don't you and Alice go in the livingroom? I will clean up in here. Then we can have dessert. *Ja?*"

If Alice didn't know better, she'd swear Greta was trying to play matchmaker. They should sell tickets to this show. At any rate, Greta was not getting her way. "I can't leave you with this mess. I'll help."

"No." Greta started clearing the table. "You need to rest your ankle. Go. I will take care of this."

"In that case." Rick stood and pulled out Alice's chair. "Shall we?"

Alice scowled at Greta's back, but since she wanted to talk to Rick, she ambled into the living room with Rick following behind. Nothing like a limp to lure the opposite sex.

She sat on one end of the fern green low-back cushioned sofa. Rick sat on the other end.

The people he'd hired decorated this room to perfection like they had the others. The blue and green-flowered chairs matched the flowered drapes and had the same shade green as the couch. The walls were painted blue instead of having old-fashioned wallpaper. The shiny brass lamps on the glass inn tables and the brass starburst clock hanging on the wall between golden candlestick holders added to the modern look. All very chic.

"I was surprised to see you in shoes." Rick pulled on the collar around his neck. "I mean... I figured the doctor would have you in flats for a while longer since you just got rid of your crutches."

"He does." Alice twirled her wedding ring on her finger. She wasn't ready for this. It felt too much like a date. "A little early for my Mary Janes, but I didn't think it would hurt anything for a few hours."

The silence stretched through the space between them until it became uncomfortable. "I should help Greta." Alice started to rise.

"I knew your husband." Rick said it quietly, almost like a whisper.

A lump formed in her throat as she sat back down. "How?"

"During the war. He talked about you often."

She blinked. "Why didn't you tell me you knew him?"

"I planned to." He shrugged and leaned forward, resting his elbows on his knees. "The subject never came up."

"Were you in his unit when he... at the Battle of the Bulge."

"I was with him when he died. Yes."

Alice's throat grew thick.

"He didn't suffer." Rick scooted to the middle of the sofa and placed his hand on hers. "He died a hero."

She wiped away a stray tear. "Thank you."

He gazed into her eyes. "He always described you as sensible, so I know you'll reconsider using the blacksmithy for your quilt tour scheme, especially after what happened with Lois."

Heat rushed through her, and she pulled her hand away. "Quilt tour scheme? Is that why you came over here, why you told me about Joe?" She stood, took a deep breath, and exhaled it.

"Now, calm down." Rick stood and grabbed her arm. "I brought up your husband because you keep twirling your wedding ring."

"I will not calm down. How dare you use Joe to try to influence me? Joe supported me. He loved me."

The vein in his neck throbbed. "He did love you. He wouldn't have let you go on with this harebrained idea. He'd want you to move in with your brother where you could be taken care of, where you'd be safe."

She pulled away and limped across the room, heart racing, as she tried to get some distance between them. She blinked to keep from crying and turned to face him. "You don't own me, Rick Morrison. I am going to have the quilting tour, and it's going to be a success for Alice's Notions and for Burning Bush. I think Jonsey's blacksmith shop is the perfect place for the tour headquarters."

Rick took two steps toward her and pointed his finger in her face. "Well, let me tell you something, doll. It's bad enough you having this tour. If you use the blacksmith shop, I'll... I'll revoke your lease."

"Maybe you'd better leave."

"Fine." He grabbed his hat, marched toward her, grabbed her into his arms, and kissed her.

Tingles went through her, and she leaned into the kiss for a moment before pushing him away.

Rick stomped down the stairs and slammed the door on his way out.

Chapter Twelve

Alice swayed a bit, sorry now the crutches were out of her reach. A thousand emotions stirred inside of her as she drew her fingers to her lips, sensations she didn't want to feel again without her husband. Nobody had ever made her so angry before while leaving her confused and shaky causing her soul to need crutches — except Joe.

Rick wasn't Joe. Joe wouldn't have kissed her to win an argument. The pressure of Rick's kiss still clung to her lips as she remembered all the times her husband did sway her anger with his kisses. "Oh, Joe. What am I going to do?"

Greta came in, dishcloth in hand. "Herr Morrison?"

"*Ja.*" Alice wiped her cheeks with her hands. "I mean, yes, it was him." She bit her lip. "I mean, he left."

Greta's raised brows made her feel like she needed to have her head examined. Maybe she did. When Greta strode back to the kitchen, Alice made her way to the sofa and sank into it. What just happened? How did Rick stir her emotions with one kiss? She knew one thing. She'd never let it happen again.

"Greta?"

"*Ja?*" Alice's roommate turned off the kitchen light with a flick and joined her in the living room. "What happened? Are you A-Okay?"

"A-Okay?"

"Is an American expression. *Ja*? Did I not say it right?"

"Yes, you said it right. My ankle hurts a little, but I'm fine." Alice pulled off her shoes and propped her foot on the coffee table. "What was all that business about your hat?"

"Mein hat?"

Alice blew out a sigh. "With Rick. He gave you a new hat, and then all but accused you... oh." As far as she knew, she was the only one who'd seen Rick pick up the feather. Unless Rick had told Greta earlier about the feather on the floor of the blacksmith shop, her roommate couldn't have known.

"Alice? Are you... how is it... set-up over this? This gift? I will return it."

"No! Oh, no, of course I'm not upset, Greta. It's just... are you sure you tossed the feather on the grass by church?"

"What is the trouble over a feather? I will go look. I do not want any trouble."

"Please, Greta, I didn't mean... I just can't imagine you throwing anything away." She grimaced. "You're usually so thrifty."

"Is good to make do, yes, but the feather was broken, and I feel terrible about it, now." Greta raised her brows and smiled. "At least someone else can use my old hat, *ja*?"

Alice smiled weakly. "*Ja.*" It was silly to suspect Greta of something because of a broken feather. It might have been a feather from a bird flying through the shop. There were open places in the roof. More proof Rick was all wet.

"Why did Herr Morrison leave? Was he unhappy about something?"

Alice rolled her shoulders, shutting out the fear and passion he'd sparked earlier. "He thinks he owns this town. I don't get it. Why doesn't he want something good for Burning Bush, something he doesn't have anything to do with?"

"You speak of the quilt tour?"

"Right, but there's more. He keeps trying to run my life, tell me what to do." She snorted. "Huh! Go and live with Pete! Ridiculous!"

Greta gasped.

Alice willed her heart rate to slow to a steady beat. "Oh, don't worry. His bark is worse than his bite."

Greta followed the gasp with a hand to her throat. "He bit you?"

"No, no." Giggles eased her edginess and prevented her from explaining the idiom for several seconds. "I'm so glad you're here with me. I'm sorry I wasn't friendly right away."

Greta's expression fluctuated between hilarity and dismay. "Prejudice is hard to control. It caused great harm in my country when powerful men were allowed to have their way."

Alice mulled Greta's comment over. Powerful men who would do anything, even plant an unwanted kiss, to have their own way. Men like Rick Morrison.

*****

Andrea Collins, a woman in her early fifties who had the charm and grace of Ethel Barrymore, came to the next meeting of the Ladies Sewing Circle and Burning Bush Quilt Tour Committee. Mrs. Round also brought two other women Alice had yet to meet.

A place as small as Burning Bush shouldn't have any strangers, but Alice had been gone a while. So many new people had decided to make this dying town at the base of the Appalachians in West Virginia their new home. Burning Bush wouldn't become a ghost town, if she had anything to do with it.

Mrs. Toliver rapped the gavel three times. The chairwoman had managed to avoid her for all of last week, and must have only slipped into the shop a second ago.

Alice shook hands with Jennifer Garett, the woman in a faded blue dress, and Rosemary Lance, and invited them to sit. Greta carried over two more slat-backed chairs and set them up. This time, Greta was sitting with them.

It was a good thing they were moving to a new place for these meetings. The shop was cramped with all the newcomers.

Rosemary perused the goods. Hopefully she would become a customer. "I noticed you have a large inventory of craft supplies." She picked up a skein of yarn. "Have you ever considered supplies for basket weaving?"

"It's crossed my mind," Alice said, "but nobody around here weaves baskets."

"I do," Rosemary said. "It's a passion of mine."

Ideas for a basket weaving class and baskets to display items in the shop flittered through Alice's mind.

Mrs. Toliver interrupted her thoughts clearing her throat and banging that horrible gavel of hers. At least this time, Alice thought to set her bread board on the counter to avoid any more dents.

Alice and Rosemary took their seats. "We'll talk later."

Mrs. Toliver announced the agenda for the day, which consisted of deciding whether or not to move into the blacksmith shop. "All in favor?"

She didn't even wait for the ring of "ayes" to finish echoing before she rapped again.

"The next item on today's agenda is adding a parade. As the entertainment chair, Mrs. Round, this will be your responsibility. My nieces, of course, will participate. All of them. Meeting adjourned." She draped her purse over her arm and walked out.

The bell hadn't stopped jingling when Greta made a face at the door. "She was not so talkative today."

"No, she wasn't." Alice glanced around the room at the other puzzled committee members.

Mrs. Round's chin trembled. "I have my report all typed up. It took days because I kept making mistakes. I talked to Deputy Tyler about the barbershop quartet singing and even checked with the Montgomery High School Band. I never thought about a parade."

Alice wanted to hug the poor woman. What could she do to salvage the day? She stood and clapped her hands.

"Ladies, thank you for coming. The meeting of the Burning Bush Quilt Tour Committee may be adjourned, but the Friday Ladies Sewing Circle isn't. Please, have some refreshments, and bring your chairs into a circle. Let's get to know one another."

Two hours later, it appeared most of the oddness of the earlier tour meeting was forgotten as smiling ladies put away their individual projects and trickled out of the store. Alice promised to meet with Mrs. Round later to help her with ideas for the parade, and Rosemary had made several purchases and offered to teach a basket-making class.

Alice still hadn't figured out what had put a bee in Gwendolyn Toliver's bonnet, but something was up with that woman.

Chapter Thirteen

Alice's lips were clamped around four straight pins when the bell over the shop door announced an arrival. She looked up from her kneeling position on the floor hopeful it was a customer so she could stand up straight and get rid of the pins.

Tailoring wasn't her favorite activity, she much preferred designing a dress from scratch, but she'd need every dime she could get if Rick Morrison carried out his threat to cancel her lease. Fitting the Toliver nieces in new ginghams for the upcoming festivities wasn't her idea of fun, but she was paid well for her services.

Mrs. Toliver charged into the store not long after opening, gadded on about needing her nieces' dresses fitted, left the pile and one girl, then sailed right back out, calling, "I'll return in an hour." She did, exchanging one child for another. Three times.

On the radio, Frank Sinatra and the Pied Pipers finished crooning *I'll Never Smile Again* reminding Alice of all she'd lost. One kiss from Rick Morrison couldn't change that.

It had been a week since it happened. The next morning, he left for one of his mysterious trips, so she hadn't been able to talk with him about it and see if he intended to carry out his threat. *As Time Goes By* began playing, and Alice suppressed a chuckle when Louis Armstrong sang "a kiss is just a kiss." She would never let Rick's kiss become more.

Mrs. Toliver bulldozed into the shop with nieces in tow, bearing her usual generous smile and trailing a rather serious-looking fellow along in her wake. "Well, well, don't you look charming? How are we coming along?"

Lulu jerked around at her aunt's appearance causing Alice to prick her finger on a pin in the girl's hem. "Ouch." She spit out the pins and stuck her finger in her mouth.

"This hem is too long," Lulu said, folding her knobby-elbowed arms across her flat little chest.

"Lulu, darling, aren't you just precious!" Mrs. Toliver held out her arms to the twelve-year-old ringleted little demon. Lulu had not been precious to Alice when she complained about the style of dress, demanded three more ruffles along the hem, and described Burning Bush as out in the boondocks. Even Greta had escaped, two hours earlier, during the tirade of the oldest niece, seventeen-year-old Tanya, who refused to wear apple green checks and demanded Alice order moss green gingham instead and make a new dress.

"Uh, ma'am? Do you need a hand?"

Alice accepted the stranger's firm grip. On her feet, she raised her eyes from a broad chest up the throat, along a beautifully sculpted jaw, and straight nose into the smoky eyes of... *wow.*

"Thank you." Alice almost wished she still had her crutches to lean on. This man could sweep her off her feet.

"Alice, dear, may I introduce my nephew, Lucien Wendell Holmes? He's the girls' older brother, of course, my brother Stanley's brood, God rest his soul."

"How do you do?" Alice replied to Lucien's self-conscious grin. How did the horrid Toliver nieces get such a dreamboat for a brother?

"Lucien, Alice."

Alice ignored Lulu's smirk and playful "ew." The other nieces giggled. Tanya let out a snort.

Lucien gave his sisters a narrow-eyed warning before turning to Alice and replacing it with a heart-melting smile. "It's a pleasure to make your acquaintance, ma'am. Please, call me Luke. All my friends do. Aunt Gwynnie's the only one who ever gets to call me Lucien."

"Luke." Alice stuck out her hand to shake his.

He took her by surprise when he took it and brushed his lips along her knuckles.

Lulu snickered.

"My aunt has said so many nice things about you, but she never mentioned what a beauty you are, and so accomplished. She told me all about your quilt tour. I think it's brilliant."

"Lucien is in security, Alice. He agreed to help us with the tour, and show us how to keep everyone safe and happy. Isn't it wonderful? Then people like Rick Morrison can't object."

"Now, Aunt Gwynnie," Luke said, "I agreed to give you a few ideas."

"Of course. Change your outfit, Lulu, and the rest of you, come along. Alice, surely you can close up for lunch, can't you?" Mrs. Toliver glanced around the shop. "Or your servant can keep an eye on things -- if you trust her. Where is she?"

Every muscle in Alice's body tensed. She forced herself to count to ten before she said anything. "Greta is not my servant, Mrs. Toliver, and I do trust her. My employee stepped out to buy refreshments for the meeting tomorrow."

"Yes, Alice, of course. I misspoke." Mrs. Toliver directed Lulu to the changing room at the back of the store and ushered the other girls outside. "Wait by the car, ladies." She turned her attention back to Alice. "Well, then, it's time to see what's been going on at HQ." She winked. "Headquarters, you know. So nice of Rella Jones to let us in her father's former shop." She called out to the back. "Hurry, Lulu, darling."

Lulu darling promenaded from the back of the shop wearing her own clothes and dragging the gingham along the floor. At least the floor was clean.

Alice placed her "Back shortly" sign on the front door of the shop. Curious as she was about HQ, Lucien Holmes and his strong physique, square jaw, and smoky Dana Andrews eyes competed with her good sense about anything else: the wisdom of closing shop for an hour, what Greta would think when she returned, and even how this turn of events with proposed security would affect her precarious relationship with her landlord. If he realized how careful they were planning the tour, surely he wouldn't kick her out.

She slid across the front passenger seat of Mr. Toliver's '42 Chrysler Town and Country. Mrs. Toliver squeezed in next to her forcing her to scoot to the middle. Closer to Luke.

The expensive barrel-back station wagon had plenty of comfortable room for the nieces. The girls chattered in back like a gaggle of geese as Mrs. Toliver gave terse directions to Lucien.

"Straight on through there, dear."

"Watch from the right!"

"Pull up over there."

The four-minute ride to blacksmith shop became a cacophony of noise worthy of Time Square when the announcement came the war was over.

"Coming?"

Alice stared at Luke's hand offered once again to help her out of the car. He held on to her arm as they walked toward the banner-bedecked entrance of Jonsey's. She could get used to such considerate manners.

Luke didn't look like the kind of guy who would threaten a girl one minute, then kiss her senseless the next. He was so chivalrous and, well, safe in a dreamboat sort of way. Luke Toliver was a gentleman.

"How long have you known your aunt?" Alice asked.

He laughed as they stepped across the threshold of HQ. "All my life, ma'am."

The twinkle in his hazy, dark eyes reflected her ridiculous question, and the resulting heat of embarrassment made her wish the floor would open up and swallow her. Alice decided to reclaim her dignity by ignoring herself.

That's when she noticed the changes in the blacksmith shop. No longer did cobwebs overwhelm the place. Everything had been swept clean, and a litany of noises filled the air as both men and women patched the holes in the walls and cleaned windows that hadn't been broken. "Lois! Look what you've done with the place. It's amazing!"

Lois stood near a large table covered with maps, designs, and color swatches. She wore trousers and a red plaid Pendleton, and with her hair all waved and pinned, no one would have guessed, a few days ago, she'd been the victim of a frightening attack on this very spot.

"There you are!" Lois gave one more direction to one of the neighbors who wielded a hammer and a length of bunting. "Just tack it up over the broken window for now."

Lois took Alice's hand and reached up to plant a kiss on her cheek. "By next week, this place should be ready to hold our meetings. How's the ankle?"

"Not bad, but I'm still wearing flats for a while," Alice said, pointing to her penny loafers. "Did you meet--"

"Lucien?" Lois tossed a look over Alice's shoulder. "You bet I did. Mrs. Toliver explain it to you?"

"Luke."

"Luke," Alice spoke in tandem with him.

Lois was oblivious.

"About the security? Not really. So, is this where the money from the council is going?"

"Yes." Lois grinned. "Mrs. Toliver and I are keeping it in check, though, don't worry. We've got plenty left for advertisements in the newspaper and signs if the girls help paint them."

"The nieces?" Alice shuddered at the thought of a paintbrush in Lulu Holmes's hand.

"Mrs. Toliver has been working on the block designs," Lois whispered. "I know you wanted to do that part--"

"What part?" Mrs. Toliver's exuberant question was tinged with a bit of defensiveness. "Surely you don't think I'm trying to take over your little project, do you? Why, I'm just trying to make the tour better."

"Of course we know you're trying to help," Lois said. "You have such a good eye for color..." Lois's voice faded into the din of hammering and sawing and cheerful chatter as she drew Mrs. Toliver outside.

"She can be a battleship matron when she gets an idea," Luke said.

"She has been working hard on making the tour a success." Alice bit her lip. No way she was going to voice her concerns to Mrs. Toliver's nephew no matter how irritated she was. "Your aunt's even gone to visit other communities where quilt block tours have been done."

"She's dedicated, I'll give you that." Luke nose wrinkled in an adorable way. "What's this about her taking over your job?"

Alice's face warmed as she led the way outside. "We're all in this together."

"Of course." Luke placed her hand in his. "You're the one with the quilt business. You must know more than the others about designs and so forth."

"Owning a shop doesn't make me an expert." Alice looked up the road to the half dozen buildings in Burning Bush's small business district. Alice's Notions was in the center of it all. "Even if I am able to keep my business from closing."

"Oh, anything I can do to assist you?" He flashed a dimple. "I am in the protection business, you know."

Luke's smooth features under slicked dark brown hair somehow gave Alice hope. "I don't know how you could help. My landlord isn't too keen on this whole tour business. Or women entrepreneurs."

"The man must be blind if he didn't notice your gender when he rented the place to you."

Alice giggled.

"There must be another reason he's reconsidered," Luke said.

"I signed the papers before I hurt my ankle and picked up a roommate."

"I see. Roommate?"

"I signed up to sponsor a refugee," Alice said. "With Joe, my husband, gone, I wanted to help someone else recover from the war. Maybe I just wanted some company. Greta is staying with me until she gets on her feet."

"Aunt Gwynnie told me about your husband. I'm sorry for your loss."

"Me, too."

"Greta? So she's your servant girl?"

Alice wrinkled her nose. "No. I already told you, Greta is not a servant. She's a refugee."

"I don't mean to offend, but I understand she's from Germany."

"Well, yes."

"I can understand your landlord's concerns. It's hard to forget what the Nazis did during the war, and there's no way to know if she wasn't a part of the atrocities that happened."

Alice studied the patch of dandelions near her toe. "I felt the same way, until I got to know her."

"There you are!" Mrs. Toliver sang, as she came around the building, trailing Lois and the ginghamed girls. "Lucien, you simply must return Mrs. Br--I mean,

Miss Alice, to her shop. Better yet, take her out to lunch first. Right, Alice? We'll stay and help Lois. The girls' hems can wait another hour. Tootleoo." She waved her hands at them and dashed back inside the shop.

Lois winked and nodded her head, giving permission.

Turning her head away from Luke, Alice grimaced on her way to Mr. Toliver's car. Having lunch with Luke was appealing, but Mrs. Toliver's interference somehow made her feel like a charity case.

As Luke opened the door for her, Alice said, "There's no need to do anything but drive me back to the shop. I'll have lunch with Greta. She'll be wondering where I am."

He slammed the door, rounded the car, and sat beside her. "It's up to you, but I was looking forward to a luncheon engagement with such a beautiful and talented woman." He started the car, and faced her with raised brows. "Are you worried I might not be the trustworthy sort? I could give you references to vouch for me?"

What could it hurt?

"I know we just met, but I am in the security business, you know. If you'll accompany me, I promise to be a perfect gentleman."

Alice glanced toward the shop. Mrs. Toliver was standing by the door and had the oddest smile of satisfaction on her face as she stared at them.

Chapter Fourteen

Alice and Luke sat in the booth in the back of Daria's Diner facing away from the jukebox, the one where she and Joe always sat on their dates. Hopefully nobody would see them there. She didn't want Rick keeping tabs on who she ate lunch with.

Any hope to remain invisible disappeared when Sheriff Jenner strode back to the jukebox. He slipped in his nickel and chose *Laura*, the theme song of one of Alice's favorite movies with Dana Andrews, the actor Luke resembled.

Sheriff Jenner nodded. "Mrs. Brighton. I don't think I've met your escort."

Alice didn't bother to respond.

Luke extended his hand and smiled. "Lucien Wendell Holmes. Gwendolyn Toliver's nephew, but please call me Luke. Always happy to make the acquaintance of a lawman."

Jenner shook Luke's hand. "Another Toliver, huh." He pointed his thumb at his chest. "Sheriff Jenner. I hope you're not here for this quilt tour nonsense."

Luke shrugged. "Guilty as charged. I'm in security. My aunt asked me to ensure the safety of the tourists during the festivities. I'd like to schedule a meeting with you later this week to discuss the particulars, so I'm sure we'll meet again."

The muscle in Sheriff Jenner's jaw twitched. "I'm sure we will. You look awfully comfortable there with Rick Morrison's renter." As if to show his authority, or lack of manners, he turned and made his way to the counter without another word.

Heat rose to the back of her neck. Not only did the sheriff insult a kind man who'd offered his help, by morning Jenner would spread it all over town, and to Rick Morrison, she had a new beau.

Luke mock-saluted the back of Jenner's head and winked at Alice. She suppressed a giggle.

Daria delivered the hamburgers.

"So tell me more about this landlord of yours. Why is he causing you so much difficulty?" Luke bit into his hamburger.

Alice poured some chocolate shake out of the silver tumbler into her glass. "I can't really say. I don't know why he'd be against the tour when it could help this town so much."

"What does he do for a living?"

"He says he's in real estate, but he doesn't act like it."

Luke lifted an eyebrow.

"He acts more like he's some kind of, oh I don't know, maybe a Fed or something." She grimaced, realizing how silly she sounded.

"You mean like a spy?" He didn't sound condescending like she expected, more interested. "What makes you think so?"

"Oh, I don't know. A couple of things. He says he owns buildings in a bunch of different places, so why would he live someplace like Burning Bush?"

Luke took a sip of pop. "Maybe he likes small town life."

"Maybe." She nibbled on a ketchup-drenched fry. "Then there are all these mysterious trips he takes. He never says where he's going or when he'll be back."

"If he has real estate all over, he would need to travel."

"You're right. I'm being silly." She had a strong compulsion to change the conversation. "I'm surprised you're so much older than your sisters. Why haven't you visited Burning Bush before?"

"I'm the son of my father's first marriage. My mother died when I was six years old."

"Oh, I'm sorry." Alice placed her hand on his.

"I hardly remember her." Luke rubbed his hand over his chin. "The reason I never came to Burning Bush with my sisters before now was because... well... my father sent me to an exclusive boarding school when I was young, sort of like a military academy. After high school, I was trained at a military facility. Then the war broke out, and the rest is history as they say."

"What did you do in the war?" She took a bite of her hamburger.

"Security for a secret project, but I can't really talk about it. I shouldn't have said that much, but you're so easy to talk to. Please forgive me."

"There's nothing to forgive," Alice said.

There was a lull in the conversation while they polished off their hamburgers.

Luke wiped his mouth with his napkin. "There has to be more."

"What do you mean?"

"About your landlord. Alice, you're a classy lady from the ground up. I've only just met you, but you don't seem like the type to make baseless accusations."

"Maybe." She wasn't ready to tell him how Rick put her brother in a chokehold in two seconds flat or how he gave her roommate the third degree about her hat.

"Okay," Luke said. "If you don't want to talk about it, we'll drop it for now."

"Your aunt said you work security. Who for?"

His dimple deepened. "I'm in charge of security for a plant outside of Charleston. I took a leave of absence for a couple of months until the quilt tour is over."

She sipped her shake. "Which plant?"

"What's the biggest one over there?"

"DuPont." Her eyes widened. "DuPont manufactures products for the war department."

He shrugged. "The war's over, but DuPont produces a lot of products including the nylon for your hosiery."

"You must have some kind of security clearance to work there."

Luke laid a tip on the table and offered her his arm. "Let's just say I'm qualified to handle security for your quilt tour."

After paying the bill, he escorted her back to the shop. "I've been thinking about what you said about Rick Morrison."

The hair on the back of her neck prickled. "Yes."

"I have a couple associates from the war who work for the FBI. If you want, I can make some inquiries."

"I don't know." She didn't like the idea of spying on her landlord, but most landlords weren't as mysterious as Rick. "I suppose it wouldn't hurt."

*****

Luke held the door open for Alice as they entered the shop. Rick and Greta stood whispering in low tones by the thread counter, sharing military secrets by the looks of it.

Greta loped to Alice and hugged her. "I was so worried about you. What happened?"

Alice blushed. "I'm sorry, Greta. I should have written you a note. When Mrs. Toliver stopped by to pick up the girls, she wanted me to see what Lois had done with the blacksmith shop."

"*Ja*, I should have known it was something like that."

Rick's jaw clenched. "I stopped by to invite you to lunch." He kept his eyes fixed on Luke while addressing her. "Have you eaten?"

Louis Bellson from the Benny Goodwin Orchestra was doing a drum solo inside Alice's stomach. "Yes, Luke was kind enough to buy me lunch."

Rick's eyebrow rose slightly. "Luke?"

Luke extended his hand. "Lucien Wendell Holmes. My friends call me Luke." When Rick made no move to shake his hand, Luke rubbed it across the back of his neck and delivered a grin, more like a self-satisfied smirk. "My aunt requested my assistance with security for the quilt tour."

"Your aunt?"

"Gwendolyn Toliver."

"I see, Lucien." Rick slurred the name out to make it sound almost like a curse word.

Alice glanced from Rick to Luke, then back to Rick until Luke broke the dueling eye lock by kissing the back of Alice's hand. "I better get back to my aunt before she sends Sheriff Jenner to fetch me. Thank you for the luncheon date, Alice. We'll talk again soon."

"Thank you for a lovely lunch," Alice said.

Luke made his exit. Rick stared at the door as if it was in danger of jumping off its hinges and attacking them.

"So, what did you want?" Alice asked.

"What?" Rick said. The spell had been broken.

Alice crossed her arms and braced herself. "You must have come here for a reason." What would she do if he decided to revoke the lease?

Rick turned to Greta. "Would you mind if I talk to Alice alone?"

Greta nodded. "I have some boxes to unpack in the back." She closed the door to the storeroom behind her.

Alice swallowed and prepared for his onslaught.

He wiped his face with his hand. "Alice, I'm sorry. I shouldn't have threatened you. I'm still not keen on the quilt tour, but I was out of line."

The last thing she expected from him was an apology. Alice grabbed hold of a bolt of material lying on the counter and placed it on the shelf to keep him from noticing the surprise on her face. "Why don't you want us to have a tour?" She turned to face him. "Maybe if you could tell me why, I'd understand."

The *trust me* look crossed his face again. "I can't discuss why. If you would just believe I have this town's best interests at heart, as well as yours, I'll explain when I can."

A prickling traveled up her spine. "So I should just take you on faith. Why? Do you think all you have to do to convince me is force a kiss on me? I'm not that easy a sell."

Rick lowered his eyes. "I didn't kiss you to change your mind. I do care about you, but it has nothing to do with this."

She turned back to the material and blinked to keep her eyes from watering. "Maybe you'd better leave."

Chapter Fifteen

"I call to order the first meeting of the Burning Bush Community Barn Quilt Tour. Mrs. Morgan, you'll make note of the name change, along with the new place, on Friday, May thirty-one, year of our Lord 1946, in our new official headquarters," Gwendolyn Toliver intoned with all the personality of a salami. "All rise for the Pledge of Allegiance. Place your right hands over your hearts. Gentlemen, remove your hats."

The gentleman in question, Luke, winked at Alice as he put his hand over his heart and faced the flag pinned to the east wall of the smithy. He'd not worn his fedora indoors, naturally, as good mannered as he was. Alice had better watch herself before she became smitten.

"Mrs. Morgan, you will please read the minutes of the last meeting," Mrs. Toliver said.

Alice put up her hand to guard her mouth and whispered to Luke, "What's up with your aunt? She seems a little out of sorts."

"Poor dear's tired. She's been traveling a lot. Research," he whispered out of the side of his mouth, his cherubic expression never leaving his aunt's face. Alice received the brunt of Mrs. Toliver's glare.

"Yes, Mrs. Brighton? You have something to share? Some new information, perhaps?"

Alice slunk a few inches, feeling like she was back in high school history class. "I'll wait my turn."

"Very good."

Alice wasn't the only one who jumped when the gavel came down. At least this time she was using it on the anvil and not Alice's counter. The reports were next. Mrs. Round had managed to make contact with the band leaders of the local communities as well as the fire departments from Montgomery, Oak Hill, and Kingston who were always happy to drive their trucks in a parade.

"The mayor," Mrs. Round nodded at Mrs. Wilson, "will lead the parade, followed by the Holmes girls on their bicycles--"

"Blowing their horns," Luke whispered.

Alice stifled a giggle, earning another black look.

"The Burning Bush Men's Quartet will provide a lunch time program," Mrs. Round said. "We plan to put up some picnic tables by the river, as I have discussed with the chairman of the Refreshments Committee, Mrs. Gorman." She nodded and smoothed her skirt to sit, but then stood straight again. "I want to thank Mrs. Lance for joining my committee."

"Very good," Mrs. Toliver said. "Mrs. Gorman, have you contacted the high school about donating the use of the tables and chairs?"

Bernice pressed her lips together and stilled her knitting needles. "Am I next?"

Mrs. Toliver rapped. "Yes, you may report."

As Bernice informed about the tables and chairs and who would be supplying cakes and pies for the bake sale, Mrs. Toliver leaned forward against the great anvil serving as her table. She used her left hand for the gavel. Before today, she'd written her notes with her right hand. Alice was certain of it. Mrs. Toliver hadn't removed her gloves today, soft yellow ones creeping past her prominent wrist bones.

"Next, Security! Mr. Holmes, are you prepared to report at this time?"

Alice yanked back to attention as Luke rose. "Good afternoon, ladies. Thank you for allowing me to be part of your tour committee." He swiveled in a circle to cast a charming smile at each lady present. "So far, Aunt, uh, I mean, Chairwoman Toliver," a few chuckles echoed in the little room, "I am currently engaged in driving all the roads in this lovely community, paying particular interest to traffic patterns and times of day when vehicles are using the roads, and the general condition and safety of said roads. I may need the aid of someone who was born and raised in the area to be my guide." He rocked back on his heels and shared his smile with Alice. "That's all for now."

Were there really a couple of "aw"s? Alice rolled her eyes though she smiled back when he met her glance as he sat. Her sister-in-law sat with her pen poised over her pad, dreamy, eyelashes fluttering.

Condition and safety of the roads? Brow furrowed, Alice was in the act of facing him when the rapping of the gavel called her notice forward. "Final report. Mrs. Brighton."

Alice pursed her lips and rose. "Thank you, Madam Chairwoman. Since you still have my file, I tried to recreate my notes for as many as fifteen stops--"

"We won't need that many," Mrs. Toliver said.

Alice forced her jaw to relax. "The more the merrier. Anyway, I'm not turning down--"

"How many barns are there in Burning Bush?" Mrs. Toliver asked, sugar-sweet.

"As far as I know, only two actually downtown."

Lois tittered.

"Of course the tour will encompass our beautiful community, as you so aptly stated in renaming the committee, Madam Chair--"

"Security demands we have no more than eight stops, Mrs. Brighton. It simply won't do to have more. We would be unable to control the traffic." Chairwoman Toliver pounded the gavel. "I suggest you discuss the matter outside of the main meeting. Now, if there are no further--"

"Mrs. Toliver!" Alice called out. "I thought the function of a barn quilt tour was to get out and about and see the barns of our community. Visitors would return to--"

"See here, Mrs. Brighton. You are out of order, according to..." She held up a little green and white striped book, *Mr. Robert's Rules of Order*, and scanned the room. "I will now ask for a motion to adjourn." She nodded at Mrs. Jenner, practically pulling the words from the woman.

"I move we adjourn."

"Is there a second?"

Silence covered the room and Mrs. Toliver glared at each woman.

"Fine, I'll second," Mrs. Wilson said.

"All in favor say aye." She rapped the gavel before anyone could answer. "Motion is carried. Mrs. Morgan, please note the time in the minutes. Good day, all. Thank you for coming." The last phrase faded as she clutched her pocketbook to her right side and winced, white-faced, and marched out.

Alice stared at the door with her mouth open. "What's the matter, Luke? Your aunt looks out of sorts."

Luke clutched her shoulders and gave them a squeeze. "Aw, swell of you to be so concerned, but she's fine. Tired, like I said. No need to worry."

Lois approached them with a puzzled look.

Luke beamed at Lois. "Say, why don't you tell me about Burning Bush where you grew up?"

"I didn't grow up here, Alice did," Lois said.

He took both of their arms and led them outside. "Well, you live up there on the hill on Mockingbird Road, don't you? I'd be honored if you two charming ladies would be my guides."

Lois giggled. "I don't know. I'm married, you know."

Luke splayed his hand across his chest. "I meant nothing improper, Mrs. Morgan." Charm dripped from his smile. "Although your husband is a very fortunate man. I only thought you might act as a chaperone and provide me with much needed information about your mountain."

"I suppose it would be all right." Lois turned as red as her lipstick.

Alice stepped in front of her to break the spell. "I believe my sister-in-law needs to get home, and I must get back and open the store."

His warm smoky eyes looked almost apologetic. "Maybe another time." He offered to walk Alice back to the shop, but she declined.

As much as she enjoyed his company, she needed time to sort out all the details of the quilt tour meeting and figure out Mrs. Toliver's strange behavior. Something wasn't as it seemed.

She opened the shop door, and as the bell above it rang, Deputy Eddie and Greta backed away from each other. If the guilty looks on their faces were any indication, they'd been conspiring to overthrow the government.

"Thank you for stopping by, Deputy Tyler." Greta started arranging the bolts of material. "I will see you soon."

"Yes, of course." Eddie glanced around like he was trying to figure out what to do next. "Well, see you around." He darted out the door.

Mrs. Toliver wasn't the only one acting strange. "Greta," Alice said. "What's going on?"

"I do not know what you mean." Greta moved from the cloth bolts and started arranging the skeins of yarns. "I am minding the store like you asked."

Alice crossed her arms. "You know what I mean. What was Deputy Eddie doing here? Why do you look like you were caught with your hand in the cookie jar?"

"I am not eating cookies." Greta moved to the spools of thread. "Would you like me to bake cookies?"

Alice placed her hand on the thread. "This isn't about cookies, and you know it, sister. What's going on between you and Deputy Eddie? He acts like he knows you."

"Yes, we've met." Greta's face flushed. "He was just stopping by... to visit."

"Why?"

"He is... how you say... being neighborly."

Before Alice could ask another question, Rosemary walked into the store with her basket weaving supplies. Alice twirled a loose curl and wondered how many more mysteries she would have to solve before the day was over?

Chapter Sixteen

"Mrs. Toliver, I thought we had an understanding." Alice stood on one side of the anvil untying her bundles of sampler blocks. Women had shared their favorite patterns this way since the early days of quilting. She had collected a number of them from her mother and her New York City neighbors.

"You've got it all wrong." Mrs. Toliver's usually carefully combed curls today twirled more like crispy grass around the edges of her decade-old cloche hat. "The girls are delivering the patterns this afternoon. We must move along if we're to be ready on time."

Alice drew in a deep breath, searing her lungs. After stalling for weeks, holding up plans, not ordering paint, and not following through on their contacts with the farm families who agreed to be part of the tour, Gwendolyn Toliver rushed to the finish line in a race all by herself. Gee, wonder who would win?

"Grandmother's Flower Garden is a perfect block for the Collins's barn," Alice said through her gritted teeth. "She wants to do that pattern." She held up the block of pieced hexagons, arranged in a burst of colors radiating from a six-sided center scrap of yellow material. "It was the last quilt her dear late aunt sewed, and we chose colors to match her flowers."

Andrea Collins, who lived near the Pete's house on Mockingbird Road, had been Mamie's best friend, not Gwendolyn Toliver. The quilt tour was starting to break through Mrs. Collins' grief over her only son dying in the war, and Alice wasn't about to disappoint her no matter what Chairwoman Toliver said.

"Lucien has already reported the dangers to the sheriff, and I quite agree. You of all people must understand the safety of our dear guests is of utmost importance." Mrs. Toliver flexed her right hand and tugged on her gloves. Red polka dots today. "A palette of tasteful colors will unify the whole tour."

Lulu giggled from outside the window. A car door slammed.

Alice took in a sharp breath through her nose. "Pete already purchased the paint." She softened her tone. "I already gave Andrea Collins the pattern. Her and everyone else on our road." *Since you never did anything about it.* "Colors should draw the eye. It's important to make each block unique."

The chairwoman shook her head hard enough to shift her hat.

"Mrs. Toliver, won't you tell me what's going on?" Her breath hitched at the sight her puffy, purplish ear. "What happened to your ear?"

Mrs. Toliver yanked the hat down again and leaned over their impromptu desk. "Bee sting. Don't change the subject. We had an understanding." Her words slurred through bared teeth.

"Well, it wasn't with me."

"Hear, hear." A muscular shadow filled the doorway of Quilt Tour HQ. "What's all this gibber-gabber from my two favorite gals?"

"Luke!" Alice straightened, wondering whose side he would take.

He walked over to his aunt and put his arm around her shoulders, an affable grin planted on his handsome face. His dark gray eyes sparkled with something more than laughter. Of course he'd choose family.

Alice sighed and put a hand to her hair, adjusting a bobby pin to make sure it was straight. Why hadn't he told her about his safety concerns? Especially since it was her family's road?

He whispered in his aunt's ear, and whatever he said made an immediate difference. Mrs. Toliver's alarming red cheek color began to fade, and she nodded several times.

"All right, then, Auntie?" he finally said. "You go on, then. I'll take care of things here."

With one last acid look at Alice, Mrs. Toliver slumped out of the building.

Luke rubbed his hands together. "Put me to work."

"Wait just a minute. What going on? Why did you not report any concerns to the last meeting?"

His impossibly cute dimple deepened, making him even more charming. "Let's just say I saved us both from a rapidly escalating danger. Now, where were we on the parking situation?"

Alice moved both her hands to her hips. "There's something fishy going on, and I want to know what it is."

"Don't worry so much." Luke took her hands in his. "I promise everybody's going to profit from this." With a squeeze of her hands, he turned and pulled her back to her desk. "Show me the route again."

Alice pulled her chilled fingers from his. "I don't like secrets. Half the committee is made up of people who live along Mockingbird Road. They drive it every day, and it's perfectly safe. If what you said to your aunt affects our tour, I have a right to know."

"I'm telling you to trust me. The road is safe for you, maybe. Everything's under control. I can handle my aunt, and your landlord."

Taken aback, she narrowed her eyes. "What do you mean? Handle Rick?"

He glanced left and right, then leaned close. "Come out with me, and I'll tell you."

She fought the desire to step back when his breath tickled her ear. "Come out? Now?"

He chuckled and stepped back. "Tomorrow night. I'm asking for the pleasure of your company to see a special combo band coming into the Montgomery on tour. We can get some dinner, maybe dance." His dimple was back. "I hope I'm not being too forward, but ever since our lunch together, I've been trying to find a way to ask you out for a date."

She shook her head a bit, dazed. "Uh... I don't..."

"You're a special woman, Alice. Give me a chance to show you how special." His grin never slipped. "I'll be at your place at eight o'clock."

"I suppose it would be all right."

He leaned closer. She didn't pull away.

Lois rushed inside, waving a newspaper clutched in her gloved hand.

Alice's face warmed, and she stepped back.

"Look! We made the front page." Lois thrust the page in front of her. "Hiya, Luke," she tossed his way.

"I'll check in with the committee later," Luke said. "Officially, that is." He fit his gray fedora at a rakish angle over his brow and bowed slightly. "Ladies." He strolled out the door.

Lois giggled. "What a dreamboat."

"Lois!"

"I know, I know. I'd never do another thing to hurt Pete. I just think the two of you would make a good pair." She started humming under her breath.

Joe had hummed in Alice's ear as they danced on the balcony of their New York apartment. She shook the memory away.

"You both have such beautiful hair," Lois said.

"Lois!"

"Hey, it's not a crime." Lois laughed. "So, anyway, take a gander." She pulled off her pink gloves and pointed at the bottom corner of the front page.

Alice squinted. "Where?"

"Down there. See? We got our ad all the way over in Charleston." Lois' grin was infectious. "They were going to charge us extra for the front page, but Mr. Toliver knew the op ed guy." She folded the Charleston Gazette, rubbed her fingers along the creased folds, and set it on the table. "Who's op ed? Is it someone I'm supposed to know?"

Alice giggled. "Oh, Lois."

Lois's cheeks turned a pretty shade of pink, almost matching her silk head wrap.

For the first time since she'd entered, Alice took a good look at her sister-in-law. She wore gray pants, a pink cotton plaid shirt, and black penny loafers. "What's with the trousers? This is the second time I've seen you in them."

Lois pinked up again. "They're all the rage since Katherine Hepburn started wearing them." She wrinkled her nose. "Pete agreed with me. It's not like we're back at the shipyard, wearing those coveralls." Lois looked down the length of the narrow gray legs. "Maybe if I was more comfortable, I'd get used to the farm."

"Uh-huh." Alice could just picture the look on her brother's face. "As long as we continue to do our patriotic duty and not let those hosiery plants go out of business."

"Mr. Toliver was boring me to death with facts and figures." Lois lowered her voice and stuck out her gut. "The Gazette is the way to go. Not the Montgomery Herald. Did you know there are five -- count 'em, five -- hosiery plants in Charleston? All silk. Employs three thousand people."

Alice chuckled. "Now there's something we could use here in Burning Bush."

"Three thousand factory workers?" Lois smacked the paper on the anvil. "If they can't handle guests for a barn quilt tour, there's no way they'd allow a whole factory to be built here. The DuPont plant in Belle is close enough. Let's quit talking about this boring stuff and get down to business. How'd Mrs. Toliver take the news?"

Alice bit her lip. The war may be over, but there were still too many little fights going on. Lois was going to be so disappointed. "Something else came up. Mrs. Toliver..." she made a point to emphasize, "somehow decided the tour route we'd all agreed on at the last meeting was all wrong. She said it was too dangerous to drive Mockingbird Road up the mountain and took it off the map."

Lois blanched. "That's our road. Pete came home with paint and supplies last night."

"She said it was too far away--"

"It's not!"

"I know. Luke came in while we were discussing the matter. He said something to her, and she took off, so we didn't get to finish the conversation. He said not to worry, but I don't know what he means."

"All the work we've done." Crystal droplets rolled down Lois's cheeks. "We're on a real road. It's not fair. She can't keep us out, can she?"

"I'm not sure what's going on, but if I'd just seen the White Rabbit, I'd say things were getting curiouser and curiouser."

Lois sniffed. "It's not curious. It's just mean. What am I supposed to do now? Pete's already unglued over this outfit," she stuck a pant leg out and waved at it. "I can't tell him we've wasted even more money."

"Not to mention our neighbors." Alice handed Lois her handkerchief. "Mrs. Collins was so looking forward to the tour. It's the first time I've seen her smile since... well, since her son died. You know how she loves quilts."

Lois wiped her eyes and looked around the empty room, whizzing past the maps tacked to the walls, color swatches, and rolled patriotic bunting. "I seem to be missing people. Like my committee to work on the brochure. The meeting was supposed to have started ten minutes ago."

Alice sighed. Dust motes swirled in the rays of light beaming through sparkling clean windows. She and Greta had spruced up the peeling sills and lost glazing the other night. If nothing else, this little shack might be a rental deal for Rella Jones.

"Am I late? Of course I am. I'm so sorry," Mrs. Jenner sang out as she rushed through the door, pulled off her chiffon scarf, and scurried around. She set her purse down, picked up some papers on the anvil, studied them, and set them back down.

Lois stared with her mouth open while Alice collected her wits. "Uh, yes, hello. I... we... weren't sure if anyone was going to come, what with the tour being changed and the girls out delivering the patterns and stops. Did you want to change committees? Lois is on publicity, you know."

Mrs. Jenner kept shuffling through the papers on the anvil.

"Can I help you find something?" Alice turned to her sister-in-law and made slashing motions across her mouth, hoping to pull Lois out of her daze.

"What?" The sheriff's wife peered at her. "Oh, I was just looking for something to do." She straightened and put on a strained, overly bright smile.

If a white rabbit hopped in, checked its pocket watch, and pulled a fish out of its hat, Alice wasn't sure she'd be alarmed. She would have even welcomed Rick Morrison if he could explain why everyone in Burning Bush was off their collective rockers.

With a questioning look, Lois took Mrs. Jenner's arm and led her away from the table, toward the door. "The publicity meeting is canceled for today, Mrs. Jenner. The regular committee meeting is tomorrow. You should come back then."

"I...told... er, was told--"

"Come back tomorrow," Lois said in her soothing voice. "Things are a bit of a mess, and Alice and I have to... have to..."

Alice stepped up and took the woman's other arm. "We have to drive the route again. For Mrs. Toliver. To check on... on..."

"The length," Lois supplied. "Mileage. You know, for the map we're going to have printed."

"Right," Alice said. "For the map."

By now they were out on the road and directing Mrs. Jenner toward her house by the river.

"Bye," Alice said.

"Yes, bye now, Mrs. Jenner. Thanks for dropping in."

The girls turned toward each other. Alice clutched her sister-in-law's elbows. "What do you suppose that was all about?"

"I bet her husband sent her to spy on us." Lois checked the area around the shack then followed Alice back inside. "From what I heard, he bullies her into doing what he wants. Bernice says he hits her sometimes where it doesn't show. Poor dear."

"You shouldn't be spreading rumors. You don't know if it's true." Even as she chided her sister-in-law, she couldn't help thinking the stories sounded valid. Mrs. Jenner did act brow beaten, like an abused housewife. "Besides, it's none of our business."

"I guess not. I still feel sorry for her. Pete and I have our problems, but he would never hurt me."

Alice tried to dismiss the anger stirring toward Sheriff Jenner by reorganizing the shuffled pages back into their respective stacks. Blocks and colors and paint samples in one pile; refreshment committee lists in another, and separate piles for entertainment and publicity.

She held the page with the proposed route stops in her hand, studying it. There was no way to make all the barns in their area line up into a neat one-way parade route. Some backtracking was necessary.

True, there were only three roads in Burning Bush, and not all the farmers' barns could have a quilt block painted on it. A few of the old-timers and bachelors hadn't wanted anything to do with the tour. Of the twelve sites, well, now eight if Gwendolyn Toliver got her way, four were on her parents' road.

"Alice, what should I do with these?" Lois held up the sample quilt blocks for their road.

"Nothing for now." Alice grabbed her purse. "Let's check out the route again, like we said. I've got a hunch about something."

*****

The following morning, at the next meeting of the Burning Bush Barn Quilt Tour committee, Alice and Lois were prepared for a battle as fierce as Iwo Jima.

"So you see, Mrs. Toliver," Alice said, pointing to her enlarged copy of the routes and quilt block patterns at each stop, "if you take away the blocks on Mockingbird Road, the tour will not only miss a valuable legacy of quilters in our community, the route will be lopsided and too short. No one will want to buy a program or stick around for the picnic or bother to come back."

Gwendolyn's mouth stayed pruned.

"The merchants will be unhappy if no one visits them," Janice said. Her husband worked part time at the grocers, besides running their farm. With the baby on the way, they needed extra income. "Since our farm is at the base of the hill, we could give directions, as well as sell cold drinks and such."

"Drivers only have to turn at the Morgan's. It's all been worked out for weeks." Alice was not about to get down on her knees and beg, no matter what, but she started to see red. Andrea Collins had already started painting her block, and Pete and the Gormans had also spent time and money on this project.

"The sheriff has put his foot down," Mrs. Jenner declared. She'd arrived on the heels of Gwendolyn Toliver, and until now, hadn't uttered a word. "He says we can't have so many stops. Besides, your road is too dangerous." Mrs. Jenner straightened her little pudding figure and looked Alice right in the eye. "You know what happened out there when your parents drove off the road. You don't want the same thing to happen to anybody else, do you? I'm surprised at you, Mrs. Brighton, I am. You don't seem to care about--"

"Enough, Mrs. Jenner!" Lois stood. "Alice does too care about... about everything, and every one!"

Alice blanched. "Lois, thank you," she managed to rasp out.

The eight ladies, eight and one-half with Janice, sat on wooden folding chairs borrowed from church. Bernice had given her report already and wasn't having near this amount of trouble. She'd convinced half the town to bake cookies, cupcakes, or pies. Mrs. Collins, who agreed to make ten apple pies, even offered to make sweet tea and coffee for everyone.

Bernice's knitting needles stilled. "I thought this was all worked out. Eight stops aren't nearly enough."

"We did have it worked out," Alice said.

"You might have thought so." Mrs. Toliver unlocked her lips long enough to growl. "Henry says it's impossible. Sheriff Jenner agrees. If anyone else is hurt on that road, we could be responsible."

"Pete, and Jeff, and the others drive it nearly every day," Lois said. "They've never so much as hit a bush."

Alice blew out her frustration and plastered the sweetest smile she could manage on her face. "Won't the extra security ensure safety? Surely Luke can handle finding a way to make it safe."

"Lucien agrees with me."

Alice let out a groan. Later tonight, when she and Luke were having supper, she would get him to see her side. After all, he wasn't from around here. He didn't know the whole situation.

"Oh, dear." Mrs. Round said. "We're at a stalemate? Perhaps Pastor Round could come in and say a few words."

Alice's eyebrows rose of their own accord. Janice Felton held her great stomach.

"Are you all right?" Alice rushed to her Janice's side, grateful for the diversion.

A wink from Janice. "No, we're all right, we're fine, thank you. No need to call anyone."

Alice nodded and gave her a pat on her arm. "Let's adjourn for now. There may be another solution. They already installed a guard rail where my folks, where the accident happened. Perhaps we can put up a warning sign at the most dangerous places." She was willing to do anything to include her friends and family on this tour. They deserved it.

The women departed in groups of twos and threes. The unlikely duo of Mrs. Toliver and Mrs. Jenner whispered at each other on the way out the door.

"I have to run along, too," Lois said. "Pete's taking me to the club in Montgomery." She looked worried for an instant. "I'd ask you to join us, but it's sort of a date." She giggled. "Even though we're married. We never got a chance to have much fun."

"Sure, sure, you two kids have a swell time. Don't worry about me." Wouldn't Lois be surprised to see her and Luke later?

After tidying up the chairs and the reports, Alice locked the door. Jiggling the keys, she turned to leave and smacked right into the hard chest of... she looked up the skinny black tie to... Rick Morrison's chiseled handsomeness.

Their mutual apologies over, Rick took her breath away again.

"So, I hear the club has a special tonight. Some combo outta the big city. S'posed to be top notch. If you're up to it, how about taking me dancing tonight?"

Alice barely got her wits in order and had not had time to frame a reply, let alone open her mouth, when a car door slammed and whistling interrupted her.

"I thought you could use a ride," Luke Holmes said, giving Rick an unenthusiastic appraisal. "My aunt said the meeting was over."

Chapter Seventeen

Alice gulped.

Rick stepped in front of her like a caveman defending his territory. "She's already got a ride, Lucien."

Luke's characteristic grin slipped. "You?"

Rick's shoulders squared. "Yeah, me. So maybe you ought to mosey on along and do whatever it is you do."

Alice stepped out from behind Rick and blew bangs out of her eyes. "Wait just a cotton pickin' minute. I didn't say I'd accept a ride from either one of you."

Both men puffed up their chests and circled each other.

"Alice," Rick said without taking his eyes off Luke. "Who would you like to give you a ride, me or this fat-head?"

"Alice." Luke took a step toward her. "Do you want this ill-mannered oaf to drive you home or the man you have a date with tonight?"

Rick's face fell. "Tonight?"

Luke's grin reappeared. "I'm escorting her to that new dance club in Montgomery. The Charlie Spivak Band's playing, tonight only."

It was the first time she could remember Rick looking so unsure of himself. "Luke." She had an overwhelming desire to help him save face. "Rick offered to take me home before you got here, so I'll ride with him."

Luke's lips pressed together. "As you wish. I'll be there at eight." He kissed her on the cheek and headed toward his automobile, a brand new shiny black Cadillac. The door slammed as he got in and zoomed away.

She never thought of it before, but Luke's job at DuPont had to pay a lot. His Cadillac cost twice as much as Rick's Fleetmaster, not to mention his expensive double-breasted Esquire suits and silk ties. Lois was right. Luke was a sheik.

Rick cleared his throat and offered his arm. "Shall we?"

She looped her arm through his and strolled to his car.

He didn't say anything on the way back to the shop, which only made her feel worse. She'd rarely seen Rick at a loss for words. His pensive stare reminded her of Joe when he was trying to work something out in his mind. When her late husband had been in one of those moods, it would sometimes be hours before he'd talk again.

They pulled up to the curb beside the shop, but he didn't make any move to get out of the car. "Alice." He kept a tight grip on the steering wheel. "I'm sorry about... well about the kiss and about asking you out. All you had to do is say you were seeing someone, and I would have backed off. Why can't you dames ever be honest?"

"I'm not seeing Luke."

"Yeah, sure you're not."

"Rick, look at me."

He turned toward her. His stony expression didn't cover the hurt look in his eyes.

"This is our first date, and it's none of your business if I go dancing with another man. You're my landlord. It's not like we're engaged or anything."

He flinched.

She placed her hand on his arm. "Why are you acting like this?"

He tilted his chin. "I know I'm being a jerk. You're free to do whatever you want. It's just--"

"What?"

"I was engaged once. I really carried the torch for that dame."

"What happened?"

"She ran off with some 4-F clown while I was off fighting for our country." Rick shrugged. "She wrote me a Dear John letter six months after I shipped out."

How could she stay annoyed after hearing the heartbreak in his voice? "I'm sorry for what happened to you, but what does it have to do with me going on one date with Luke?"

"Nothing at all." Rick snorted. "It's just Joe asked me to look out for you, and I don't like Holmes. He's a punk."

"Just how well did you know my husband, and why didn't he ever talk about you in his letters?"

His face turned as red as the apple she had for lunch. He got out of the car and opened the door on her side.

She crossed her arms. "I'm not moving one step from this car until I get some answers. I swear you act more mysterious than Humphrey Bogart in *Casablanca*."

His shoulders slumped. "Please, Alice, there're some things I can't tell you." She didn't budge.

"I'll make a deal with you." He delivered a lopsided grin, causing her heart to beat faster no matter how much the man annoyed her. "Come to supper with me, tomorrow night. We'll go see the new Lana Turner movie playing in Montgomery."

He did know how to tempt her. "What makes you think I want to go out with you no matter how much I want to see *The Postman Always Rings Twice*?"

Rick let out a sigh. "Because if you do, I'll tell you how I know Joe."

Alice raised her eyebrows. "Fine." She got out of the car and made a beeline to the store.

He followed close behind and opened the door for her. "I'll pick you up at five tomorrow."

"If you don't spill your guts, it'll be the last date we ever have."

He nodded, a strange look on his face, a little like a lost puppy.

A warm glow went through her. She hadn't felt this way in a long time, and she would have done anything to squelch her attraction to Rick. Luke was a perfect gentleman and too handsome for his own good, but he didn't make her heart beat faster like Rick did when he kissed her, or now. She cleared her throat. "If you come inside for a minute, I'll get you the rent payment."

"You can wait. I mean if you don't have enough to pay me now."

Alice chuckled. "I have enough. Despite opinions to the contrary, this quilt tour has been good for the shop and the town." He followed her inside.

The place was empty except for Greta who was sitting at the sales counter writing a letter, but it was always quiet this time of day. Greta looked up. "How did the meeting go?"

"Horrible." Alice rubbed her temples. "Mrs. Toliver's trying to change the route. She wants to remove Mockingbird Road, and Sheriff Jenner says we can't have the tour unless we do. Not only does it cut out Pete and Lois, three other families with avid quilters won't be included. At this rate, the only stops will be in the holler."

Greta hurried to Alice's side and gave her a hug. "I am so sorry. Did you tell her why it would not work?"

"Yes." Alice blew out a sigh of frustration. "She's not listening."

Rick stepped to the counter and leaned against it. "Did she say why she wanted to change the route?"

"She mentioned my folks' accident and said the road's too dangerous. It doesn't make sense. They died during a snowstorm, and guardrails have been put in place since."

"That's odd," Rick said. "It's not like you can drive anywhere in West Virginia without going up at least one mountain."

"The money is in my office." Alice led Rick and Greta to the back of the storeroom, opened the cash box under her desk, and handed him the envelope with the rent payment.

"I made supper," Greta said. "Herr Morrison, would you like to stay? There's enough for three."

Alice turned to him and shook his hand. "Thank you for driving me home." She had enough of Rick and his Dick Tracy spy codes for one day. "I need to get ready for my date. You understand."

He nodded, a look of disappointment crossing his features. "Thank you, anyway, Greta. I'll take a rain check. You sure hit the spot in this bachelor's stomach. Food from you... your cooking..." Wrinkles drew his eyebrows together. He turned away and thumped out of the office.

"Rain?" Greta said. "It's not raining. I do not understand this. He wants to come next time it rains?"

Alice followed Greta up the stairs into the apartment as she explained the idiom. She got halfway up the staircase and stopped. "You go on, Greta. I forgot to lock up."

She turned the corner from the staircase. Rick stood at the counter with his back turned to her, reading Greta's letter. She pulled back until he finished and walked out the door. When the car door closed, she came out of her hiding spot, locked the front door, and pulled the shade.

Her heart pounded. She picked up the letter and read it. It was written in English and was to Greta's mother. Most of it sounded innocent enough, but a couple of lines troubled her.

> *I found Flight Officer Eddie Tyler here and made contact. He's promised to not tell anyone we know each other or how. I believe I can trust him. They don't know who I am yet. If I'm discovered, all will be lost.*

Maybe the feather Rick found did come from Greta's hat. She had become Alice's closet friend next to Lois, but Greta was German. Maybe she was involved in all this intrigue.

*****

Alice didn't say much as she sat at the table with Greta and ate the knodels her roommate was so good at making. Maybe if she came right out and confessed she'd read the letter, Greta would confide in her. Then she'd have to admit she was a snoop.

"You said you have a date," Greta said. "If it is not with Herr Morrison, is it with Herr Holmes?"

Alice took a sip of pop. "He's taking me to a dance club in Montgomery. Charlie Spivik and his band are playing there."

"Oh." Greta started clearing the dishes. "I am surprised Herr Morrison did not ask you."

"He did. Luke asked me first, so I'm going with him."

"He is beautiful."

Alice chuckled. "Men aren't beautiful. They're handsome, but you're right. Luke Holmes is a real sheik."

Greta's eyes widened. "You have sheiks in the United States?"

"No... no. It means he's really handsome, more than most men."

"More than Herr Morrison?"

Alice carried her plate to the sink. "Kind of. I don't know."

Greta raised an eyebrow. "If you like Herr Morrison, why do you let Herr Holmes court you?"

"Because he's not like Joe."

"Your husband?"

Alice nodded and grabbed the dishtowel off the hook. "I already had the romance of a lifetime. All I've ever desired was to be Joe's wife and mother to his children. I can't go through that again. My feelings for Luke aren't the same. He's nice to look at, and I enjoy his company, but he's polite and safe, like Burning Bush. He doesn't cause my heart to race. Rick is more like New York City, excitement, confusion, and a hint of danger around every corner. For the record, I don't like Rick Morrison all that much."

Greta sprinkled dish soap into the sink. "Staying away from danger is not always the way to be safe. You cannot always sweep under the floor. *Ja*?"

"Under the rug." Alice dried a plate. "All I want is to run this quilt shop, and get the tour going. If I stay away from romance, I'll keep my heart protected." Maybe Greta had done some things to stay safe. Maybe that's what the letter meant.

She glanced at the clock. "Oh, no. I didn't realize it was so late. Greta, could you finish up here?"

Greta nodded, and Alice rushed to the bathroom to get ready for her safe date with the sheik of DuPont and try to put Rick Morrison's broken heart and puppy dog eyes out of her mind.

Chapter Eighteen

"Say, Luke, this sure is a swell car," Alice rubbed her hand along the black leather seat. "Nice. Is it yours or did you borrow it?"

"I just thought you deserved the best," Luke replied with a serious kind of smile.

"Oh," Alice said. "Thank you. You didn't have to go to any trouble."

"It wasn't. Would you like me to turn on the radio?"

"You have a radio in your car." Alice tried not to show she was impressed but failed miserably. He certainly had the automobile to go with his image. Maybe it was a company car.

Luke delivered a self-satisfied grin as he reached for the knob. "It's standard with one of these." Benny Goodman and his band blasted *It's Gotta Be This or That* through the speakers.

As the drive to Montgomery stretched on, the Cadillac cruised over ruts, making the ride feel smooth. Alice had been so excited about this night. She was looking forward to hearing the band and going dancing, something she hadn't done since before the war, but now she wasn't so sure. This was the first date she'd ever had since Joe died.

It was a warm night. She toyed with the handle of the window, trying to decide if blowing her hair out of the curls she and Greta made would be worth getting some air.

He must have noticed. "Would you like to put down the window? I can slow down if you're worried about wind damage."

"I have a scarf," she said, pulling the chiffon from her clutch. "You don't have to slow down."

"Good. I like to go fast."

She hoped he only meant when it came to cars. She cranked the window down about four inches, enough to be comfortable. A large rut jarred the automobile and jostled her to her left, closer to Luke.

He reached out to steady her, and when she tried to straighten herself away from him, he kept his arm around her shoulders. "Don't want you to get hurt," he said, with his eerie smile planted on his face.

She twisted her wedding ring. Maybe she shouldn't have accepted his invitation. At the next stop sign, when Luke needed to work the gears, she slipped back on the wide bench seat. "There sure is a lot of room in here."

"Too much," Luke said.

All Alice could think about was this was too soon even if Luke was a safe date. Joe had only been dead a little over a year.

Luke pulled into the parking lot of the dance club. Couples dressed in their finest made their way toward the club. At least she wouldn't have to put up with alcohol causing problems the way it did in some of the nightclubs in New York City. West Virginia was a dry state, but the thought of dancing close to a man other than her husband gave her an empty feeling in the pit of her stomach.

"You know my ankle's still pretty sore," Alice said. She waved and greeted a few neighbors she recognized.

Luke reached for her hand, and she waved at a few people she didn't know just for something to do to keep her hands out of his clutches.

His growing unrest and frown let her know he wasn't crazy about her attitude. She wasn't being fair since she agreed to this date, so she tried to smile at him. After all, he could have gone out with any single woman in Burning Bush, and he asked her. She allowed him to take her arm and lead her inside.

Cigarette smoke and the clinking of numerous beverage glasses vied with the band playing *Stompin' Room Only*. Clarinets and drums sparred with a swanky saxophone, and Charlie Spivak's trumpet, combining into a cacophony making small talk difficult. All right by her. She wilted with relief when Pete waved them over to a small table. They waded through dancers to get to her brother.

"I'm so glad to see you," Alice said. "Where's Lois?"

Pete nodded toward the back hall. "Ladies. Who's this?"

Somehow she didn't mind her big brother sizing up Luke.

"Luke Holmes," Luke replied tightlipped, not bothering with the friendly "Lucien, my friends call me Luke."

Pete's slight frown didn't loosen Alice's tongue, so he introduced himself. "I'm Pete Morgan, Alice's brother."

Luke's mouth relaxed into a smile as he stuck out his hand. "Well, now, I'm delighted meet Alice's brother."

"My wife, Lois," Pete said as Lois joined them.

Lois had dressed for the occasion with her emerald green off the shoulder satin gown, matching high heels, and pearls. Her hair was flipped up in a pompadour. She must have spent hours fixing it. She giggled and leaned into Pete. "We met."

At Pete's raised brows, Alice decided she was thirsty. "How about something to wet my whistle?"

"Sure," Luke said. "Then a dance."

After he'd sauntered away, Pete muttered, "Where'd you pick up that guy? He the one you've been gallivanting all around town with?"

"Pete! Gallivanting?" Alice asked. "Where'd you hear such a thing?"

"And, you, Lois," Pete said. "Where'd you meet him? Why didn't you tell me? What else--"

"Stop it," Alice said.

Lois took a step away and balled her fists. "Peter Alan Morgan! Don't you dare go accusing me of--"

"Thanks, Luke," Alice cut in when her date returned. She set the glass down and grabbed his elbow, grateful for any excuse to escape Pete and Lois' latest argument. "Let's dance." A bit of guilt nudged her at his surprised eager smile. "My ankle, though. Watch it."

"Of course. I'll be careful."

He took her hand and raised it shoulder high, gathering her waist close. Alice's ankle twinged a bit at the first back step, but she could manage. As long as he didn't try anything too fast.

"For a second there," Luke said in her ear, "I wondered if there was any man in town you didn't know."

She stiffened. "What's that supposed to mean?"

He chuckled. "I must be the most fortunate fella in town to be dancing with you for tonight."

"I don't know about that."

He squeezed her hand. "You're a special lady, so beautiful. I don't mind telling you I think I'm falling for you."

Whoa, this was moving way too fast. She tried to take a step back.

"You need someone to watch over you. Protect you." He squeezed her tighter against him. "You know, like the song."

Other couples brushed by them as they stood in the middle of the floor under the revolving mirror ball. She felt more nauseous by the moment and pushed back from him. "I told you, I don't need anyone's protection."

Luke stood rigid like the ferocious stone lion guarding New York City's public library under the lights, with his shiny hair, stern countenance, and smoky gray glare. "I think you do, a lonely war widow keeping company with a dangerous sort like Morrison. You have no idea what you're dealing with."

Chapter Nineteen

"What are you talking about?" Alice stopped dancing and disentangled from his arms. "I changed my mind having you check Rick's credentials. You have no business--"

"I'm making it my business." Luke tugged her arm as he led her off the tiny square floor, outside.

"Hi, Alice!" Bernice Gorman waved. She and her husband Ralph met them near the entrance. "Have you been inside?" Bernice asked as she touched up her auburn curls. "It's been so long since Ralph took me out. I'm so excited. Are they any good?"

"Oh, they're wonderful, Bernice. You'll love them." Practically vibrating with her fury at Luke, her curiosity about what he thought he knew, and relief at the interruption, Alice's stomach wound up in knots.

"Aren't you the fella from DuPont?" Ralph asked. He stuck out a hand to pump Luke's. "Ralph Gorman. Live next door to the Morgans. My brother works at the plant. Overheard Toliver talk of you in town. Nice to meet you."

Luke's enthusiasm didn't quite match Ralph's, but he returned the hearty handshake. "Lucien Holmes, but my friends call me Luke. Pleasure to make your acquaintance."

"Alice, is it going to work out with the quilt tour?" Bernice asked. "I know it hasn't been that long since the accident, but surely everyone knows how safe our road is by now. I have to send Ralph out to pick up the paint for our block soon."

"There have been some... developments, Bernice," Alice said. "I'm not sure this is the best place to talk."

"What developments?" Bernice rushed on as Alice's second sentence vanished into the night.

"Uh..." Alice looked at Luke, hoping he'd take the blame.

"Sheriff Jenner has some concerns Mockingbird Road is not suitable for safe travel. It's been removed from the barn quilt tour," Luke said in a grave voice. "We believe it's for the best."

Alice narrowed her eyes. He offered an excuse but passed the responsibility like a hot grenade. How could she have ever been attracted to him? She wished she'd never agreed to this date.

"The best!" Bernice cried. "Now see here, young man--"

"Well, now," Ralph cut in. "What say we go on in, leave these two lovebirds alone?"

Lovebirds! Alice took in a sharp breath, ready to spout denial like the river.

"We've been planning this for weeks," Bernice said. "Surely there must be something you can do. If you would just tell the sheriff we're safe, he would believe you."

Ralph took her arm. "If both the sheriff and the security expert say it's too dangerous, then we have little choice."

"I'm so sorry, Bernice. I'm doing all I can to work it out," Alice told her. "I'll call you tomorrow."

She rounded on Luke's dark chuckle. Her bum ankle picked that moment to give out. She stumbled and fell against him. He grabbed her shoulders, and she struggled to free herself.

"Hey, there, now," he scolded and gently set her on her feet. "I meant it when I said I wouldn't want you to get hurt."

She took a cautious step back. "Why didn't you tell the truth about the quilt tour? You see how much it means to them."

"I did tell the truth. It's too dangerous."

"I'm driving out there tomorrow." Alice swallowed at the thought of getting behind the wheel of an automobile, but she'd manage it somehow. "I'll prove it's safe."

When he took another step toward her, she backed away.

"I'm telling you, Alice, you're not safe anywhere, not with a man like Morrison around. He's a spy. Worse, he's a double agent. Now let's get back inside before the Gormans do any more damage to our reputations." He chuckled again. "Lovebirds."

A sick feeling lodged in the pit of her stomach. Rick, a double agent? She followed him back inside.

*****

Alice sat rigid as Luke drove them home from the dance. The evening had been a botched job, as far as she was concerned. Her ankle thrummed from her stupid attempt to run when the band slid into the last song. *I'll Be Seeing You.* No way was she dancing to their song with anyone but Joe.

Luke, who had turned out to be the fastest, smoothest talker she'd ever met, had convinced Ralph skipping Mockingbird Road would somehow work in Bernice's favor, and she'd earn a bigger profit from selling her cookies in town instead of at their tour stop. Bernice wasn't buying it.

If that wasn't bad enough, he wavered between making declarations of love to Alice and flirting with every other woman at the dance, married or not. When he told her sister-in-law she should be in the movies because she was prettier than Lana Turner, Lois giggled and Pete announced it was time to go home.

Alice had been ready to leave with Pete and Lois long before the last song, but she needed to grill Luke about his stunning announcement about Rick.

When Luke had caught up with her in the parking lot after the last song, Ralph Gorman kept them there another half hour running his hands over the Cadillac, examining the engine, and talking about tires and fuel. They finally managed to get away.

"You know what I'm going to ask you about." Alice crossed her arms and stared into the black night, too angry to look at Luke. She anchored her good foot under the seat so she wouldn't be sliding all over the place every time he spun the big car around the bend. "So you might as well just come and tell me how you happen to know Rick Morrison is a spy. Oh, right. Not just a spy, but a double agent."

She batted his hand when he reached for the radio's dial. "Oh, no, you don't, mister."

"Bossy, aren't you?" Luke asked with another of those infuriating chuckles.

"I like a feisty lady."

The scent of his brilliantine hair gel now mixed with something sweeter. Cloying. Luke patted his coat pocket. A thumping sound confirmed Alice's suspicion he had a flask with him. He'd done more than slick his hair before they'd left the club.

She blinked her eyes. How could she have been flattered by him?

The only reason she didn't find her own ride home was because she needed to know the truth. If Luke had evidence about Rick Morrison and his activities, it be her duty as an American to put a stop to it. Just what evidence could he have?

Flashes of Greta's words and Rick's constant surveillance buzzed in her conscience. She needed to know what to do.

All right, Joe. For you. I'll play this out, and you won't have given your life in vain. I'll do what I can to foil the enemy's plans. Just help me, my love.

As much as she hated it, she needed to play along, flirt a bit.

She took a deep breath and faced Luke. "Pretty funny, wasn't it? Bernice thinking we were lovebirds."

He gave her a smooth gaze before returning his attention to the road.

A few sweaty seconds later, she tried again. "Come on, Luke, I'm sorry. I've just been so worried about all the details about this quilt tour. I want to make a good impression on your aunt, you see, and I don't think things are going so well."

He snickered under his breath. "Don't worry yourself, my dear. Things couldn't be better. Believe me."

She ignored the dear remark and held her breath as she shifted a few inches closer to him. "Aren't you going to tell me about spies?" She laced her tone with honey.

He lifted his right hand off the steering wheel and cupped her shoulder. "What do you want to know?"

Inwardly groaning, she steeled herself. "Tell me about my landlord." She didn't have to pretend to shiver. "Maybe I should find a new place to live."

"We've been watching him," Luke said. "You're safe where you are as long as you listen to me and do what I say."

"Who's 'we'?"

Luke gave her a sidelong glance. "The men who work for me."

"How do you know he's a double agent?"

Luke stopped the car on the side of the road by the Kanawha River, the spot where the trees thinned out. With a full moon shining low in the sky, the view was breathtaking. The hills on the other side of the river looked almost blue in color.

If only she could be here with Joe.

"I know I've been vague about this, but I am trying to protect you and everyone in Burning Bush. Please trust me." Luke's smoky eyes pleaded with her. He almost reminded her why she'd been attracted to him. Almost. "If I tell you about Morrison, you have to promise to not say anything. Loose lips sink ships, you know."

She placed her hand on her heart. "I won't say a word."

His voice lowered to almost a whisper even though there wasn't another soul around. "I checked with my army buddy from the FBI."

Crickets chirped. An owl hooted. Her heart beat faster. "Go on."

"Morrison's not FBI, I can tell you that much. There was no record of him employed by any government agency."

A deep sense of relief went through her. "Thank God."

Luke placed his hand on hers. "He's not in the real estate business either."

Alice's heart throbbed so hard she could feel it in her throat. "Of course he is. He owns buildings all over West Virginia."

His gaze grew more intense. "Alice, the property in Burning Bush is the only place he owns, and nobody knows what he does for a living."

She shook her head trying to make sense of it. "Maybe he just wants to keep his business private."

Luke's low chuckle was back. "I'd say. Did you know he worked in Military Intelligence during the war?"

Remembering Rick's chokehold on her brother, somehow it didn't surprise her. "So, lots of men did, even you."

"My friend says the Bureau's been watching him. His parents emigrated from Russia when he was a child, and there's evidence he might have been talking to the Soviets toward the end of the war."

Her stomach hardened. "Why would a Russian spy want to come to a sleepy little village nestled in the hills of West Virginia?"

"Think, Alice. DuPont's only an hour from here. The Russians want to get their hands on a way to make atomic bombs, and, this part is top secret, we have the plans.

Alice gasped.

"DuPont was in charge of the plutonium at Oak Ridge, Tennessee for the Manhattan Project, you know."

"Then why didn't he set up in Charleston, some place closer." Her voice came out thin, raspy.

"Dupont's only one of many targets," Luke said. "There's the Ordinance Works Plant in Mount Pleasant, army facilities all over West Virginia, railroads, barges on the Kanawha River. Burning Bush is the perfect spot for Soviet spies. They already have evidence of some operatives nearby."

"What evidence?"

He moved closer so his lips were almost touching her ear. "Of course, this whole operation is top secret. My friend in the FBI only told me on the sly because we're army buddies, and since I'm in security, he thought I could be of assistance. He told me to keep my eyes open and report anything suspicious."

A knot lodged in Alice's stomach. "Then why tell me." She pressed against the door of the car.

He placed his arms around her. "I care about you. I don't want you hurt by someone like him."

She held back a sob. Rick wouldn't do something like this, would he? She didn't know him very well, and he was pretty mysterious. She may have just met Luke, but he was the nephew of the Tolivers, people she'd known since she was a little girl. He had to be telling the truth.

Besides, he worked for security for the military and at DuPont. If anyone would know things like this, it would be a security man. Wouldn't it?

"Don't worry, my love." Luke pulled her closer to him and kissed her. She was so shocked by what she'd just learned, she let him plant his brandy-tasting lips on hers. "You'll be all right, but you need to do what I say."

*****

Alice didn't bother with the lights after she locked the shop door behind her. Luke drove off, and her rubber knees gave out on the stool at the counter.

"Perfect. Go out with the guy," He had told her when she revealed her plans for tomorrow. Probably today already. He'd given her a set of questions to ask, and some coded words in Rick's answers to memorize.

She would never sleep. She downed a couple of aspirin hoping it would knock the pain from her ankle. She leaned over to touch it.

If she'd stayed on her crutches, she would never have gone through a night like this, but then she would have never learned the truth, the man she had feelings for was a traitor.

Anger fired in the pit of her belly. What happened to this country? Had all the good men been taken by the war machine? She held up her clenched fist and vowed again not to let Joe and all the others like him have sacrificed themselves for nothing.

Yes, there were plenty of good men, men like Pete, who were honorable, truthful, decent.

"I'll do whatever I have to, Joe, for democracy, and for the brave men who fought and died to preserve our freedom. For you, Joe."

Chapter Twenty

Alice blinked as she was jostled out a deep fog.

"What is wrong? Why are you here?" Greta shook her shoulder again.

She yawned and lifted her head from the store counter. "Oh, my goodness." She looked at her watch. After nine o'clock already. "I must have fallen asleep. Could you open while I get cleaned up?"

"Of course." Greta stared at her with a held-back grin.

Alice ignored it and made her way upstairs. How could she ever suspect Greta of anything? She was her friend. It was those who wanted to hurt others, take away liberty, and property, and humanity, and life who deserved to be punished. No matter who they hurt. Greta had lost so much more than she had.

Could her friend be trusted with a secret as big as Rick being a double agent? No, definitely not. Judging by what Greta had said about her life in Germany, there was no telling what she'd do to Rick. There was also the mysterious matter of Greta's letter.

Alice would deal with this herself. Once she had enough evidence, she'd go to President Truman himself to see justice done, and she knew just how to start. She hurried over to the telephone and dialed Rick's number.

"Good morning, Rick, This is your tenant, Alice Brighton."

"My tenant, Alice Brighton. Let me see."

Alice couldn't stop the smile growing at the sound of his teasing voice, despite her determination to make sure he faced the firing squad. If he was guilty.

"I have so many tenants. Would you be the Alice Brighton in Gorse Ridge? Or the Alice Brighton in Triumph's Hollow?"

"Silly," she said. "You men are all just a bunch of kids at heart, aren't you?"

"Say, you're not going to cancel on me tonight, are you?"

"No." She twirled the phone cord. "Why would I cancel?"

"Just a... never mind. So, what's so important you needed to call? Plumbing backed up? Window stuck? Stove broken?"

This time she couldn't keep the laugh inside. "No, no. Nothing like that. I planned to take a little drive this morning, and wondered if I could meet you."

"Can't wait to see me, can you? I'm flattered."

"Could be," Alice said. "So, can you?"

"I'm sorry, but I have some appointments I can't get out of. I can take you somewhere at five."

A flutter of disappointment prodded her heart into an extra beat. "I just wanted to make a point anyway. No need to involve you." *Yet.*

"Where did you want to go?"

"Oh, just out to my brother's place."

"I heard Sheriff Jenner is thinking about recommending the county abandon Mockingbird Road." There was an edge to his voice.

"Ridiculous. It's on a direct route to Kimberly, Beckley, and White Sulphur Springs."

"The clerk put a notice on the next board meeting about it," he said. "Wants to build something called a bypass."

"A what?"

"The government wants to build a larger road to Beckley and White Sulphur Springs, but it won't go through Burning Bush."

Alice felt as though she'd been turned to stone. "What about all the businesses in Burning Bush? What will happen if no one comes here? What will happen if no one stops to eat lunch at the diner? Or... or..."

"Don't worry your pretty little head about it," Rick said. "It will actually benefit Burning Bush."

Alice gnawed the inside of her mouth as she tried to figure how rerouting traffic away would help the town. Even if it did, the farmers out there needed a way to get their animals and crops to Kingston. The Copper Coal Company Store was located there and depended on the farmers in Burning Bush. Pete, the Gormans, and the others would suffer financially if the road was condemned.

"Alice, you still there?"

"I'm sorry," she said. "I was thinking of something."

"I was just saying I'll see you at five."

After they hung up, Alice dressed in a hurry so she could help Greta with the customers. Ever since the plans for the barn tour started, the store had been doing well, especially on Saturdays. People from Montgomery, Kimberly, Oak Hill, Kingston, and as far away as Beckley, were coming to her shop to buy their patterns, fabric, and quilting supplies.

As a steady stream of customers came through, Alice couldn't keep her mind on business. She kept thinking about what Luke had told her last night. Rick didn't seem like the type to betray his country, and he knew Joe. At least he said he did, but the government trusted Luke with security for DuPont, and he had friends in the FBI. He had to know what he was talking about.

It was all so confusing.

Alice glanced up at the clock. Almost lunchtime. "Greta, could you watch the shop for an hour? I need to drive to Pete's house to check something out."

Greta's eyes widened. "You drive?"

"What makes you think I don't know how to drive?"

"I did not know you owned an automobile. Since I have been here, you have never driven."

Alice placed her hands on her hips. "Even if I don't drive, I have a license. I own a green deluxe Plymouth. It's parked out back in the garage." Joe loved that automobile so much she couldn't bear to part with it. "Besides, I'm a good driver." At least she used to be before her folks' accident caused her insides to knot up every time she got behind the wheel.

She'd be able to do it this time. She had no choice. Something was making everyone want to detour Mockingbird Road. She was going to find out what.

*****

Alice put the clutch in gear and started up the road past the Feltons'. So far, so good. Now the hard part. Pete's farm was half way up the mountain. She'd concentrate on getting there first.

"I can do this, Joe. You always said I could do anything I put my mind to."

She blew a strand of hair out of her face and clutched the steering wheel tighter as she passed the Collins'. She tried to keep her eyes focused on the road, but when she reached the spot where her parents went over the edge, she glanced down.

Her foot slipped off the clutch, and the engine sputtered.

The straight precipice down to the town below caused her heart to race. Sweat beaded on her forehead.

The guardrail was so small. It wouldn't keep a car from going over the side.

She gazed over the edge. There were only about six inches between her and the road.

Trying to slow her breath, she started the car back up and pressed in the clutch but couldn't bring herself to take her foot off the brake. "I can do this. I can."

Her stone foot was too heavy to lift. Her death grip on the steering wheel couldn't budge. She couldn't bring herself to go any further. Maybe the sheriff was right. Maybe the road should be condemned. They could build another road bypassing the mountain.

She couldn't believe she'd once driven this way every day. Her father taught her to drive on this road. "Pappy."

The day she heard about the accident was etched in her mind. One month earlier, the US Army had informed her Joe had been killed in action at the Battle of the Bulge in service to his country. They had offered their deepest sympathies at her great loss. Great loss didn't begin to describe it.

Mamie had called her when she'd heard. As soon as they could get train tickets, she and Pappy would come to New York to be with her and to meet Pete's new wife, but with the transportation problems the war caused, it never happened. Poor Bernice Gorman had to call long distance to tell her the news about Mamie and Pappy.

There she was, stuck hundreds of miles away in New York City, after another great loss, and it took two whole days before she could get a single train ticket home. They wouldn't even let Lois come with her. Even then, she'd only managed a seat because of the circumstances. Her parents were dead, and with a brother fighting in Japan, she was the only one who could bury them.

Tears ran down Alice's face as she remembered the day she got back. She drove Pete's truck to the spot where her parents were killed, and she'd frozen just like she did today. She didn't know how much time had passed before Bernice found her there and drove her to the old farmhouse where she'd grown up. She hadn't driven since.

A chipmunk, curious about her car, caused some stones to roll down the hill under the guardrail, their echo magnified like thunder as they bounced.

One thing she didn't understand was why the accident happened. There was nobody else involved, and Pappy knew this mountain better than anyone. He'd never had a problem driving it before, and if the roads were too icy, he'd use tire chains or not drive at all. Maybe a deer leaped in front of the car and he'd swerved to miss it. What else could it be? Not a chipmunk.

She pressed in the parking brake and got out of the car. Wrapping her arms around herself, she gazed over the guardrail. A blue jay landed on the lower branch of an oak tree by the road. Hemlocks, spruce, and ash dotted the landscape. In the valley, the train stopped at the water tower in the village of Burning Bush to refuel. Boxcars carried steel, coal, and timber. At the far end of town, barges traveled the Kanawha River on their way to Charleston or further to the Ohio River.

One reason she came home after the war was she missed the beauty of the countryside. After her parents' funeral, when she returned to New York City, she hated it. The busy sidewalks and the crowds made her feel so alone and scared. It was worse after the war ended when Pete took Lois away. She'd felt so alone.

Quoting scripture helped during that awful time. The only way she got through it without falling into a deep pit of despair was to hold on to God. She got back in her car. *Joe's* car. If God kept her from falling then, He could help her drive up this mountain now no matter how afraid she was.

"Lord, please give me the resolve." She pressed on the clutch and stepped on the gas. The Plymouth groaned as it slid backwards for a moment before it gained purchase on the road and continued climbing.

"Be strong and of a good courage, fear not, nor be afraid of them."

She made it past the barrier.

"For the Lord thy God, He it is that doth go with thee."

Around the curve.

"He will not fail thee, nor forsake thee."

The automobile reached the area where the hill evened out. Alice quoted every verse she'd memorized when Joe died. Before she knew it, she'd arrived at the farmstead halfway up the mountain.

When she talked to Mayor Wilson and the council at the town meeting, she needed to remind them this road was the shortest way to Kingston, Powellton, White Sulphur Springs, and Beckley. To drive in a circle to Montgomery then around the mountain on the other side would add at least an hour to the trip, maybe more. She had to convince the town the road was safe. It would destroy the farmers' livelihood and turn Burning Bush into a ghost town. Maybe warning signs would help.

If she could persuade them, then it would be easy to get back the barn tour stops on Mockingbird Road.

A blue Fleetmaster was parked next to the Gorman house, next door to Pete's. What was Rick doing there? She almost stopped to satisfy her curiosity but decided to drive on. She would ask them about it later. They weren't involved in whatever Rick was up to. She trusted them even more than she did the Tolivers.

Bernice would tell her the truth.

*****

Pete leaned against the kitchen wall with his arms crossed. Lois banged pots and pans then reached for Mamie's old tin coffee pot. She filled it from the kitchen pump, and set it on the coal stove.

Alice lowered herself into a chair at the oak table her father had built years before. She'd walked in on another fight.

Lois swiped at a tear running down her face. "I'm sorry I can't get you something else, Alice. Since this brute of a husband of mine doesn't have time to put in any modern conveniences, like plumbing and electricity, I burn everything I make."

"Maybe if my wife learned how to cook instead of gallivanting around meeting pretty boys and running this quilt block tour of yours, she'd learn how to cook."

"I do so know how to cook." Lois plopped in the chair beside Alice. "I know how to cook on a gas stove and on an electric stove. I don't know how to cook like the pioneers. This is the twentieth century."

Alice stood. "Will you two stop it for a minute? Pete, all she's asking is for you to put in a few modern conveniences."

Pete swiped the back of his neck with his bandana. "You know how busy this time of year is for me. She's asking for the world."

Alice placed her hand on her brother's. "When will you get around to it? Every time of year on a pig farm is busy, except winter. Then it will be too cold."

"What if we do have a baby sometime? How do you expect me..." Tears rolled across Lois's red cheeks.

"You heard Doctor Brenner. It's probably not going to happen." Pete stormed outside letting the screen door crash shut behind him.

Lois skirted into the bedroom and slammed the door.

Alice poured herself some coffee and sipped it, hoping it would soothe the lump in her throat. Maybe she should just leave, let them work it out on their own. She could talk to Pete about the road some other time, but she really wanted him to speak at the town meeting about how closing it would hurt the farmers.

Lois opened the door and came back into the room with a powder blue suitcase in one hand and a matching train case in the other. "Will you drive me to the train station in Montgomery?"

"Oh, Lois, no."

"I'm leaving Pete. This time for good. I'm going back to New York on the next train headed east."

Alice stood and started toward her. "Lois, calm down. You don't mean it."

"I do! I don't know what I was thinking when I agreed to marry him. We didn't even know each other! He's just a hillbilly."

"Now, hold up there! Pete's my brother. He comes from good stock. Maybe stubborn, but good." Alice stepped between Lois and the door and placed her hands on her hips. "Maybe there are things going on neither of us knows about. Men are good at hiding their feelings from us, you have to admit. Maybe it's not just time keeping Pete from... ah... modernizing things."

Lois stared at the floor, her gloved knuckles clenching the handles of the suitcase.

"Don't you remember how much you love him? He adores you."

Lois sniffed.

"We grew up here. This is just the way it is. Maybe it's hard for him to change things."

Lois tilted up her chin.

"You've given up a lot, I know. We're always the most comfortable with what we know." Alice waved her arm around the kitchen. "This is what he knows best. After all he went through in Okinawa."

The suitcase dropped to the floor.

"He had to kill or be killed." Alice swallowed. So many soldiers, like Joe, didn't come home, and the rest were altered forever.

"We had to change, too, right, Lois? We had to do the things the men couldn't do because they were gone. Remember the time we had to replace the pipe under the sink at our flat because there was no one who could come?"

This time Lois smiled wanly. "I can't seem to stop making a fool of myself!" She sat at the table and dug a handkerchief out of her purse. "To be honest, I'm afraid. Afraid of... you know. I might not be able to give him another baby."

Alice's eyes watered. "The doctor didn't say it was for sure."

The women held each other and cried.

Lois stepped back and wiped the tears off her face. "You're right. How could I be so demanding, when Pete is making a huge effort, at least for him."

Alice studied here sister-in-law's delicate face. It had to be hard for Lois, being raised in an upscale Manhattan apartment with all of the modern conveniences at her fingertips. The only trees she'd ever seen were in Central Park, and she'd never seen a pig until Pete came home from the war. "You're doing your best, too."

Lois looked around the kitchen. "Women have been cooking like this for hundreds of years. Why can't I?" She straightened her thin shoulders. "I will not let a little coal and iron come between me and my man."

Alice dissolved into snorts of giggling. "Atta girl. I'm sure Bernice would give you lessons if you asked."

Lois frowned, looking again like a lost little girl. "She's tired of me asking for things."

"This time you're not asking for a handout. You want her to help you become self-sufficient."

"Right." Lois inhale. "I know Bernice was excited about the quilt tour. She talks about it all the time." Her expression turned wistful. "I guess I'd hate to miss it too after all the work we've put in. Do you think Greta could give me cooking lessons?"

Alice narrowed her eyes. "You trying to steal her away from me?"

Lois laughed. "Yes." Then she sobered. "No. Maybe she and I should change places for a while. Pete's always going on about her cooking." She made a wry grimace with her lips. "Talk about men and their secrets. Maybe she'll give me the recipe to Pete's heart."

"Come back into town with me. We can talk to her."

Lois looked at her suitcase with a bit more longing than Alice liked. "Could I stay a few days?"

"Only if Pete agrees."

"Okay. I'll ask him," Lois said. "So, why did you come up here again?"

Chapter Twenty-One

With Lois beside her, Alice regained her courage and turned the car around, bumping back down Mockingbird Road. Lois whistled and kept exclaiming how beautiful everything was. Alice sweated.

"I think it will be good for Pete to be alone for a couple of days, don't you?" Lois asked. "Give him time to miss me."

"Um, sure." Alice double-pumped the clutch and let her foot off the brake after she negotiated a turn.

"You're not looking too good. Want me to drive?"

"No," Alice said.

"Okay, then, simmer down. You're doing fine, kid."

She didn't feel fine at all. She gripped the steering wheel tighter.

"I've never seen you so nervous, not even when handsome Luke had you in his arms. Mmm-mmm. I wish I could have danced with him."

"Lois!"

"Ha! Knew you'd come out of your coma. So when's your next date?"

"Tonight," Alice muttered.

Lois whistled. "Fast worker."

"No, not with him. With Rick."

"Your landlord. Alice, what's going on?"

"I wish I knew. I really wish I knew." She shifted into a lower gear. "It's not a real date."

"No? Tell."

Alice risked a glance at her sister-in-law's puppy-eager face then decided to pull off the road. She had to trust somebody. There was too much espionage, and heartache and worry, and confusion bottled up inside. The two of them roomed in New York together and consoled each other while Pete and Joe were at war. Lois was the one who helped Alice through her grief. There was nobody she trusted more.

"It's a secret." She took Lois's hands and stared her in the eye. "You cannot tell anyone, not even Pete. It's a matter of national security."

Lois's baby blue eyes couldn't have gotten wider as she nodded. "Okay. I promise. Spill."

Alice closed her eyes and clenched Lois's hands. "Rick Morrison might be a double agent, and I've been asked to help gather evidence."

Silence. Alice opened one eye.

Lois was smiling. "Ninny! How could you believe that about Rick Morrison? Why, it's more likely Pete is a spy. It's always the person you least suspect. So, tell me about your date."

"I have this information on good authority."

Lois snorted. "Whose? Who can you trust nowadays anyway? Besides, what would spies have to gain in a puny little town like Burning Bush?"

"That's just it. Burning Bush is right in the middle of the action."

"Could have fooled me." Lois folded her arms and sat back. "What action?"

Alice explained how Mockingbird Road led to important military sites all over West Virginia.

Lois tsked. "If you want to know who's playing who, don't you think the ones who want to close the road are at the bottom of your little dilemma?"

*****

Greta had acted pleased to see Lois, but the glint of determination in her eye comforted Alice more than words. If anyone could talk sense into Lois, it was her boarder. Greta even offered to give up her room for the next three days, but Lois refused insisting on taking the couch.

Alice left Lois in Greta's capable hands and started getting ready for her date, but her nerves were twisted tighter than a permanent wave.

Get a grip! You want to find out the truth, right?

As well as prove to Luke, Rick... was what?

Lois had a point. What if Rick agreed with Luke about the road?

While Alice applied mascara, there was a knock on the door. Greta's "I will answer it," trailed from the other room. It was too early for Rick. She slid a robe over her slip and nylons as Greta climbed the stairs carrying a box from the flower shop.

Rick was so sweet thinking of having flowers delivered before their date. Warmth danced across Alice's cheeks. Of course, they might have been from Pete trying to make things up to Lois.

Greta handed them to Alice. "The boy said they are for you."

She took the flowers into the kitchen and set them on the table while Greta and Lois hovered around her.

Lois stroked the box. "Aren't you going to open them?"

"Give me a chance," Alice said as she fumbled with the bow. Long-stemmed roses. Rick must have spent a fortune on them. She read the card and couldn't help the disappointment sweeping through her.

"Well." Lois raised her penciled eyebrows. "Who are they from?"

Alice let out a sigh. "The sheik of Burning Bush." Only after last night, Luke didn't seem like such a dreamboat.

Lois squealed. "What's it say?"

"Thank you for a wonderful evening. I look forward to many more. Affectionately, Luke."

"Affectionately." Lois swooned into the kitchen chair. "Pete hasn't bought me flowers since the morning..." She blushed. "When he came to wake me after the incident at the blacksmith shop."

"You must get ready," Greta said as she grabbed an empty milk bottle from the cupboard under the sink. "I will put these in water."

Alice sauntered to the bathroom. The flowers gave her a new problem to worry about. As soon as she had the opportunity, she needed to let Luke know she wasn't interested in any more dates. The only reason she even considered seeing him again was for patriotic reasons.

She tucked her white silk blouse into her blue straight skirt while reciting the code words Luke had taught her. She was supposed to get answers about Rick's other properties and about a certain man named Drake. Luke had refused to reveal

Drake's importance, saying only he was. Infuriating. If Luke couldn't trust her, then why was he romancing her with roses, let alone getting her to spy on Rick? Did this make her some kind of a double agent too?

Or a double-crosser. Rick had been plenty nice to her. Alice pinned on her blue, felt, skimmer hat matching her blue suit and blotted her red lipstick. If Rick was guilty, he'd get what he deserved. She wouldn't let his adorable smirk keep her from doing her duty, but if he wasn't, how would he ever forgive her betrayal?

"Bye, girls! Don't wait up for me," she called and hustled down the steps, their giggles and good wishes following like a vapor.

Rick was waiting already, leaning on the side of his car, hands in his pockets, staring at the sidewalk.

"Must be something good down there," Alice said.

He jumped.

"Didn't mean to scare you." She laughed a nervous titter.

He grinned. "Not used to dames being on time." He dodged her playful swat to his elbow. "Here, let me get the door."

Alice settled into the Fleetmaster. It might not be as luxurious as Luke's new Caddy, but it felt more real. More honest.

"Swell evening," Rick said as he pulled away from the curb. "How was your drive this morning? Sorry I had to miss it."

"It went well," Alice said, determined not to admit her fears or that she'd seen his car at the Gormans'. "So, what did you do today? Tell me about your business. The meeting." She studied his profile. Would she know if he was lying?

He glanced her way then back to the road. "I'd rather talk about us."

"Us?"

"Us and Joe."

Alice unclenched her hands. "Right. You were going to tell me how you knew my husband and why he didn't mention you in his letters."

"He wouldn't have." Rick slid to a smooth halt at the last stop sign out of Burning Bush and shifted gears. "A lot of what he wrote you was made up."

Alice's throat closed. As he stopped the car, she coughed and gripped the door handle. Her world spun. The door opened, and she tumbled into Rick's arms.

"Hold on, now," he said as she struggled. "I'm not going to hurt you."

"I don't know what you're talking about!" She wrenched herself away, swung her purse his direction connecting with his shoulder, knocking him off his feet. She fell to her knees in the grass on the side of the road. Her hat lay next to her, and she reached for it with shaky hands. "This was a mistake. I'll just be going home now."

She gripped the door handle and pulled herself upright. She shook out her skirt and tried hard not to think about the state of her hair.

Rick just sat there staring up at her with a puzzled look on his face.

"What's the matter with you? Don't tell me I hurt you." She reached for her hat.

He leaned back on his elbows. "No, I'm not hurt. Not as much as you are, apparently."

"Your lies couldn't hurt me. I won't let you get away with your nefarious plans." She stopped, horrified she'd let anything slip out.

"Nefarious?" Rick got to his feet, laughing. "I'm just trying to do what's right for my new home."

"New home?" Alice turned and tramped off in the direction of her shop. To her eternal annoyance, he kept pace.

"Burning Bush. I don't want to see it all jazzed up, like some tourist haven. What'd you think I meant?"

"Oh!" Alice slung her purse along her arm. "Of course, Burning Bush." She stopped and glared up at him. "We're not going to change everything with the barn quilt tour. It's not permanent."

"Things rarely are." He reached for her hand. "Please."

It cost him, she could see.

"Please, come back to the car. Let me explain."

A red haze covered him, and her jaw clenched. "Brother, there's nothing you can say to fix calling my Joe a liar."

"I never said any such thing."

"You said, and I quote, 'A lot of what he wrote to you was made up.'"

Rick put up his hands in a mock surrender and stepped toward her. "Besides the fact we couldn't reveal our true locations and missions, did you really want to hear how we were taking fire?" He pulled back his sleeve to reveal a white scar snaking across his forearm. "What happened when we got too close?" He closed his eyes, and his Adam's apple bulged.

She melted. "Joe?"

"Joe stepped in front of... He saved my life." He looked away. "I didn't deserve a friend like him."

"Sounds like my Joe."

"We weren't pals at first, you know." Rick took a deep breath, and she gave him space.

A man couldn't fake this emotion. She was sure of it. Something had broken inside of Rick back then. Down deep, she knew Joe's letters had been too cheerful, but she had accepted it, believing he was trying to avoid the censors and keep her from worrying too much. She'd let him get away with it of course. There wasn't anything else she could do. When Rick opened the car door, she got in, fixed her hair, and pinned on her hat while he got in the driver's side.

The pieces started fitting together, both before and during the war. "Joe wasn't just a tech sergeant, was he?"

"It took two years for him to rise in the ranks," Rick answered, without giving anything away. "Tech Sergeant, highest grade, MIS. Yeah, he was all that, and more."

"MIS?"

Rick wiped a hand across the back of his neck. "Military Intelligence Service."

She nodded, knowing deep inside he was telling the truth. Even though Joe had never said anything, she knew.

"I was his lieutenant, but it could have been the other way around." He shook his head. "I wasn't even green yet, but he made it work."

Alice placed her hand on his arm. "I always thought he could do anything. He was something special."

"Yes, he was." Rick's jaw twitched. "I can't tell you anything about our missions."

"I know."

He stared at the steering wheel and spoke in quiet tones. "I still have nightmares about it."

She nodded. "I know you can't say anything else, but could you tell me...at least, a little bit, about... about... you know." She couldn't bring herself to be any more specific.

"They were going to kill us. Joe was the brave one. I couldn't say a word, but there he was cracking a joke." Rick turned and took her hands. "He told me about you, and he was right about everything. I'll never be anything like him, but he made me promise to check in on you."

Alice squeezed his hands. "So you have. Come on, Lieutenant, we have a show to catch."

She left Luke's code words by the side of the road.

Chapter Twenty-Two

Supper at the Blue Room and the new Lana Turner movie had been wonderful. Alice was surprised at Rick's insight into the theme of the movie in their conversation in the car afterwards. Sin will always be punished, and the truth will come out. The postman always rings twice.

She and Rick had so much in common, including their faith and their love of movies and swing music. She enjoyed hearing more about Joe. Rick mentioned little things, like when Joe helped him play a joke on the cook. They'd gone into the mess hall in the middle of the night and turned everything upside down.

They would have gotten away with it if the cook hadn't threatened one of the privates he'd suspected with KP duty. Joe had confessed, and he and Rick spent the whole day cleaning the mess hall and peeling potatoes. They could have ordered the cook to forget about it since Rick outranked him, but Joe insisted on making things right.

Somehow, listening to the stories, she felt closer to Joe and closer to Rick at the same time. It was hard for her to believe Joe could trust someone so much if he was a traitor.

They entered the Montgomery Diner where they'd stopped to get dessert on the way home. Rick selected the song *Sentimental Journey* on the jukebox, and they sat in a booth near the back.

It looked like most eateries in West Virginia, with red checkered tablecloths and a black-and-white checkered linoleum floor.

The waiter, a man in his early twenties with purplish scars on his face, probably a wounded vet, stopped by the table and dropped off the apple pie both of them ordered.

Alice took a sip of her Coca-Cola. "So where were you born?"

Rick wiped the corners of his mouth. "Akron, Ohio. My pop worked for the Quaker Oats Company. Worked there until the day he died."

"Oh, I thought you were..." She stopped herself before she said something about him being born in Russia. She'd make a long-distance call to the Quaker Oats Company and the court of records in Akron on Monday no matter how much it cost. It would be easy to check his story.

"You thought what?"

"Nothing." She ate a large bite of pie before he could say any more.

They made small talk until Rick ate another forkful, leaned back in his chair, and gazed at her with those dreamy hazel eyes of his. "How's Greta getting along? Is she a help to you?"

"Greta has been wonderful. I never thought I would get along so well with a German girl, but I feel like I've known her my whole life."

He took a sip of coffee. "Has she made any friends — other than you, I mean?"

"No, not really. She seems to know Deputy Eddie Tyler, but I don't know from where."

"Isn't he the fighter pilot who got shot down over Germany?"

Alice nodded. "From what I hear, he walked over sixty miles until he got to allied territory without ever getting captured. He even got a medal for it."

Rick steepled his fingers in front of his mouth. "Hard to do without help. Has Greta made any other friends?"

"Pete and Lois think she's swell, and Bernice likes her, but most of the people in Burning Bush won't give her a chance."

"Prejudices from the war run deep. I can understand."

"I was just as bad," she said. "When she first got here, I almost sent her packing."

"What changed your mind?"

Alice smirked. "My sprained ankle. I had to give her a chance if I wanted to keep the shop."

Rick nodded. "That's when I tried to talk you into moving in with your brother, before I knew how stubborn you could be." She delivered a playful slap on his arm, and he winked. "What does Greta think about all this talk of closing Mockingbird Road?"

"She doesn't understand it any more than I do. What about you? Do you think it should be closed?"

"I don't see any reason for it. The tour would be too short without it." Rick's brow furrowed. "Who's behind this? I know Sheriff Jenner wants it closed for safety reasons, but somebody has to be egging him on."

Alice took another bite of apple pie to hide her relief. Somebody understood. Unless he had a spy reason for keeping the road open. "The Tolivers seem to be the ones who came up with the idea of leaving out Mockingbird Road. Then Luke latched on to it, saying the road was unsafe. Next thing I know, the sheriff wants to condemn it. He's even using my folks' car accident as an excuse. I asked the mayor for a town meeting. He scheduled it for Friday."

The waiter stopped by the table, and Rick paid the bill. "How'd you like to go exploring with me after church tomorrow?"

"Exploring?"

"We could go for a drive up the mountain, you know, check out what all the fuss is about."

"I don't know if I can." She'd agreed to meet with Luke and report what she found out from Rick, but she hadn't really found out anything yet. Somebody was lying, and she was starting to believe it wasn't Rick. "I'll meet you after church."

The truth would come out either way just like in the movie they watched. The postman always rings twice.

*****

Rick escorted Alice to the door, and there was a moment of hesitation. He leaned in to kiss her, his warm breath against her cheek, and she wasn't at all sure she didn't want him to.

He cleared his throat, stepped back. "Thanks for going out with me tonight."

Alice flushed as she fumbled to get the key in the lock. "I had a good time." *Unlike last night.*

"Here, let me help." He wrapped his arm around her and placed his hand on hers as he turned the lock.

Tingles flittered along her shoulders and fingers where they touched.

"See you at church tomorrow." His warm breath tickled her ear. He tipped his fedora and headed toward his car.

Her stomach fluttered as she swept into the shop.

"So, how was it?" Lois asked. She and Greta surrounded Alice like the GIs besieging Hitler's bunker. "Was he as dreamy as Luke?"

Alice giggled despite herself. "Luke who? Rick's taking me for a drive after church tomorrow."

"He's some fast operator," Lois said.

"I do not understand," Greta said. "Operators work for the telephone company, do they not?"

"No, silly. It's an expression. It means he's moving in fast."

Alice unfastened the pin in her hat and followed Greta and Lois upstairs. "You two weren't waiting up for me, were you?"

"Partly," Lois said. "We wanted to see how your date was."

Alice raised her eyebrow. "So what was the other part?"

"Not tonight." Greta headed toward her bedroom. "I must get sleep. *Guten nacht.*" She closed the door behind her.

"Lois, what's going on here? You two are acting like a couple of conspirators."

Lois shrugged. "I made some coffee. You want some?"

Alice followed Lois into the kitchen and poured two cups as they sat at the kitchen table. She took a sip and raised her eyebrow at Lois. It tasted more like Greta's coffee. "You made this?"

Lois snorted. "Don't act so surprised. Greta taught me how. She's been working all evening teaching me how to adjust my recipes so I can cook on a coal stove like her aunts back in Germany, and how to thread a needle, and even how to bake bread from scratch. I'm not good at it yet, but she's putting me through homemaker's boot camp. Maybe I'll be able to do more than boil water and char the pork roast when I go back home."

Alice dropped her jaw. She never knew her sister-in-law to be so enthusiastic about homemaking skills. "Why?"

Lois wrapped her hands around her cup and stared at her coffee. "Greta told me what it was like being part of the underground in Germany. Did you know her parents knew Dietrich Bonhoeffer? They were in cahoots with him or something."

Alice took in a sharp breath. She'd heard of Bonhoeffer and how he was hanged for being involved in a plot to kill Hitler. She never dreamed Greta would be mixed up with someone like him.

"Anyway, she told me how they had to do without so the rations would be enough to feed the Jews they were hiding and how her father and brothers were executed as traitors to the Third Reich."

"They were executed? I thought they died in battle or something."

"That's what she said. Anyway, I got to thinking about all Pete did in the war and what he went through, and I'm squawking about indoor toilets and cook stoves."

Alice took another sip of coffee. "Sort of puts things in perspective, doesn't it?"

Lois swiped a stray tear. "I love Pete. I've always loved him. I haven't been very nice to him. I wanted my own way instead of trying to see where he's coming from. Well, not anymore. I've asked God to forgive me, and I'm going to try to be the best pig farmer's wife ever."

"Hmm." Alice studied her. "What about the indoor plumbing?"

"From now on," Lois vowed, "I don't say a word about plumbing, or stinking pigs, or outhouses, or an electric stove, or anything. I'm going to be a regular pioneer."

"What about the other problem?" Alice's cheeks grew warm. "A baby?"

"Doc Brenner didn't say I couldn't get pregnant. He just said it might be difficult. I'm going to do my part and leave the rest in God's hands. You'll see. I'll be on the nest in no time." Lois smiled, wistful. "What better way to honor all the sacrifices of the soldiers than by bringing a new life into the world?"

Alice laughed. "You must have had some talk with Greta."

"It was." Lois stood and yawned. "I better get some beauty sleep. See you in the morning."

Alice stayed up long enough to wash the cups. She gazed out the window over the sink. A starry night. One thing for sure, Lois wasn't going to turn over a new leaf right away if she knew her sister-in-law.

"Oh, Joe, I miss you so much. I wanted to have your baby, but how would I have handled being a mother, all alone? I don't know who to believe or what to do. I wish you were here."

Chapter Twenty-Three

Alice rolled over and groaned. After eight a.m. She crawled out of bed, nightmares still lingering about telegrams, spies, and traversing up Mockingbird Road. She swiped her hands through her curls. This afternoon, she'd climb the mountain again. No wonder she hadn't slept well. At least this time, she wouldn't be driving.

She yawned and opened her bedroom door. Lois's lighthearted chatter, interspersed with Greta's more serious tones, drifted down the hall from the kitchen. The smell of coffee made her stomach rumble. She made her way to the bathroom to apply a generous portion of pancake makeup to cover the circles under her eyes.

As she dressed for church, she considered ways of telling Luke she had another date with Rick instead of meeting him to give her report. She hadn't found out anything proving Rick was a traitor anyway.

Akron, Ohio! Hmm.

Luke might have been mistaken about Rick. If the FBI had any proof, Luke wouldn't need Alice to spy on him. As much as she wanted to believe Rick, she needed to check out his story to be sure.

Another thing she and Rick had in common now was nightmares. Alice was certain hers hadn't been as bad as his, but when she was falling, falling forever like her folks, from the side of the road, it felt terrifying. She shuddered at the thought of the scar on Rick's arm.

What if he was a traitor? Could that be the reason Joe was killed? Alice slapped her hands on the cold enamel sink and gave her reflection a fierce stare. "For Joe! I can do all things. I have to find out the truth no matter where it leads. I must."

She helped herself to the coffee and joined the girls at the chrome kitchenette. "Good morning! What's cooking?"

"Hey, good lookin'." Lois grinned. "You're sure chipper! I was just telling Greta it was about time we starting banging pots to wake you."

"Who, me?" Alice raised her cup. "I'm never late."

Greta scraped back her chair and hustled to her feet. "We have some eggs left."

"I didn't burn all the toast this time." Lois giggled at the look Greta gave over her shoulder.

"My lessons have not gone all kaput."

Lois snuggled her chair closer to Alice. "What are you gonna say to Luke about going driving with Rick today? Are you going to tell him right in church?"

Alice groaned. "I don't know. I have to pick the right moment."

Greta set a plate of steaming scrambled eggs and dark toast on the table.

Alice closed her eyes and inhaled. "Mmm, thank you, Lord, for this food, and my friends, and even my family. Amen."

"I can see his face now," Lois said. "He'll turn--"

"Lois!" Alice lifted a forkful of eggs. "I'd rather think about what it will be like seeing your husband."

"Oh that!" Lois leaned against her chair back with a huff. "Much as I'd like to let him stew a couple more days, Greta is right. A wife's duty is at her husband's side." She beamed at Alice. "I'm a new woman just like I told you last night."

Alice chewed then waved her fork. "Uh huh. If Greta can make miracles like this happen overnight, just think what she could do in a week!"

Greta wrapped her hands around her cup and frowned. "I have seen miracles, never created them."

*****

They hadn't been late, but Alice was glad to slip into the pew with seconds to spare before the piano started. She still had to come up with the right words to say to clue Luke in on her driving date without arousing anyone's suspicion or sending any male someone off his rocker.

Although she only peeked once, the intensity of Luke's gaze burned her left cheek. Rick shared a hymnal with Greta, thank heavens, which left her and Lois together. Pete might be here somewhere. They'd been late and rushed in so fast she hadn't had time to look too closely.

Alice squinted at the words while desperately working through her excuse. She risked a sideways glance at Rick. If only she could figure out a way to talk to Luke alone.

Lois tugged her sleeve. She blushed realizing she was the only one still standing and plopped into the pew. Everyone stood again for the blessing, and Alice's cheeks flamed again. She hadn't even noticed church was over. She bit her lip. Showtime.

"Excuse me for a few minutes, won't you?" she said in the general direction of Rick and the others. "I just... um, want to freshen up. Be right back."

Rick nodded. "I'll meet you outside."

Relieved Rick wouldn't be privy to their conversation, Alice caught Luke's attention and motioned toward the back of the church. When he met her there, she checked to see who might be listening.

Only a few neighbors stopped to chat before taking advantage of the sunshiny morning. "Luke, real fast, now, I don't have a lot of time and I can't talk long, but I have to cancel."

Luke's eyes narrowed. "Wha--"

"Shh! I didn't get the information you asked for. So he... we... I mean..." Alice took a deep breath and faced front. The sight of the cross hanging on the wall behind the altar, the same cross she stared at when she kneeled there as a little girl and gave her life to God, the cross overshadowing her vows to Joe, calmed her rushing pulse. Thank you, Lord. She let out the breath, and smiled at Luke. "I'm going to talk to him some more today."

His scowl made her heart jump a beat, but she wasn't going to let fear stop her this time. "You understand, Luke, don't you? I have to go now."

"Now wait j--"

Alice didn't wait to hear what he had to say. She took off through the door and headed for the willow tree on the front lawn of the parsonage where Rick and

Greta were talking. Rick's gentle smile made her breath hitch.

Lord, I'm begging for a sign. I love my country. Who do I trust?

By the time her frantic prayer was over, she'd reached Rick. He put out his elbow, and she took it forcing herself to look only forward and not back at Luke.

In the sunshine, she blinked, and blinked again, at the sight of Lois and Pete holding hands and whispering to each other. Lois giggled. Greta strolled to Deputy Eddie's side and looked on from a few paces away, a little smile playing at her lips.

Alice followed Rick toward his car, but clutched his forearm tighter when the mayor and Mrs. Wilson stepped in front of them. "Good morning, Mayor Wilson. Mrs. Wilson. Lovely day."

"Yes it is," chirped Mrs. Wilson.

"Alice, I wanted to remind you of the special meeting you called for Friday," the mayor said, "to finalize the route for your barn quilt tour."

"My tour?" Alice splayed her hand across her chest. "It's for the town. Mrs. Wilson, surely you don't--"

"There, there, dear." Mrs. Wilson patted her arm. "The mayor is doing what's best for us, you know." She waved a funeral home fan in front of her face.

Mr. and Mrs. Toliver joined them. "Ah, good, Alice," Mrs. Toliver said. "Just the person I needed to see." She pursed her lips together and adjusted her oversized purple hat with more flowers than Mamie's flower garden. "I certainly didn't expect to find you on the arm of Rick Morrison. Does Lucian know?"

Alice inhaled sharply. "Mrs. Toliver, you have no-"

"Mayor," Mrs. Toliver said, "you've informed them of the route changes?"

"We've been informed of the meeting." Rick put his hand over Alice's. "There's sure a lot of flapping going on over one little event."

Alice studied Rick's expression, his beautiful lips quirked in his infamous smirk. "Such a load of malarkey. Makes a man wonder what the fuss is really about."

Mrs. Toliver endured his stare for only a moment before she batted her funeral fan back and forth at the speed of bongo drums. She turned her back to them. "Come, Henry. We must be on our way."

Henry Toliver offered a cold nod to all and followed his wife. Luke caught up with the Tolivers and flashed a look toward them, not bothering to hide his disdain.

Lightheaded, Alice bit off a ragged nail.

Tipping his hat, the mayor said, "See you at the meeting," and strolled away with Mrs. Wilson trotting to keep up.

Rick nodded at Greta, and Greta flicked a glance at Alice and strolled away with the deputy. What was that all about?

After Rick closed the door of the car, Alice put her hand on his arm before he could start the engine. "Wait. What's going on? I get the feeling I'm in some Bogey movie, and I'm not sure what country I'm in."

Patting her hand in a patronizing way, he smiled. "I'd stick with my gut if I were you. You got great instincts, Kid. I'm not about to tell you which way to leap." He started the car and pulled onto the road, slowing for pedestrians then speeding up again. "Joe always said you were one of a kind, and he wasn't kidding."

He tilted his head toward her then faced forward again. "Trust yourself, Alice. I think you already know which way the wind is blowing. Now, why don't you sit back and relax? I'm planning to enjoy our little drive."

She pressed her lips together and studied the clutch purse on her lap. Life was supposed to be simpler when she moved back to Burning Bush life, but it was becoming more complicated by the minute.

What had Luke said? Maybe Rick wasn't a real estate tycoon, after all? Start with that.

"So, Rick." She cleared her throat. "Tell me, how many properties do you own? Uh, what's it like, being in charge of so many rentals? You sure travel a lot. You must be busy."

His knuckles tightened on the steering wheel before he slipped his arm across the seat behind her shoulders. He smiled at her, lazily, almost laughing. "My company keeps me busy. We've talked about this before."

He chuckled low, under his breath then returned his hand to the wheel as the road got steeper. "Lucien whispering things in your pretty little ears?" He glanced at her and chuckled again at the heat coloring her cheeks. "Don't believe every canary singing its little heart out. You know what a canary's job is, don't you? To test the air in the mines?"

Alice bristled. "So?"

"Canaries are the first to go when they sniff something bad."

Chapter Twenty-Four

Alice hadn't said a word since Rick's statement about the canaries. It sure made him sound like a spy, or a secret agent, or something. Her gut said he wasn't a bad guy. He knew Joe. That had to count for something. Maybe her first suspicion was more on target. He might be some kind of G-man.

None of it made any sense. If he was FBI, Luke would have found out when he checked Rick out with his friend. Maybe Rick wasn't telling the truth about knowing her husband. After all, Joe never mentioned him in his letters. Besides, Luke was the head of security for DuPont, and he was Mrs. Toliver's nephew. He had no reason to lie.

Rick smirked as he headed up the mountain. "Have you figured it out yet?"

Alice flushed. Was he a mind reader too? "Figured out what?"

"Why they want to close Mockingbird Road?"

"Oh." She let out the breath she didn't realize she was holding. "I don't understand it."

The Fleetmaster climbed higher as her pulse raced. They drew close to the spot where Mamie and Pappy died.

Rick parked on the side of the road and turned off the car. "Why don't we get out and look around?"

Alice nodded, and Rick opened her door. She scooted her feet onto the gravel berm.

He placed a hand on her elbow and held onto her as they peered over the edge. "I see they put a guardrail up where it happened. Has there ever been another accident up here?"

As she stared over the cliff where her folks' Model T plunged them to their deaths, she swallowed the lump in her throat. "No, they were the only ones. It doesn't make sense."

He stepped over the guardrail. "What doesn't?"

"My folks lived on this road all of their lives. They'd been up this hill thousands of times. They didn't drive it if conditions were bad. It just doesn't add up they would be up here on a snowy day, let alone miss a turn."

"No, it doesn't." Rick climbed to the safe side of the guardrail and stepped into the middle of the road. He crossed his arms and examined the pavement. "Not much traffic up this way. What about deer?"

"I guess it's possible, but the deer usually don't come up this way. They tend to stay in the woods closer to the river."

He paced across the width of the road as he counted his footsteps. "Plenty of room for two cars to pass, a wide berm, pavement intact, a guardrail around the curve, very few deer, and only one accident. I can't think of a single reason to close this road." He spun and strode to the edge. "It's not like you can close every mountain road in West Virginia."

"Exactly."

"Alice, you stand your ground no matter what the Tolivers try to pull. Don't you let them push you around."

She blinked back the tears. He understood.

He stepped closer, wrapped his arms around her, and kissed her. This time she didn't pull away. In her heart, she knew she had nothing to fear from him.

Drawing back, Rick gazed into her eyes with his *trust me* look, warming her heart. "I'll be out of town a few days, but don't worry. I'll be back for the meeting on Friday."

As they headed back into Burning Bush, Alice scooted closer to him. He placed his arm around her shoulder, and she leaned her head against him. She hadn't felt like this since Joe was alive.

He's a double agent, Alice.

Luke's words startled her, coming into her thoughts uninvited. What if she was wrong? How could she fall for a traitor?

By the time they reached her shop, Alice had talked herself out of believing Rick was a spy at least five times. Then Luke's words would haunt her, and she'd have to start working it out all over again. She didn't let on to him, but she had made a decision. She would call Akron, Ohio first thing tomorrow.

Rick followed her to the front stoop. "So, how about a cup of coffee?"

"I'll give you more than a cup of coffee." She fished in her clutch for her key. "Greta is planning a feast."

He rubbed his belly. "Thanks for taking pity on a poor bachelor. I was planning on a baloney sandwich for Sunday dinner."

She chuckled. "A grown man needs more than baloney."

"Wait." Rick reached for her hand. "Remember what I said? Trust your instincts."

"I will." With a long last look into his eyes convincing her he was the good guy, she opened the door and stepped inside. "Greta? We're home." No answer. "She's probably in the apartment."

She climbed the stairs with Rick close behind and stepped into the kitchen. "Greta," she called out. There were no pots on the stoves, nothing in the oven. "Greta!" Dinner hadn't been started.

Rick grabbed her arm. "Alice, stay here."

She tried to pull away. "Something's wrong."

"Don't move." He turned toward the door and pulled a big black shiny pistol with a wooden grip from a holster inside his suitcoat.

Alice swallowed. "What are you... what are you doing with a gun?"

"Shh," was the only answer she got as he skulked into the hallway.

Her heart pounded. A door, probably from one of the bedrooms, thumped. A second door crashed open. She almost peeked out to see what was going on, but Rick returned before she had a chance.

He holstered his weapon. "Nobody here. Are you sure she wasn't going anywhere?"

"No, she said she'd..." Alice gulped down the lump in her throat. "She said she'd make supper for us. Rick, what are you doing with a gun?"

He leaned against the doorpost. "Doll, I can't tell you. Not yet."

"Where's Greta?"

"I don't know." Rick took her in his arms. "I'm going to find out."

"I'm going with you."

"No, you're not," Rick said.

She pulled away and delivered a glare she hoped would show him she wouldn't take no for an answer.

He rubbed the back of his neck. "What happens if she comes back? You need to wait here for her."

"She's not a child. She can stay here on her own. We can check later to see if she made it back okay."

"You have got to be the most stubborn dame I've ever... " He blew out a loud sigh before grabbing her elbow. "Since I can't stop you, let's get going."

*****

There weren't too many places Greta could be on a Sunday. Daria's Diner was closed. So were the grocer, the gas station, and the roller-skating rink, but Rick seemed to know where he wanted to look first.

Alice placed her hand over her stomach as his Fleetmaster raced toward the river on the edge of town. "Do you think she went for a walk by the river?"

He glanced at her but didn't say anything.

The only building out there was the smithy shop, the headquarters of the quilt tour.

He jerked the car to a stop and left it running as he got out and pulled his gun. Before closing his door, he leaned in. "Stay here."

She scooted out of the car and slammed her door. "No."

He tapped his fist against his forehead. "Fine. I don't have time to argue, but you better stay close behind me and do everything I say."

Alice nodded and followed as he inched the door open. He flashed a look toward her to stay put and burst through the door. A moment later, he motioned her to come in.

She stepped inside. Greta lay in the middle of the floor unconscious. "Greta." She ran to her.

"She'll be fine." Rick surveyed the room.

Greta groaned and reached for her head.

"It's all right." Alice pushed the hair away from Greta's face. "Just lay there. We'll get you help."

"No! We'll take her back to the apartment. It doesn't look serious, just a bump to the head."

Heat flashed up Alice's neck. "She's hurt. She needs a doctor, maybe the hospital."

He knelt next to her and grabbed her shoulders. "Nobody can know about this. Got it?"

She nodded, but she didn't get it. She didn't understand him. "What if she has a concussion or something?"

"We'll make do."

Greta moaned and pulled into a sitting position. "What happened?"

Rick grabbed some papers scattered across the anvil, and after scanning them, folded and tucked them into his inside suit pocket.

Alice patted Greta's hand and tossed a glance toward Rick. "What are those?"

"What?"

117

"The papers you hid in your pocket."

Rick shrugged his shoulders. "Just the security plans to the DuPont Factory near Charleston."

Chapter Twenty-Five

After Rick helped Greta up the stairs to the apartment, he left again in such a hurry Alice didn't even get to say goodbye. Or get a goodbye kiss. She sat on a chair next to Greta, who lay in the narrow bed with a cool cloth across her forehead. After giving her some aspirin, Alice prayed Greta didn't have anything serious, like a concussion. The bump over her ear looked pretty sore and swollen, but an ice bag had helped.

As Greta dozed, Alice watched the clock, determined to wake her every two hours according to the Red Cross directions she'd remembered.

Lord, what's going on? What was Greta doing with the plans to the DuPont factory?

Trust your instincts, Alice. Trust.

Trusting was not her strong suit.

Greta moaned and moved her legs.

Alice leaned over and turned the cloth on her forehead and patted her arm. "There, there." Maybe she hadn't done the right thing by trusting a German girl. Whatever was going on, it looked like Greta was in the middle of it.

Five p.m. She removed the cloth and nudged her friend's shoulder. "Greta? Greta? Wake up for a minute, there's a dear. Wake up and tell me your name."

"You already said mein name. Greta Engel." The girl groaned and tried to lift her head. "I'll just get a sip of water."

"You're not going anywhere. I'll get some water and more ice. Stay put."

In the kitchen, Alice chipped more ice for the bag and ran a glass of water. She settled the ice bag against her friend's head and replaced the cool cloth. "Oh, Joe, what am I going to do? Who do I trust?"

Greta moaned. "*Vielen dank.*"

Alice went to the tiny window overlooking the river. "I thought the war was supposed to solve the problems, not make new ones. It's over. Why can't everything just be normal?"

"Wars never solve anything."

She turned at the sound of Greta's weak voice. "What do you mean?"

Greta scooted up on her pillow and pressed her pale hand against the ice bag on her forehead. "Where there is hate, there is always jealousy, envy, strife. Remember Pastor Round's message?"

Alice shook her head, the heat of embarrassment on her throat about not paying attention in church, and the reason why.

"We are all sinners, and nothing will be right in this world. Even Christians can't agree how to treat each other."

Alice sat in the straight wooden chair by the bed. "Amen, sister. How are you feeling? Does it hurt very much?"

"*Ja.*" Greta reached to touch the ice bag. "Thank you for rescuing me."

"Rick didn't want me to call the sheriff, or a doctor. I hope we're doing the right thing."

Greta pressed her lips together and closed her eyes. A tear escaped and rolled along her temple.

Alice dabbed it with her hanky. "There, there. I'll call the doctor no matter what."

Greta grasped Alice's wrist. "No. Rick is right. This is my fault."

She had to know. "Greta, what were you doing there?"

Below, the door to the shop crashed open.

"Mrs. Brighton!"

Alice exchanged a look of fright with Greta. In the excitement, she must have forgotten to lock up. When the wounded girl tried to rise, Alice pushed her back. "No, you stay here. Don't you even peep. I'll take care of this."

"Mrs. Brighton, please come down!"

Alice headed to the stairs. "I'm coming, Sheriff. What's all the fuss?" With shaking fingers, she locked the door to the apartment and settled the key in her bra. She gathered a deep breath, smiled, and walked down the steps pretending nothing had happened.

She stopped short at the sight of the men behind Sheriff Jenner.

"Luke!" She looked from him to the sheriff and Deputy Eddie to Frank Summers. "What can I do for you gentlemen? We're normally closed on Sundays, but we just received a shipment of quilt batting. Candy, perhaps?"

"Mrs. Brighton, this is no laughing matter," Jenner said. He twirled his hands together. "Where's your girl?"

She tamped down a quiver from her stomach. "Why, Sheriff, you know I don't have any children."

Luke stared at her with such hard eyes, the hair on the nape of her neck rose.

"Just go bring her down, Mrs. Brighton."

Alice squared her shoulders and returned the sheriff's frown. "Not until I know what this is about."

"Lucien, here, has a complaint against her." Jenner waved him forward. "Go on, then, tell Mrs. Brighton what you told me."

Luke's lips were white. He unclenched his fists and set them on his hips. "That German spy was--"

"I beg your pardon!" Alice's fury quelled her fear. She paced right up to Luke and stuck her nose close to his. "For your information, Greta Engel is no spy! In fact, she was accosted this afternoon. It's lucky Rick and I--" She grinned at the rage on Luke's face. "--found her when we did."

What had she ever seen in Lucien Wendell Holmes to make her want to spend even a second in his company? She stepped back and pointed at him. "If anyone's a spy, Sheriff, it's him!"

Jenner stepped between them. "Now, everybody get off your high horses and calm down." He threw his hat on the counter. "What's this about Miss Engel being accosted?" He eyed Luke up and down as if considering the best way to capture a rabid coon.

The shakes returned. Alice had done what Rick ordered her not to do, told about Greta. She folded her arms. "Perhaps I was a little hasty. Greta had an accident, yes, but she'll be fine in the morning."

"Where did this accident take place?" Jenner was not giving up easily. "I'll need to speak with her in any case."

"Sheriff." Concern etched Deputy Eddie's features. "If she's hurt, maybe this isn't the best time." He turned to Alice. "Is she all right? Maybe we should get Doc Brenner."

"No need. She'll be fine after a good night's sleep. You can see her tomorrow." Alice started to shoo the men away, but Frank Summers, who had been quiet till now, straightened from his slouch against a shelf of bolted yellow and red calico fabric.

"I saw Greta sneak into the smithy."

Alice summoned every ounce of courage. "So? I doubt the word 'sneak' is accurate. We're using the building as headquarters for the quilt tour committee, and Greta is on the committee. She can go there whenever she likes."

"On a Sunday?" Summers snorted a bourbon-scented waft of air.

Alice wrinkled her nose and fanned her hand in front of it. "What's it to you?"

"I told you, Sheriff," Luke said. "Arrest that spy! She stole something of mine."

"Yours!" Alice cried. "What were you doing there, anyway? Greta would never steal anything, certainly not--"

At Luke's triumphant smirk, she amended lamely, "Anything not belonging to her." She narrowed her eyes and pointed at Luke's chest. "What, exactly, were you doing there?" She glanced at Summers. "On a Sunday?"

Luke glanced away and straightened his tie and smoothed his hair. "If you recall, I happen to be a member of the committee as well. I have every right to visit headquarters anytime, as well as anybody else. Just so happens I was doing double duty."

"On a Sunday?"

"I often work on Sundays. I'm conscientious about my career, and I needed a quiet place to work."

"What were you working on?" Alice asked him.

"It's none of your concern, but my very important papers were stolen, and she took them. All the same, nothing ever changes. We may have defeated Hitler, but--"

"Now see here," Jenner cut in. "Mrs. Brighton says Greta was there, and we'll talk to the young lady. There's no need to start up the war machine."

"She's probably some Nazi war criminal," Summers said. "Better talk to her now, before she escapes."

"Pshaw! Escape to where?" Alice replied. "You have my word, you can come back tomorrow, and we'll be here. If she's feeling up to it, you can see her."

"Sheriff, I demand you arrest that German girl right now," Luke said. "By tomorrow who knows what those two will have cooked up?"

Uh, oh. Even Alice backed up at the way Jenner's countenance could have sent lightning bolts. "Demand?"

"Tomorrow will be too late. I need those pl--papers now. Who knows where she put them? Who she's called."

Sure now Rick had picked up Luke's missing papers, Alice had a few questions of her own, starting with, "If you were there, how did the papers get stolen, and why do you think Greta would do such a thing?"

Luke tugged at his tie. "I'm not the one who needs to be interrogated here."

"You never did say how your papers got out of your sight," Jenner said.

"I heard a noise," he muttered. "I went to look, and when I came back, they were gone."

"Rick and I didn't see you when we were there."

"When was this?" Jenner asked her.

"Two thirty. The only person there was Greta, unconscious on the floor, where she... she had tripped and fallen, hit her head. Hard. We took her home."

"Unconscious?" Deputy Eddie stepped toward the phone. "I'm calling Doc Brenner."

"She doesn't want a doctor." Alice blocked the deputy's path. "She'll be fine."

Eddie tilted his head, looking torn about what to do. "She might have a concussion."

Maybe the deputy was right. The only reason Alice didn't get Doc Brenner right away was because Greta and Rick insisted. "If she gets any worse, I promise I'll call."

"Where's Morrison now?" Jenner asked.

Even Luke turned to hear her response.

"I don't know. He's just my landlord."

Jenner's attention focused back on Luke. "You said you were only gone to check on a noise."

"Yes, well, when I saw Frank here, we decided to get a cup of coffee."

"Where? There's no place selling coffee on a Sunday," Alice said.

She bent her head at the look of remonstrance from Jenner. "Boys?"

Luke's expression said he didn't appreciate being called a boy. "We went to my aunt's house. She invited me to stop by when I needed a respite if it's any of your concern."

"The kraut woman must have gone in to steal the plans when we were gone," Summers said, earning himself an acid look from Luke. "We went in to warn to--er, tell Luke here I saw someone coming."

"Plans, eh?" Jenner asked. "Had a lookout, did you?"

"Just part of my profession. As the head of security. I can't let those plans get into the wrong hands." Luke stood a little straighter and tightened his tie. "Now, Sheriff Jenner, if you can't handle this, I could call the FBI since this is a matter of national security."

The sheriff jutted his jaw and stared Luke down for a moment before turning to Alice. "I'm sorry, Mrs. Brighton, but it looks like we'll have to disturb Miss Engel this evening, after all."

"No need. I am not disturbed." Greta, pale but composed, came into the room wearing Alice's fuzzy pink bathrobe.

How long Greta had been there listening? "Let me get you a chair." Alice strode behind the counter and hefted the wooden chair.

None of the men came to help her, so much for chivalry, but the deputy did rush to Greta's side and offer her an arm as Greta, white-faced, sank onto it.

"Miss Engel, you had an accident?" Jenner asked.

"I hit my head. Here." She lifted her hair from her ear to show them the angry, purple bump.

Alice watched the other men out of the corner of her eye. Summers gloated, she was sure. One suspicion confirmed.

"Perhaps we should call the doctor," Jenner said.

"*Nein.* I will recover. You had questions?"

"What were you doing at the shack earlier today?" the sheriff asked.

"I was going to surprise Alice with a new block for the quilt tour. I stop on my way home from church. Then, bam, I fall down."

"Super, Greta. We needed some fresh ideas, especially if we add the other stops on Mockingbird Road, once the council approves the route." Alice raised her brow at the sheriff who appeared not to have heard. He was fingering his badge and nodding to some inner thought. "Sheriff? We should let Greta go back to bed."

"Ask her about my papers," Luke said.

Jenner shot him a stern look. "Miss Engel, did you see anything unusual at the shack?"

Alice wondered what made the sheriff use those words.

"*Nein.* Nothing I did not expect to see."

"No papers, they looked like blueprints?"

"I do not know 'blue print.' What it means? Printed fabric?"

"Never mind." Jenner whirled and grabbed his hat. "We're sorry to have bothered you ladies on a Sunday evening. Miss Engel, Mrs. Brighton, if you see Morrison, tell him I'm looking for him, won't you?"

"I don't know when I'll see him again," Alice said with a glance toward Luke, "but I'll pass along your message."

Summers followed a fuming, muttering Luke out the door.

Sheriff Jenner nodded. "Ladies, sorry to have disturbed you." The bell gave a jangle as he left.

Deputy Eddie stood there a moment longer and opened his mouth to say something, but he pressed his lips tight and exited without saying it.

Alice locked the door tight and pulled the shade. "Greta, what on earth is going on? Who are you, really?"

Greta stood and melted onto the floor.

Chapter Twenty-Six

Greta hadn't said another word about what happened yesterday. When she collapsed after Sheriff Jenner and Lucien's mob left, Alice had decided she needed the rest more than another interrogation. When Alice woke her this morning, she still had a nasty knot and a pounding headache. If she wasn't better by the end of the day, Alice was going to ask Doc Brenner for a house call no matter how much Greta protested.

Since Alice had opened the door at ten, a steady stream of customers had come through She glanced at the clock as she cut three yards off a bolt of dotted green cotton for Bernice. It was already eleven thirty. She didn't ever remember the shop being this busy..

If Greta had been there to help, she might have been able to pull herself away to make the phone calls. If she didn't find time soon, Summit County records in Akron would be out to lunch.

Bernice paid for her yard goods and left. Alice locked the door behind her and hung the "Out for Lunch" sign on the window a little early.

Taking a deep breath to calm her nerves, she dialed zero for the operator. When she reached Summit County Records, she asked the clerk to look up the birth certificate for Rick Morrison.

"Date of birth?" an older woman's voice asked.

"I'm not sure. Maybe sometime between 1910 and 1920."

"Could you be more specific, ma'am?" The voice sounded annoyed.

"No, I can't. You have his name. I'm sure you can find the birth certificate."

"Is the name on the certificate Rick or Richard?"

"I don't know." Alice bit her lip. "Can't you check both?"

A groan on the other end of the line. "This might take some time. Can you call back after lunch?"

Calculating on her fingers how much all these long-distance calls were going to cost, Alice agreed and hung up. The next call she had the operator make was to the Quaker Oats Factory.

A male voice answered. "Quaker Oats. How may I help you?"

"I'd like to talk to the person who handles employment records."

"One moment, please."

She twirled the receiver cord around her fingers while she waited.

"Hello, this is Mrs. Frances in Personnel. May I help you?"

"I hope so. I'm calling to find out if you had a man named Morrison working there in the 1920s and 30s."

"First name."

Alice twisted the cord tighter. "I don't know his first name." Maybe she should have waited until she found the certificate. Rick's father's name would be on it.

"Ma'am, Morrison is a common name, and I have dozens of file cabinets of records to look through."

"I understand." Alice leaned against the counter and rubbed her forehead.

"I'll call again when I know more."

"Happy to be of service." The phone clicked.

She blew out her frustration as she hung up the receiver. There had to be a way to check out Rick's story. "What next, Lord?" She had an idea and dialed zero. "Operator, could you give me the DuPont Factory in Belle, West Virginia. I don't know the number."

It only took a couple of minutes to get to the switchboard at DuPont and then the security department.

A man answered. "DuPont Security. May I help you?"

"Yes, I'm calling from Burning Bush, West Virginia, and well..." She wasn't sure how to say this without sounding crazy. "Who's the head of your security department?"

"Mr. Benjamin Graves. Would you like to speak to him?"

Alice twirled the cord. "Graves? I thought Lucien Wendell Holmes was the head of security."

"Lucien Holmes?" The voice had a tinge of uneasiness. "No, ma'am."

She gave the cord another twist. "Does Lucien Holmes even work there?"

A pause. "Maybe you should talk to Mr. Graves about this."

Her stomach churned. "Have any plans to your factory been recently stolen?"

"One moment, please."

Alice rubbed her hand across the green cotton bolt as she waited.

Another man's voice came on the line. "Ma'am, this is Mr. Graves. You're calling from Burning Bush? Is that outside of Montgomery?" The voice sounded older and had a rough quality to it.

Alice struggled to find her voice. "Yes."

"You're asking about Lucien Wendell Holmes? Around six-foot tall, one hundred seventy pounds, dark brown hair, brown eyes?"

Her heart raced.

"Is Mr. Holmes in Burning Bush now, ma'am?"

"Yes. I don't understand. He's been here for about a month. Does he work there?"

"Ma'am, what's your name?"

She hung up the phone. Took some deep breaths. Tried to convince herself there was nothing to be afraid of.

Work, work, work, Alice. Don't think about it.

After putting away the bolt of material she'd cut for Bernice, she sat at her quilting frame and picked up the needle. Her hand trembled as she set it back down. Had Luke stolen the plans from DuPont? Maybe he was the double agent, the traitor. Or maybe he was undercover investigating a spy ring in Burning Bush. Mr. Graves did seem to know who he was.

A snort escaped her lips. A spy ring in Burning Bush. "Joe, have you ever heard of anything so ludicrous." The whole world was crazy, and she'd come home to escape the insanity, but she had a sneaking suspicion, even in Burning Bush, she was the only sane one left.

She couldn't concentrate on the quilt and decided to have lunch and check on Greta. After making sandwiches, she went to Greta's room.

Her roommate looked better. She'd propped herself up on pillows and some of her paleness was gone.

Alice set the tray on the nightstand. "How are you feeling?"

"Much better. My head still hurts, but I don't feel sick to my stomach anymore."

"Good." Alice handed her a sandwich and sat on the chair beside the bed.

"You did not have to make lunch. I could have managed." Greta took a bite.

"You don't have to wait on everybody all the time. I take advantage of your cooking because I don't enjoy working in the kitchen, but I do know how to cook, and I can still fix us something to eat. You need your rest." Alice checked out the bump above Greta's ear. "You could have been killed."

"I was in little danger."

"Greta, what happened?"

"I told you. I wanted to surprise you with a quilt block and went to HQ as you call it. Then I do not know until you and Herr Morrison found me on the floor."

Alice raised an eyebrow.

"You do not believe me?"

"Where's the quilt block?"

Greta bit her lip. "I lost it... at HQ."

"You didn't have a quilt block or I would have seen it." Alice took a sip of pop while she tried to find the right words. Maybe it was better to just come out with it. "You're lying to me. You and Rick are in the middle of whatever's going on."

"I am not in the middle of anything."

"You trust me, don't you?"

"*Ja*, I trust you. You are a good friend."

"Then why won't you tell me the truth?" Alice grabbed Greta's hand. "Are you in some kind of trouble? Because if you are, maybe if you talk to me, I can help you."

"I am not the one in trouble." Greta set her sandwich down and placed her hand on her head. "My head hurts. I need to close my eyes."

Alice blew her frustration out in a heavy sigh. "Fine. I still plan to call Doc Brenner this afternoon to come take a look at you."

Greta started to argue, but Alice put her hand up to stop her. Greta sank into the pillow.

Alice stood and pulled the blind "After I make sure you're all right, we are going to talk about this. You mark my words."

Greta's eyes were closed, and she made no response, so Alice closed the door softly behind her and made her way to the kitchen to finish her lunch while she tried to figure out what to do next.

Pounding on the shop door interrupted her thoughts, and she went to see who couldn't wait until lunch was over for her to open.

When she unlocked the door, Sheriff Jenner stood on the other side. "Mrs. Brighton, we need to talk."

"Come in, Sheriff. What would you like to talk about?"

Sheriff Jenner didn't waste any time storming inside like he owned the place. "For one thing, where's your landlord? Where's Rick Morrison?"

"I don't know." It was the truth, but Alice struggled to appear calm. "I told you yesterday, my landlord doesn't share his personal itinerary with me. All I know is he's out of town on business. He'll be back for the meeting Friday."

Jenner's brow furrowed. "Ah, yes, the meeting to try to get Mockingbird Road back on the tour."

"Yes, Sheriff. I still don't understand why you would want to close the road. We've driven on it for years."

The sheriff, who normally had an answer for everything, wrinkled his brow. "Mrs. Brighton, I must ask you one more time. When you and Mr. Morrison found Greta, were there any papers lying around?"

Alice swallowed. She didn't want to lie, but she needed to find out what was going on before she told Sheriff Jenner anything. "I was so worried about Greta... You understand. At the time, she was my only concern."

Sheriff Jenner crossed his arms as if he could see right through the deception. "If you see your landlord, tell him I need to see him."

"I will, Sheriff."

Jenner tipped his cap and left.

She closed the door and waited a moment to make sure he wouldn't return before calling Summit County Records. She spoke to the same clerk she'd talked to before. "This is Mrs. Brighton. I called earlier."

"Yes, Mrs. Brighton. I remember you."

"Did you find Rick Morrison's birth certificate?"

"Well... sort of."

Alice twirled the cord. "Did you or didn't you?"

"Well, ma'am, it's like this. I've never run across anything like this before, but I found the certificate in a sealed envelope."

"I don't understand."

"You see, ma'am, the records are there, but they've been sealed by order of the State Department."

Alice dropped the phone.

Chapter Twenty-Seven

Alice sank into the chair at the counter. Joe had said something in his letters, something important. What was it? She grabbed the shoe box she'd kept in the storeroom and went back to the counter.

On top of all the letters, pictures, and momentos was a telegram. She took it out and thumbed through the coorespondance until she found it, the last letter he wrote. She'd received it two days after the telegram from the US Army.

She held it tight to her chest then reverently opened it. Tears watered her eyes as she read about his undying love for her, how much he missed her, and all the plans they had for the future. She mulled over one paragraph.

I miss you so much. I can't wait to see you, to touch you, again. It's all
I think about. If something ever does happen to me, I've told my friend
Bear to contact you. You can trust him.

Someone placed a warm hand on her shoulder. It startled her so much, all her self-defense training from her years working in the shipyard came back in a rush. She jumped up from her seat at the shop counter, twisted, and chopped at her would-be assailant.

"Ow! What did you do that for?" Her brother hunched behind the counter with his arms over his head.

"Pete?" She must have forgotten to lock up after Jenner had left and had been so deep in thought she'd been oblivious to the bell ringing above the door. "For goodness' sakes, you know better than to sneak up on a girl." She took a deep breath as she struggled to regain her composure.

"I sure hope you don't treat all your customers this way." He held up his arm and flexed his wrist, puzzled look creasing his brow.

"Only pesky brothers who sneak up on me with no warning." She straightened the basket of spools on the glass counter. "Lois knows those moves, too, you know."

"I'll have to watch out."

"Customer? You?" she said over her shoulder. "Don't tell me you've come in to make a purchase."

"Nah. Lois just asked me to stop in here and find out if you have any material for curtains. Since I was coming into town and all." Pete helped himself to a candy bar.

"Sure. I didn't know you needed new curtains." She cocked a brow at the candy display. "Help yourself."

"Thanks. Not needed. Wanted," Pete said between chewing. "Mamie's are faded, and Lois thinks she can sew now." He held out his left elbow, which was covered by a paisley patch fastened by large red stitches on to his twill shirt.

Alice laughed. "Yes, well, Greta showed her how to thread a needle and make basic stitches the other day."

"Speaking of whom," he emphasized the "m," glanced out of the shop window, and lowered his voice, "I heard she had a little accident."

A shimmer of trepidation crossed Alice's shoulders. "Oh? Who told you?"

Pete flushed. "Um, don't tell Lois, but I stopped for a bit of Daria's roast beef at the diner, you know? Summers was there, spouting off about how he was involved in an investigation. So, how is she?"

"She got a heavy bump on the noggin, but she'll be all right. Now, don't go around spreading rumors."

"Who, me? I'm not some old biddy." He reached for another bar of chocolate.

"Uh-uh, mister. Not without money. Don't let me keep you from your errands." She put her hand under his patched elbow and escorted him to the door. "Tell Lois I'll talk to her later about the curtains. Bye-bye." She waved, closed the door on him, and flipped the out to lunch sign to open.

A moment later, the bell rang as Doc Brenner, a distinguished older Lionel Barrymore type with gray hair and bright eyes, showed up at the shop announcing Deputy Eddie Tyler had told him about what happened and asked him to look in on Greta. The doctor's hearty presence was a welcome respite from her worry over Greta's injury. Greta insisted on getting up from bed and meeting the doctor at the kitchen table.

"Tsk, tsk." Doc set his bag on the floor of the kitchen and brushed aside Greta's hair. He checked her pupils and asked a few questions. "Well, I don't see there's much I can do," he said. "You've been getting good care. Just keep with the compresses and aspirin."

Alice showed him out on her way back down to the shop.

"If she complains about loss of vision or hearing or has a sudden, severe headache, call me," Doc said. "Otherwise, make sure she rests today. If she feels better, she can go back to work in the shop tomorrow."

"Thanks, Doc. Much obliged."

He tipped his hat then strode down the street.

Alice stood in the doorway for a moment, soaking up the atmosphere. After filling up at the water tower, the train's chugging sound through town caused a couple of squirrels to make a dive toward the nearest elm tree. A row of baby geese followed their mother as she crossed Main Street heading toward Kanawha River. The elm, oak, and walnut trees standing on the mountains encompassing the town were now green, evidence it was already the middle of June. How could such beauty surround so much deception?

Yellow wildflowers in the grass across the street were too tempting. She strode toward them, inhaled their fragrance, and picked a few to decorate the shop. Her mother always had wildflowers in a vase on the table this time of year.

A delivery boy stopped by with a box of flowers. Alice opened them. A dozen long stemmed roses. She opened the card from the sheik of Burning Bush.

> *To my dear Alice,*
> *I'm sorry I upset you, but I'm concerned about you.*
> *Love, Luke.*

She threw them in the trash.

The rest of the day was a blur of customers. Just before closing, a surprise customer made the bell jingle.

"Miss Spencer! Welcome. What can I do for you?"

Violet Spencer had to be in her early forties. She'd been Alice and Pete's teacher when they were kids in Burning Bush Grammar School, a one-room schoolhouse at the head of the holler beside the church. A spinster, Miss Spencer never found time for sewing or quilting before and always bought her clothes ready-made from the department store in Montgomery. A quick and flustered cornflower-blue-eyed glance at Greta's bridal display made Alice take a discreet gasp. Well, love could happen to anyone.

A pleasant half hour later, Alice had helped her pick out a pattern and material for a wedding gown, and discussed a few other details.

"I'm so pleased for you, Miss Spencer. You have my best wishes. When is the happy day?"

Miss Spencer gathered her pocketbook, straightened her little pillbox hat, and grabbed both handles of the bag in front of her. "We thought the Fourth of July."

"That's the weekend of the Quilt Tour. Are you sure you want such a busy date?" Perhaps this was Miss Spencer's way of letting her know the guest list was going to be severely limited.

"I heard the event might not happen after all."

"Who told you that?" Alice cringed. The tone of her voice sounded angrier than she intended.

"I don't like to tell tales out of school." Miss Spencer came closer and whispered even though there wasn't anyone in the shop who might overhear. "I ran into Mrs. Toliver at the grocer's, and she told me how you were so far behind in assigning quilt blocks, you might have to cancel the whole thing."

Alice wished Mrs. Toliver had been in the shop right then so she could school her. The nerve. She plastered on a fake smile. "I assure you, Miss Spencer, all will be ready in plenty of time. You might consider changing the date of your wedding."

Miss Spencer raised an eyebrow the way she used to when she caught Alice talking in class. "I believe I'll keep the date as is for now."

On Tuesday afternoon, Greta was well enough to hold down the counter at the shop, so Alice went to the committee headquarters to do some work on the tour. First, she stopped at Daria's Diner and made a big to-do about ordering a sandwich to go, which she planned to eat at the former smithy. All the men at the lunch counter heard. With so many people knowing her destination, she'd be safe enough.

Despite Miss Spencer's dour prediction, Alice still planned to make the event special for Burning Bush. Some of the people who'd agreed to host a quilt block stop were grumbling, and she wanted to make it as easy as possible. Putting up scaffolding and trying to create large-scale patterns could be daunting. By creating large templates, maybe she'd allay some of the biggest complaints.

Buford Montgomery Junior had been particularly troublesome and wanted to know if the paint would wash off. "I don't want no girlie colors on my barn," he'd told her with his dirt-crusted thumbs hooked behind the straps of his bib overalls covered with suspicious brown stains and smelling strongly of animal.

Alice assured him he could paint over the block after the tour was over.

"Me? I don't have time fer no foolishness. I tole the missus she could have this nonsense long as she don't get in the way and cleans up after herself."

Alice informed him his wife's block could go on the sliding doors of their barn instead of on the wall above and would be blue and red, no girlie colors, and she'd help paint over the design later.

Buford murmured his agreement. A simple butterfly design would do nicely, and had lots of rectangles and triangles, which could be used in other designs.

Alice had twelve large-scale patterns sketched out a couple of hours later. Lois, of course, already had her design, Flying Geese made of triangles, as did Bernice Gorman who was doing the Kansas City Star, all diamonds and triangles and squares. Andrea had Grandmother's Flower Garden, a difficult block made with hexagons. Janice was still dithering, and with the uncertainty of the fate of Mockingbird Road, was waiting before buying paint. If she didn't decide soon, Alice would assign the easy nine patch, a block made of nine squares.

She set the templates aside and grimaced at the stickiness of her blouse clinging to her back. Even with the door open, the air was warm.

A shadow crossed the little window to her right. She edged her patent leather handbag a little closer. She'd packed a brick in it, just in case.

The crunch of gravel under a heavy foot sounded outside.

"Hello?" She hitched her breath. "Who's out there? Come on, come and face me like a man."

"It's only me." Luke stepped into the doorway, filling the space.

She shivered despite the warmth. "What are you doing here, Luke?"

"Did you get my flowers?"

"Yes, but don't send me anymore."

"I just wanted to let you know I'm sorry about what happened the other night. I know you would never be involved with Morrison and the German girl's plots. You need someone like me to watch over you, keep you safe."

"I don't know what you're talking about."

Luke took a couple of steps toward her. "You're not the first woman to be confused by his double talk. There have been many others."

She placed her hand on her purse. "Maybe you'd better leave."

Another couple of steps. "I don't understand how you could be so un-American. First you take a Nazi into your home, then you would rather be romanced by a Soviet playboy even after I warned you he's a spy. Your husband fought and died for this great nation, and you would throw all it away over your infatuation for this infiltrator."

"How dare you bring my Joe into your schemes?" Alice huffed her anger, mingled with fear. "You have no right, none at all. You should leave."

"I'm not the bad guy here, Alice." Luke moved a little closer. "It's time you got some sense in that pretty little head of yours. You know what I want."

She tugged her purse nearer. "I'm sorry, Luke, I don't know what you mean."

He inched toward her with the same scowl on his face he wore Sunday night. "We both know Morrison has those papers, and I'm going to prove it. I want them back. They're mine."

She stood, not wanting to feel towered over. "I can't tell you anything. I don't know where they are."

He took a few more steps until he was standing in front of her.

She leaned back and grabbed the brick out of her purse. "Don't come any closer."

He laughed. "You're going to hit me?" Grabbing the brick out of her hand, he threw it in the corner. "Awfully brave, aren't you?" He placed his hand on hers and leaned in.

She shivered and pulled it away.

He blew out a heavy sigh. "Ask yourself why Morrison's gone all the time. What's he up to?" His calm tone didn't match the anger in his eyes. He moved closer backing her against the wall until she had nowhere to go. "You're consorting with the enemy."

She turned her head as he placed his palms on the wall on either side of her.

"Use your head, my dear. Where does he go? Not tending those other properties he doesn't own." His face drew nearer as if he might kiss her. "I'm only trying to protect you."

Her skin crawled. The smell of his Listerine breath turned her stomach. Rick may not be telling her the whole truth, but he never tried to scare her like this. She pushed at his chest but couldn't budge him. "I know you've been lying, and I can prove it."

His face turned ashen. "What do you know?"

She splayed her hand over her mouth. "Nothing." She couldn't tell him about the phone call. "Whatever you're up to isn't going to work."

"Why, you..." He reached to grab her throat.

"Lucian! Lucian, dearest, are you in there?"

He let go of her. Saved by Gwendolyn Toliver, of all people.

"Come out, now. You're needed at home."

Luke grabbed her shoulders and pinned her to the wall. "You have no idea the magnitude of events you're dealing with here or how much danger you're in." He leaned over and brushed his lips over her ear. "I care about you, my dear, but if you continue seeing Morrison, I won't be able to shield you."

"Lucian!"

He stroked her cheek with the back of his hand, then backed off and left.

When their footsteps had faded, Alice sank to the bench and hugged herself. She couldn't stop shaking. He'd done nothing but frighten her a little. There was nothing she could tell the sheriff to convince him to arrest Luke. If those security men at DuPont were looking for him, he'd have to do some much-needed explaining soon enough.

If only Rick were in town.

One thing for sure, she'd never let a committee member come here to HQ alone again.

*****

In the evening, Alice and Greta met at Janice Felton's house since Janice was expected to deliver any second now. Lois, who arrived just after Alice, was sticking to her resolution to become a happy homemaker and had even brought some sewing to work on during the meeting.

The only others invited were Bernice Gorman and Andrea Collins. It was a private meeting for those members of the quilt tour who would be affected by the prospective closing of Mockingbird Road. Alice insisted the Tolivers not know about the gathering. There was no way she way going to let that woman interfere again.

This Friday's town council meeting would be even more exciting than normal. Pete had contacted Senator Walter F. Burgess's office, who promised to look into the matter. He and Ralph Gorman had also invited the president of the West Virginia Farm Bureau, who promised to come and support the farmers on Mockingbird Road. Sending produce and hogs the long way around would force them to raise their prices to offset the cost of fuel. The Copper Coal Company might decide to buy their goods from another town.

Hoping to inject a little merriment into the tenseness of trying to work on Plan B for the tour, Alice brought up the news from yesterday since Miss Spencer hadn't committed her to secrecy.

"Wow," Janice said. "We all had her for a teacher. I always thought she would stay an old maid."

"Well, good for Miss Spencer," Bernice said. "Everybody deserves to be loved. Horace Trueman, the science teacher from Montgomery High School?"

"Yes," Alice said. "I loved when he was my teacher. He always made science so fun and easy."

"Teachers in love," Lois sighed. "It's so romantic."

"I think it's nice, too," Andrea Collins said. "Say, we should do a Double Wedding Ring block and serve pieces of wedding cake at one of the stops."

"Aren't they all planned out?" Lois asked.

"Pretty much," Alice said.

Bernice got up and served everyone a piece of her canned plum coffee cake. "I think we ought to paint another block on the Tolivers' garage and give them a double stop."

Alice chuckled. "That would certainly be the end of our chairlady's flower beds. Well, there's not much more we can do before Friday's town council meeting."

"Do you really think they'll close the road?" Lois squeaked. "Pete would be devastated. It would be like living on a dead end."

"I don't believe it," Janice said with a little gasp as she rubbed her stomach.

Bernice knelt by her chair and took her hand. "Is it time? Should I call Jeff to come home?"

"No, not yet." Janice wiped her brow. "Thank you. I'm okay."

Alice unclenched her fists. Were they? Were they all okay?

Chapter Twenty-Eight

Wednesday evening, as they were cleaning up after supper, Alice tried to make conversation with Greta. Her roommate hadn't said more than two words since the incident at HQ.

"So what do you think? I feel like we'll be prepared, especially with a state senator behind us."

"*Ja*," was the only response Greta gave.

Heat rushed to the back of Alice's neck, and she banged the plate she'd been drying on the counter. It shattered, ceramic shards flying everywhere.

"Oh, no," Greta said. "Did you get cut?"

Alice shook her head.

"I will get a dust pan."

"No, stop it!"

Greta's blue eyes widened.

Alice blew a curl out of her face. "We need to talk." She motioned at the chairs, and they both took seats around the table.

"What do you wish to speak about?"

"It's you who has some speaking to do, sister. I took you into my home and gave you a job. You'd still be in Germany being ruled by communists if it wasn't for me." Alice hated being so harsh, but one way or another, she would find out what was going on. "Now spill."

"I do not understand. You want me to spill something?"

Alice crossed her arms. "You're not a Dumb Dora. Tell me what I want to know."

Greta bit her lip, and Alice almost wanted to back down. Almost. "I thought we were growing close. You've become the best friend I've ever had next to Lois, but if you don't trust me enough to give me some answers, I'm going to ask you to leave."

Greta's eyes watered. "If you turn me away, they will deport me. They will send me back."

"I don't want to see you deported, but I can't let you stay if I don't trust you." Alice leaned back and waited while a myriad of reactions crossed Greta's face.

Greta let out an audible sigh. "I am not supposed to say anything."

Alice placed her hand on Greta's. "You have to know by now you can trust me?"

"*Ja*, I do, but I cannot tell you all of it."

"Let's start with how you got a visa when displaced Germans aren't on the list."

Greta raised her eyebrow.

"I did some checking."

"You checked over on me?"

"The phrase is checked up, but not just you. I've become a regular spy lately. I've been investigating everyone. The immigration Department doesn't have a clue how you got on the displaced Europeans list since Germans and Italians weren't included, but they did say you had a friend in the State Department."

Greta offered a half grin. "It was, how you say it, gratitude for my role in the war."

"What did you do?"

"I told you how my family hid Jews."

"Not enough. There had to be something more for them to let you get on the list."

"My family joined the confessing church shortly after Herr Hitler came to power. My fadder studied under Dietrich Bonhoeffer and agreed with him. We should do everything we could to drive a spoke in the wheel of the Nazi party. My brothers and fadder joined the resistance and were executed for their part. Even after their deaths, my mutter and I helped Jews and dissidents flee the country. We had a network of contacts to help them hide and get across the border."

A twinge of shame gripped Alice. She had so misjudged Greta. "You and your family sacrificed much to stop Hitler's evil regime."

Greta pursed her lips. "We are not the only ones. You sacrificed your husband, did you not?"

"Yes." Alice swallowed as she went to the refrigerator and grabbed a couple of Coca-Colas. "Other Germans were in the resistance, and they didn't receive visas."

"My mutter and I also helped fighter pilots. Toward the end of the war, there were so many flying over our farm. Some were shot down and parachuted in the woods behind our house. We would help them escape as well."

The pieces started fitting together. "Greta, was Eddie Tyler one of the fighter pilots you helped?"

"*Ja*, but I asked him not to say anything. I was told not to tell how I got my papers. They might take it away if I am found out. Then how will I rescue my mutter and sister."

"It still doesn't explain why you were allowed on that list."

Greta took a sip of pop. "We had a secret radio. What you call, pork, *nein*?"

"No. Ham?" Even Greta's penchant for mixing idioms couldn't make Alice smile.

"Yes. As the Americans marched toward our village, we would report where Nazi troops were. We even told them where a war criminal was hiding in our village. Even though I lived in what is now part of the Soviet sector, the Americans arrived first. They took me to their general. He was, how you say, a big shot, and he made sure I was placed on the list of displaced immigrants. My mutter was too ill to make the trip, but she has recovered. When I save enough money, she and my sister will join me."

Alice rubbed her hand across the back of her neck. "Did you agree to do anything for the visa?"

Greta stood and started toward the broom closet. "I will clean up the glass."

"Greta, are you a spy?"

"Spy is wrong word."

"What is the right word?"

Greta started sweeping up the broken plate. "I am not a spy." She leaned down to sweep the shards into the dustpan. "When an American agent asked for my help to stop a traitor, I could not refuse."

Alice leaned down and gazed into Greta's eyes. "Who asked for your help? Who is the traitor?"

"Please." Greta offered her a pleading look. "I have said too much already."

"All right." Alice took the dustpan and dumped it in the trash. "Just tell me one thing. Can I trust Rick?"

"I cannot tell you any more."

*****

On Thursday morning, as soon as Alice unlocked the shop and hung the open sign, Rick Morrison rushed through the door. He peeked out the window, drew the blind, and turned the sign to "Closed."

"What's going on?" Alice asked. "I didn't expect you back until Friday."

He looked distracted. "I know, doll. I can't stay long." He took her in his arms and kissed her so passionately, she almost forgot about all the craziness going on. "So how's the spying going?"

She pulled back. "I don't know what you mean."

A deep chuckle came from his throat. "I admire you having the nerve to call DuPont, not to mention trying to check up on me."

"I... what makes you think I would... I'd do something like that."

"Take it easy, honey." He pulled her close, and she took in the fragrance of Old Spice. The strength of his arms around her made her feel safe, protected, loved.

He kissed the top of her head. "I don't know what I'd do if anything happened to you. No more phone calls. Deal?"

Alice nodded. "Rick, Luke confronted me at HQ."

"Did he hurt you?"

"No, but he scared me." She gazed into his hazel eyes. "I told him I knew he was lying."

Rick turned away. "I wish you hadn't." He faced her with his adorable smirk. "Don't worry. He won't hurt you. It's the plans he's after." He patted his jacket. "And I have them right here."

"You brought them back here? Why?"

"Let's just say, Lucien's little schemes aren't what they seem."

"Schemes? He never said--Rick, if he's not working security at DuPont, who is he? Another thing, why do you know so much?"

"Don't fret. I'm taking care of everything." Rick drew close again and twirled her. "You just go on with your quilting tour." He pulled her up and, nose-to-nose, said, "The Fourth of July is going to be one mighty special celebration in Burning Bush."

Alice tilted her head to one side. "Quilts? How can you talk about the tour at a time like this? I need to know one thing before this gets any further, and I'll know if you're lying. Are you FBI? Are you one of the good guys?"

The door crashed open and Sheriff Jenner marched in with his pistol drawn.

"Morrison, I'm taking you in for questioning."

Rick raised his hands shoulder height, not nearly alarmed enough in Alice's opinion. She felt like fainting.

"Sure, sure," he said. "I'll tell you anything you want to know."

"Hands on the counter," Sheriff Jenner barked.

"You don't plan to search me?"

"Now!"

He glared at the sheriff, and for a moment, looked like he might decide to make a run for it or put the sheriff in one of his headlocks, but he didn't. He placed his hands on the counter, and Sheriff Jenner patted him down.

The sheriff pulled Rick's revolver from his shoulder holster. Alice drew her hand to her mouth. After securing the gun, he checked the inside of Rick's jacket pocket and pulled out the papers.

"So," the sheriff said. "Holmes was right. You're under arrest for stealing the plans to the DuPont factory."

The next thing Alice knew Jenner had Rick handcuffed and led him out the door.

Rick never had a chance to answer her question.

*****

Every time Alice rolled over in bed, Rick's wink, the one he'd given her as the sheriff led him away, made her choke. "Help me out here, Joe. I know there's more going on than fighting about trampled grass, barn paint, or closing roads. I think it even goes back to Mamie and Pappy's deaths, but I don't know who to tell or what to do."

How had Rick known about her calls? Did making those calls mean she was a spy, now, too? What would Pete say if he found out what she'd been up to? Should she even tell him? He had enough on his plate these days without worrying about his sister's new hobby.

Lord, show me your path.

She tried to get back to sleep but couldn't manage it. Spies, Fourth of Julys, and quilt blocks tumbled in her head.

Count quilt blocks. Just like counting sheep, it would help to put her back to sleep. Let's see. Twelve stops. Eight if Mockingbird Road was closed. The blocks were all traditional ones. The hardest one was Grandmother's Flower Garden. Andrea Collins had been planning for it since the tour was first mentioned. Bernice's Kansas City Star would be lovely. Janice Felton had agreed to the nine-patch. With Jeff helping, they could have fun with painting each little square a different pattern. They'd planned on blue, yellow, and pink in honor of Baby Felton.

Alice knew she shouldn't focus on so many of the Mockingbird Road neighbors, in case they had to go to Plan B. Thinking of Plan B raised her ire again. She tossed back her blanket and pounded her pillow. She'd never get any rest this way.

Deep, even breaths. Colors... squares, rectangles, triangles... Lois was doing Flying Geese, all triangles, like the quilt Alice had been working on at the shop. Lois had already bought her paint colors. No wonder she'd been so upset when Mrs. Toliver said she'd be assigning the color schemes.

Mrs. Jenner, the sheriff's wife, hadn't committed to anything, although she was a member of the committee and helping Mrs. Toliver. They owned one of two barns in town where they could display a block. Maybe Sheriff Jenner was giving his wife a hard time about being a part of the tour. Poor woman.

Mrs. Round wanted Steps to the Altar, a nice easy pattern with more triangles and squares. They'd paint the design on the carriage house next to the parsonage since she didn't have a barn.

The Friday Ladies Quilting Circle had not met the last two weeks. They'd planned to create two fabric quilts of the barn blocks -- one for raffle and one for display, but it didn't look like they'd be finished in time.

A door creaked. Alice rolled over again and cocked her head. Soft footsteps padded and a click sounded from the direction of the kitchen. She wasn't the only one who couldn't sleep. Donning her robe and slippers, she followed her roommate into the kitchen. Some warm milk ought to help.

Greta's back was turned as she stirred something in a pan on the stove. Her hair was held back by a kerchief to keep her pin curls from unraveling at night.

Alice didn't want to scare her and kept her tone gentle. "Greta?"

"I heard you coming. Mein mutter warmed the milk to help us sleep."

"Great minds think alike." Alice pulled out a chair at the table and sat.

Greta looked over her shoulder and sighed. "American idioms. I shall never understand them." She brought the pan of warm milk to the table and set it on one of Alice's grandmother's crocheted trivets and grated some nutmeg over their mugs.

Alice reached for hers, held the cup to warm her hands, and sniffed before sipping. "This is wonderful!"

Greta took a drink, adorning her upper lip with a milk mustache.

"You should go into business, selling this." Alice opened her arms wide. "Greta's Great Milk Drinks. Puts You Right to Sleep."

"Not to tease, I beg of you. I am tired, but I can't sleep."

"I understand. Me either. Do you want to talk about it?"

Greta gave her a worrisome, teary blink then dropped her head in her hands. "Are you not afraid for Herr Morrison?"

"Sure I am." Alice cocked her head, perplexed at the depth of Greta's sorrow. Did she have a crush on Alice's beau?

Wait a minute. Beau? Oh, how could she even think such a thing! Unless... "Greta, are you in love with Rick?"

Greta moaned. "How could you think such a thing?" She raised her head and faced Alice. "He is... he... oh! I must not discuss this!" She rose and paced back to the stove, the sink, the table, and back to the stove.

Alice walked to the stove and stood before her friend. She took Greta's hands in hers and gave them a little shake. "You once said I would know who to trust. I don't know how I know, but I just do. I trust you. No matter what's going on, I believe you think you're doing the right thing."

"I believe I am," Greta whispered.

"You want to bring your mother over here."

"*Ja.*"

"So you wouldn't do anything to hurt America, right?"

Greta tried to pull away.

A trickle of icy fear caught in her throat. "Would you?"

"*Nein, nein.* Of course not."

"Then what are you afraid of?"

"I hear... I hear..."

Alice tugged her back to the table and bade her take another drink of the cooling milk. "You heard something?"

Greta nodded and gulped. "When I was strolling past the butcher in the morning. Herr Summers -- you know, the big man with much hair? *Ja*? He was shouting. I did not stop at first. I thought poor man was in his cups. Then I heard... he said... I heard him say...Oh!" she covered her face with her hands.

"What, Greta! What did you hear? Who was he talking to?"

"He was talking... a man came out later. I hid. Around corner. Herr Holmes. He came out of butcher shop."

"Well, so what? Those two know each other, and Frank takes a nip more than he ought."

"He say... he say it's time to wake up. To wake up this country. He needed Herr Summers to take care of Herr -- Mr. Morrison now. He needed the plans returned. For the...the -- oh, I can't say!"

"Yes, you can. You mean the ones for the DuPont plant? Greta, what did he say he needed those plans for? Is Rick in danger?"

Greta dropped her hands and looked Alice in the eye. "He say Mr. Morrison cannot know about the bomb."

Chapter Twenty-Nine

Alice had tried to get more details out of her roommate, but Greta said she'd had to scurry off to keep Luke and Mr. Summers from discovering she was there. After hearing about the bomb, sleep was impossible. Alice gave up when the train stopped at the water tower around five. She dressed and tried to calm the thoughts racing through her mind by working on the Goose Tracks quilt setting abandoned for the past few weeks. Summers, the Tolivers, who else was involved in this plot? She was convinced Greta and Rick were the good guys here. Rick might even be Bear, the man Joe mentioned in his letters.

Lord, if I'm wrong about them, warn me in time.

"Breakfast." Greta's chipper voice broke through Alice's restless thoughts. As they ate the bacon and eggs Greta fixed, neither of them said a word until their second cups of morning coffee.

Greta took a sip. "What do you think we should do?"

"I don't know." Alice wrapped her hands around the mug. Even though it was a warm June day, a chill she couldn't shake seeped in. "I'll tell you one thing. As soon as I finish my coffee, I'm going to march to the jail and demand Sheriff Jenner let me see Rick. He needs to know about this."

"I will go with you."

"No," Alice said. "I might be awhile. I need you to man the shop."

Greta looked like she wanted to argue, but she didn't. "I will do my best to man the shop even though I am a woman."

Alice chuckled. "That you are, sister."

"What will you do if Sheriff Jenner does not let you see Herr Morrison?"

"Oh, he will. I'll picket on his front lawn until he does."

Greta wiped her hand over her face. "Are you not afraid of being arrested too?"

"Don't worry. This is America, the land of the brave and the free." Even as she said it, she wondered if it would always be true with communist spies around trying to destroy everything Joe fought for, men like Luke and Mr. Summers.

*****

Alice squared her shoulders as she readied herself to go to battle with Sheriff Jenner. After letting out a deep breath, she pushed open the door to the sheriff's office and gasped.

Rick sat across from Sheriff Jenner at the desk, drinking coffee and engaged in a game of checkers, instead of pining away the hours in a jail cell. He glanced up at her and winked.

"I... ah... what's going on here?"

Rick jumped the last three red checkers on the board. "I'm winning."

Sheriff Jenner scowled. "Mrs. Brighton, close the door and get in here. We wouldn't want the whole town gawking to see why your mouth is dropped open wide enough to allow planes to land."

She closed her mouth and the door and scurried to the desk. "I thought I was going to have to bring you a file or something to break you out."

Rick stood and offered Alice a chair.

She sat, grateful she didn't have to stay upright the way her knees were wobbling.

"So you were going to break me out." Rick's grin grew bigger. "How sweet."

"Are you under arrest, or not?"

"Mrs. Brighton." Sheriff Jenner took a swig of coffee. "As far as the town is concerned, he is under arrest. Got it?"

Alice stood. "No, I don't get it, Sheriff. Is Rick being charged or not?"

Rick wrapped his arm around Alice. "Sheriff, why don't you let me talk to Alice alone?"

Sheriff Jenner nodded. "I'll be outside for a smoke." He grabbed a pack of Lucky Strikes on his way out.

Alice wanted to start right in on Rick, but he delayed her inquiries by pulling her close and kissing her.

"You have to trust me, doll. You can't tell anyone I'm not under arrest. Deputy Eddie doesn't even know."

She nodded and placed her fingers on her lips where the press of his kiss still made her woozy.

He continued. "You do everything you can at the meeting tonight to get Mayor Wilson to leave Mockingbird Road open. If you can't get him to listen to reason, stall."

Alice nodded again.

"Don't worry. Lucien Wendell Holmes is going to get everything he deserves, and I'm the guy who's gonna see he does."

She was beginning to feel like one of those Nodder dolls the way she bobbed her head after everything he said.

Rick kissed her again, leaving her feeling even more off kilter. "Now, you go on home and work on your quilting tour stops, and while you're at it, give me a list of the quilt blocks and color schemes Mrs. Toliver wanted to use if she managed to get her way. It's the usual meeting day, isn't it?"

Alice nodded.

"Don't worry. Mockingbird Road will be open for business."

She started toward the door and placed her hand on the knob when she remembered why she came. "There's something Greta found out, something you need to know. She overheard Luke and Mr. Summers talking. Luke said he had to keep you from finding out about the bomb."

His brow furrowed. "You're sure he said a bomb?"

"Greta said he did. She couldn't stay long enough to hear more or they would have seen her."

"She did the right thing. These are dangerous men."

A shiver went through her. "If Frank Summers is involved, how many others? Is the whole town of Burning Bush a band of traitors? I grew up here. These are my friends and neighbors! So many men gave their lives... and what for?"

When Rick took her in his arms again, she felt safe, protected. He made her feel like they could fight off any commie. "No, not the whole town. Most of the people here are just what they seem, and I don't think Summers knows what's going on. Luke probably lied to him the way he did to you."

"You think so?"

"Knowing Summers, Luke paid him enough to want to believe what he said. There is someone else involved we don't know about yet, undoubtedly the ringleader of this operation, but we'll find out who he is soon enough."

Portraits of friends and neighbors flicked through her mind as she wondered which was a Communist mastermind betraying his country.

"Now remember." Rick lifted her chin. "Not a word about this to anyone. Maybe you'd better cancel your committee meeting, and make sure you get the mayor to leave Mockingbird Road open."

Alice bobbed her head again, but she wasn't sure how she would manage it.

*****

Once Alice tacked up the notice on the door of HQ canceling the regular tour committee meeting in lieu of the council meeting, she felt a little better. She wiped her hands and put the hammer away before locking up. She called Lois, who said she understood and offered to tell her neighbors. That took care of everyone on Mockingbird Road.

Walking home, Alice considered who else to contact. Maybe Mrs. Lance would make some calls, or at least tell her friend, Mrs. Round, and Mrs. Jenner.

If only the sheriff would talk civilly with his poor wife. She shook her head as she walked up the dusty road. Why couldn't husbands and wives treat each other with more respect? Poor Mrs. Jenner needed a real friend.

Things sure had changed. Before the war, if a man hit his wife, the men of the town would get together and give him the thrashing he deserved. Pappy had said it was the community's job to protect the women and children of Burning Bush. After one such incident, Mr. Parker, the grocer, had turned into one of the most loving husbands in town.

The bruise Alice had seen on Mrs. Toliver's ear flicked through her mind. Maybe Mrs. Jenner wasn't the only abused wife in town, but it was hard to believe easygoing Henry Toliver would do something that horrible even if he was a communist. Maybe it was a bee sting.

Alice passed Daria's, sniffing in appreciation of the morning's yeasty potato bread and cinnamon buns. She entered the shop and stopped short at the sight of Greta waiting on Rosemary Lance.

Greta! How was Alice supposed to keep from spilling the beans all day? Sighing, she gathered a huge smile for her friend and for her customer.

"Mrs. Lance! Just the person I wanted to see today. I'm glad you stopped in. Let me get settled and I'll be right back."

She took her time setting her pocketbook on a shelf in the back room and removing her hat. She patted her hair and freshened her lipstick. Greta gave her a curious stare but didn't say anything when Alice returned to the floor.

"Girls, I put a sign on the door at HQ cancelling today's regular quilt tour meeting. With all the hullabaloo about the route and tonight's council meeting, I figured we all could use a break."

Mrs. Lance nodded. "Please, call me Rosemary. I agree with you. Can I do anything to help?"

"You can call me Alice, of course. Thank you for your kind offer. I've already notified some of the committee members, but if you wouldn't mind calling your friend Mrs. Garett, and Mrs. Round, I'd be grateful."

Rosemary smiled. "Certainly. Anyone else?"

How much could Alice ask her to do without feeling like a heel? She really didn't want to talk to Mrs. Toliver, but didn't want to be obvious about it. The longer she hesitated, twirling a dangling curl and feeling foolish, the wider Rosemary's smile grew. Greta finished cutting the piece of fabric Rosemary bought and wrapped it up.

"How about I stop in at the Tolivers on my way home," Rosemary said. "I don't live too far from them."

"It would be such a rel--um, a blessing," Alice said. "Thank you, thank you. I hate to ask so much of you--"

"Don't mention it," Rosemary said. "It's been too long since anything exciting happened around here." She paid for her purchase and pulled on her gloves. "By the way, I noticed you're working on a Flying Geese quilt. My great-aunt had the same style quilt. I always loved it."

"Thanks," Alice said. "You're welcome to stop in any time, and bring your own work."

"I just might. Since Bobby had to go to work in the mine and we sent our son to live with my sister in Parkersburg, I'm alone most days."

Greta's eyebrows went up and down. Alice would have to explain about the mine to her later. "Oh? How old is your son?"

"Junior is fifteen." Rosemary paused and gazed out on to the street where the afternoon traffic was quiet, mostly housewives on errands.

"My husband never went to high school," Rosemary said in a quiet voice. "I didn't want the mine to take my son as well. I'm not a snob, and I do trust Montgomery High School. The teachers there are good, and I love Burning Bush, but if he stays here, he'll want to get a job here and..." She faced Alice and Greta with a sad smile. "I miss him so much. I wanted better for him. It hasn't been easy."

Alice swallowed past the lump in her throat. Pappy had stayed out of the mine because of his farm, and with so many men off to war, production had slowed. If Pete and the others couldn't make a go of their places, they would have no other choice to provide for their families. The only other alternative would be to abandon their farms and move away to some place like Akron to work in the rubber factories.

Pete and Jeff had gone out on a limb asking the mine president to the meeting tonight. Closing the part of Mockingbird Road going past the farms while building a bypass would threaten the ability of traffic to get to work at the mines.

Alice shivered at the thought. Coal dust seeping into a man's pores. Uncle Hadley had died of black lung, not his sister Jo's cooking. If no other businesses came to town, the men who returned from fighting would have no place to work and Burning Bush would die.

Maybe Rick and the others were right. A shop like this, catering to women, wasn't the right thing. Burning Bush needed businesses where men could work and be proud.

Alice squared her shoulders. "I don't blame you one little bit. You had the strength to do something most women couldn't. I'm proud of Burning Bush, but if we don't want it to turn into a ghost town, we have to do something about it."

"For what it's worth," Rosemary said, "I think you're doing the right thing, no matter how much trouble it's been. Something's odd about this road-closing talk, but I can't quite put my finger on it."

She patted Alice's hand, waved to Greta, and left, much to Alice's relief. The direction the conversation was going could have been very uncomfortable. Better nip it in the bud with her roommate as well.

"Greta, I trust you, Rick trusts you. I can't talk about anything. Please don't ask me what happened."

Greta's blue eyes twinkled. "Nothing? You can talk about nothing? It will be a quiet afternoon, then. Perhaps we should sing."

"Oh, Greta, if this wasn't so serious..." She squeezed her friend's hands. "Thank you. I'm so glad you're here."

"*Ja*. Me also."

Chapter Thirty

"This meeting is called to order!"

Alice steeled herself for the smack of the mayor's gavel. The murmuring around her ceased.

As she suspected, Burning Bush Community Church where the meeting was being held was full. It was the only building large enough for everyone except for the colored Pentecostal church at the base of the holler, and only whites were invited to the town meetings.

Even though it was 1946 and every colored man in town had fought for his country, little had changed with people's attitudes. Alice's pappy had always invited them over to help during hog butchering time to make sure they had meat through the winter and had stood up to the Klan when they tried to start a chapter here.

She'd never seen what all the fuss was about. They were good people trying to raise their families just like everyone else in Burning Bush. Some had even given their lives in the war. Rick had said it right. Prejudices run deep.

Mayor Wilson, who had dressed for the occasion, flipped his long coattails before taking his seat. Mrs. Wilson must have spent days airing out the ancient garment. The men who sat in the front row probably had the most to do with the formalities.

Senator Burgess was a kindly-looking man, roundish all over with smoothed white hair. The man next to him must have been from the Farm Bureau. Pete told her the bureau president was shy or something or maybe had a lisp and didn't want to talk in public, but he'd send somebody. An empty chair on the other side was reserved for the president of Copper Coal Company.

The mayor cleared his throat. "The agenda tonight deals with the safety of Mockingbird Road. It has been recommended not only should the road not be used as a part of the community barn quilt tour so kindly arranged by Mrs. Gwendolyn Toliver," he nodded toward the left hand side of the aisle, "but the road itself be declared unsafe. Mr. Holmes, you may have the floor."

Alice turned, along with a hundred others, to the Toliver pew. Mrs. Toliver blanched at the attention. She jerked her head around, but her nephew didn't step out of the shadows.

"Mr. Holmes?" At the rising crowd mutterings, Mayor Wilson used his gavel rigorously. "Well, is he not here?"

Neither was Henry Toliver, it appeared. Mrs. Toliver rose hesitantly to a crouch. With one gloved hand on the back of the pew in front of her and netting from her hat obscuring her eyes, she stammered, "He must be late, your honor."

"It was at his request this meeting be called. See here, you have inconvenienced a lot of people, not to mention Senator Burgess and..."

"Albert Wilcox, sir, representing the Farm Bureau of West Virginia," the bald, permanently tanned man next to the senator said. He wore a dark suit, shiny with wear, and blinked often.

Perfect! Now or never. Alice stood. "In light of the absence of Mr. Holmes," she said in a firm voice refuting the quaking of her knees, "I move the issue of the safety of Mockingbird Road be... be..."

"Struck," Pete whispered. "Get 'em, Sis!"

"Be struck from the records," Alice finished.

"You can't!" Gwendolyn Toliver had finally found her voice.

"If Mr. Holmes cannot be bothered to attend the meeting to support his alleged accusations--"

"Alleged! Why your own parents were killed on that road," Mrs. Toliver said. "In an accident, of course."

"There's a motion on the floor!" Mayor Wilson raised his voice over the noises of "She's right!" and "Where is he?" and "He's not from here, what does he know?" Alice could hardly hear the gavel.

"Mr. Mayor!" a new voice called. Alice and the audience turned at the sound of heavy boots clomping down the center aisle. Pastor and Mrs. Round cringed at the coal dust emanating from the large man as he passed by even though he was neatly dressed. "Mr. Abernathy, from Copper Coal Company."

Alice jumped when a hand touched her shoulder.

"Slide over," Rick whispered.

"You shouldn't be here." Alice gawked around, hoping no one noticed the entry of the man who was supposed to be in jail.

"Take it easy, doll," Rick said in a lazy, amused voice. "We have everything under control. Though you were doing a fine job, I might add. Maurice, there, will take over now. Sit." He tugged her wrist, and she plopped down next to him. Way too close. She wriggled against Pete, who only pushed back.

"No room on this side," Pete told her with a too-wide grin. He ignored her glare.

"Mr. Abernathy, welcome," the mayor said. "We have a motion on the floor. Mrs. Brighton, will you rescind so we can hear what Mr. Abernathy has to say?"

"I will." She elbowed Pete when he pretended to clap.

"You have the floor." Mayor Wilson sat.

Abernathy reached for his suspenders and hooked his thumbs behind them. Alice groaned and stopped fidgeting, ready for a long-winded speech. Rick was still as a statue, and only offered a heart-stopping smile when she glanced his way.

"I'm here on behalf of the mine president. As I'm sure Senator Burgess would have told you good people," Abernathy bowed to the senator, who saluted him, "all this bluff about closing the US highway is hooey."

"US highway?" a man's voice called out.

Abernathy stared at the crowd. "Maybe you folks plumb forgot, but your Mockingbird Road is better known as US Route 60."

"Yeah, so what. It's still dangerous."

Alice recognized the voice of the man now... Frank Summers. He must have been told to make a scene. Just like she'd been directed to hold up the discussion. She checked Rick out of the corner of her eye.

"We're not stupid, Abernathy," another man said. "The little white and black US sign with the six and the zero on it reminds us every day. We can read here, fella."

"I beg pardon. I didn't mean to imply otherwise." Abernathy rocked back and forth. "Then you need to also know, ladies and gentlemen, the SRC, the State

Road Commission, and only the SRC, is in charge of making decisions to temporarily close the road and recommending permanent closure to the Federal Works Agency. Right, Senator?"

"Correct, sir." The senator waved his hand. "Then the FWA decides whether it warrants further investigation before a final disposition is made."

"The SRC will take complaints under advisement and examine the questionable road and file a report. Has such a complaint been made, Mayor?" Abernathy asked.

"Not to my knowledge."

"Therefore," Abernathy said, "there can be no discussion of closing the road, or any portion thereof."

"He sounds so official," Lois whispered as she leaned over her husband.

Rick snickered. "With a little coaching, he does."

"You," Alice whispered. "No wonder he was late. So you told him what to say?"

"Nah, he already knew. We just helped him with a few details."

Alice raised an eyebrow. "We?"

A new commotion started as Mrs. Toliver strode to the front of the church. "Then I'd like to make a formal complaint. As long as Senator Burgess is here as my witness, I say the portion of US Route 60 between Burning Bush and White Sulphur Springs is unfit for travel and should be closed until the FWA can investigate. It's a disgrace to Fayette County." She clasped her hat to her head, but there wasn't any breeze to blow it off.

"Uh-oh, can she do that?" Pete said out loud.

"She thinks so," Alice said.

"Even if they do file with the SRC, it will be months before they can schedule any work," Rick said. "I checked this afternoon."

"What made you change your mind?" Alice asked. "You were so dead set against the tour."

With a hard look at Mrs. Toliver who stood there like a ship without a dock, he said, "Let's just say it doesn't take much to know the problems of one little quilt tour don't mean a hill of beans in this crazy world."

Alice rolled her eyes at his ridiculous misquote from *Casablanca*.

"Oh! Oh, my stars!"

"What? What is it?" Lois had leaped to her feet. "Doc! Is Doc Brenner here?"

"What's going on?" Alice craned her neck to see around her brother and gasped. "Janice!"

"Janice?" Rick asked.

"I think she's in labor."

Chapter Thirty-One

While Doctor Brenner and Jeff Felton helped Janice to the closest house, the parsonage, Mayor Wilson banged his gavel to try to maintain order. It did no good. The roar of conversation was louder than the train passing through town. Alice blew at a curl falling into her face as Rick whistled a piercing note. Everything went quiet and all eyes turned on Rick and Alice.

"Let's have some order here so Mayor Wilson can rule on all this malarkey about Mockingbird Road and we can get out of here." Rick nodded to Mayor Wilson.

Mrs. Toliver stood and strode to the podium. "You can't rule until my complaint has been filed."

"Mrs. Toliver," Senator Burgess said, "I assure you your complaint will get a full hearing, and with the docket we currently have, should be voted on in about five years."

The crowd clapped and cheered, and Alice couldn't resist a feeling of satisfaction at the look of dismay on Mrs. Toliver's face.

"Uh humm." The mayor puffed out his chest acting like he was President Truman himself. "Under the circumstances--"

"Wait!" Mrs. Toliver's eyes darted across the room as she continued in a shaky voice. "Even if we can't close the road, we still can't have the tour there. We can't. At least wait for my husband and nephew to get here."

"Mrs. Toliver, citizens of Burning Bush." Mayor Wilson pounded his gavel. "I've made my decision. The quilt tour will go on as scheduled with Mockingbird Road included. Mrs. Brighton will see to the details. Meeting adjourned."

Cheers erupted again as Mrs. Toliver dashed out of the church.

Rick turned to Alice and placed his hands on her shoulders. "I'll talk to you tomorrow. I have some business to attend to."

"What business?" she asked.

"Finding out what Henry Toliver and Lucien Holmes are up to and why they didn't make the meeting."

Alice crossed her arms. "I'm going with you."

Rick crossed his arms. "No, you're not. It's too dangerous."

"Do we have to have this conversation every time? I'm going."

"No." He took her in his arms. "This time, I mean it. You can't come with me." He pulled back. "Pete, can you take your sister home?"

"Will do," Pete said. "I'd sure like to know what's going on. I thought you were in jail."

Rick chuckled. "Just a misunderstanding. Sheriff Jenner dropped the charges."

Alice bit her bottom lip. "At least take Pete with you. You shouldn't do this alone."

"I'm not," Rick said. "The sheriff and Deputy Eddie are coming with me."

Pete raised an eyebrow. "When did you become so chummy with Sheriff Jenner?"

"Let's just say we have an understanding. Pete, do you mind if I talk to Alice alone before you take off?"

Pete nodded, and Rick motioned for Alice to follow him outside. Groups of people still stood in the front lawn of the church talking about Janice having a baby or about the quilt tour. Nobody was in a hurry to leave. Alice let Rick lead the way toward the willow tree where they could have some privacy.

After a cursory check to see if anyone was watching, he leaned in to kiss her. "Congratulations on winning the day. It looks like the quilt tour is on schedule."

She grunted. "You can't win this argument by distracting me with kisses and compliments. I want to find out what's going on."

"So you've decided which way to leap, have you?"

She shrugged but couldn't help the grin crossing her lips. "With a little help from the Almighty."

He took her in his arms. The warmth of his breath tickled her neck. "I'll have to thank Him when I say my prayers tonight."

Alice stepped back and tried to focus. "I may trust you," those warm hazel eyes, brown wavy hair and his adorable smirk made it difficult, "but I'm not letting you off the hook. You need to return the favor and trust me with the truth. The whole truth."

"I will." Rick leaned against the tree trunk. "Tomorrow, I'll come over for supper, and I'll come clean. For right now, you need to go home and let me handle this."

She bit her bottom lip. "All right, but I have a feeling the real reason you're coming over is for Greta's cooking."

He leaned in, whispered in her ear. "I'll have to exercise my constitutional right to remain silent." His breath warmed her cheek. His lips brushed hers, then he pressed them hard against her lips. He removed his mouth from hers, a soft, warm chuckle in his throat. "Her cooking isn't the only reason."

She felt woozy in his arms, and she didn't want him to let go.

He pulled back, disentangled himself from her. "I have to go." He touched her cheek with his hand, then sauntered away at an easy pace.

As Alice watched him, the pressure of the kiss still on her lips. A shiver traveled through her. She couldn't help but remember what happened the last time she allowed herself to fall in love. What if something happened to him?

"Joe, I don't think I could go through another great loss."

*****

Alice arrived home to the comforting aroma of popped corn.

"Just what I needed. Thanks, Greta." She sat at the table and conveyed the events of the evening including what Rick had said to her before he went on his hunt for Luke and Mr. Toliver. "I don't know what to think. I've known the Tolivers all my life. It bothers me they might be mixed up in this... whatever this is."

"Sometimes wolves wear sheep's wool." Greta ate a morsel of popcorn. "Clothing."

"Clothing?"

Alice chuckled. "The saying is a wolf in sheep's clothing."

Greta wrinkled her forehead. "Sheep wear wool, do they not?"

Alice was about to explain when a pounding on the door downstairs startled her. "Maybe it's Rick." She ran down the steps to answer the door as Greta's "Be careful" trailed behind.

She unlocked and opened the door.

Mrs. Toliver pushed her way in. "I hope you don't mind me stopping by at this late hour, but I must speak to you about something."

She swallowed hard, not sure she wanted to hear anything the woman had to say. "Mrs. Toliver, it is late, and I believe we said everything at the meeting."

Greta's footsteps shuffled on the stairs behind her. Hope she thought to bring the frying pan.

Mrs. Toliver scanned the room as if she expected a wild animal to pounce from behind the quilt frame or between the bolts of fabric. "I must speak to you alone. Miss Engel, I must insist you go back upstairs. This doesn't concern you."

Anger flushed Alice's face, then a sense of alarm lodged in her throat. She'd never had any trepidation at speaking with Mrs. Toliver alone before, but the look of desperation in the woman's eyes gave her pause. "Anything you have to say to me you can say in front of Greta." She motioned to the chairs surrounding the quilt frame. "Would you like to sit?"

"Yes, well, ah..." Beads of sweat dotted Mrs. Toliver's red cheeks and forehead. She sat next to the frame and started digging through her purse. "I suppose it would be all right if Miss Engel stays since you insist."

Alice and Greta sat beside her, and she pulled out a pink embroidered handkerchief and wiped her face with it. "It's warm in here, isn't it?"

"Mrs. Toliver," Alice said, "it's late. What did you want to talk about?"

"You must not allow the quilt tour to have stops on Mockingbird Road, at least not the part on the mountain."

Alice blew out her frustration. "We've already gone over this at the meeting. You lost, Mrs. Toliver. Now it's time for you to leave." She stood.

"You don't understand, dear. Please. I'm pleading with you. Don't do this."

"Why? Don't give me any foolishness about it being unsafe because I'm not buying it."

Mrs. Toliver bit her lip. "It's not safe, but not for the reasons you may think. I'm trying to help you. You just have to trust me."

"Well, I don't trust you," Alice said. "Not anymore. Something's going on in this town, and you, your husband, and your nephew are right in the middle of it. So unless you want to explain, I suggest you leave."

"Then there's nothing I can do to convince you?"

Alice didn't bother to answer except with a glower.

Mrs. Toliver clutched her purse and headed to the door. "Mark my words, you'll regret this." She walked out, closing the door gently behind her.

Alice slunk back in the chair but couldn't stop the tremble going through her.

Greta sat beside her and patted her hand. "There, there. It is not easy to stand up to her."

As her wild heartbeat lessened, Alice gave Greta a lopsided grin. "It helped having you beside me, but next time, bring the frying pan."

Greta giggled.

Another knock on the door. Alice's heart raced again. "Do you think she's come back with reinforcements?"

"Maybe we should not answer," Greta said.

"Alice, let me in. It's Rick."

When Alice opened the door, he staggered across the threshold, blood seeping through the right arm of his jacket and sweat beading his forehead. "The doctor might be a little busy right now. Could you bandage my arm?"

"What happened?"

"I was shot." He collapsed to the floor.

Chapter Thirty-Two

"Rick!" Alice dropped to his knees, but not in time to save his head from a hard smack on the floor. "Greta, call the doctor while I get some towels."

"*Nein.* You heard him. We cannot call the doctor."

"He'll bleed to death!"

"Stop." Greta took her by the shoulders and shook her gently. "You go get the towels and some water and disinfectant, *ja*? I will look. I have seen many wounds."

Alice closed her eyes, opened them, risking a glance at the ashen-faced man dying on her, no, his linoleum. She stumbled upstairs to take some clean towels from the cupboard in the hall. She glanced into her bedroom, the single bed reminding her of all she'd lost in marriage. She couldn't do it, wouldn't risk loving another man like she had Joe, if it meant losing him.

She snatched her pillow to put under Rick's head and raced to drop the supplies at Greta's feet. She rushed to the sink in the back of the storeroom, filled a dishpan with warm water, and brought it back to Greta. She averted her eyes from all the blood and skin of the man she couldn't risk loving.

What else had Greta asked for? Ah, yes. Disinfectant. Where did they keep it? The first aid kit on the storeroom shelf.

"You find disinfectant?" Greta called.

"Coming!" The bottle of mercurochrome in hand, Alice raced back to Rick lying in the middle of the shop floor.

"Not so terrible," Greta said. She knelt behind Rick with his head on her lap.

Like an electric shock, a volt of jealousy jittered in Alice's gut. "Won't he be more comfortable with my pillow?"

Greta nodded toward his stocking feet now resting on the pillow and her... "Hey! My display quilt!"

"Feet up, to prevent shock," Greta said through her gritted teeth. "Use a different blanket if you don't care for this."

"Right. Sorry. How is he?" The stress had unhinged her sensibility. She took a couple of deep breaths.

Greta tore his shirt away and started washing the blood off his arm. It looked like the bullet had plowed a shallow furrow across the skin.

A glance at a nasty boiled-over-looking scar just under Rick's collarbone from a past wound had Alice reeling again. If it had been on his left side, he wouldn't be here.

Greta followed her double take. "I have seen worse. I think the bleeding is slowing. Press your hand against the wound to stop it."

Alice's eyes widened. "You do it." She pinched herself hard. "I'll get the cotton gauze and bandages."

She hadn't been so unnerved since Joe's memorial service. Her throat ached. She grabbed the gauze and an old sheet. Snatching a pair of scissors, she cut the large sheet of gauze into usable squares then tore the sheet into strips.

When she returned, Greta had painted on the gooey dark red mercurochrome.

The bitter, antiseptic scent reminded Alice of Mamie treating her childhood scratches, and another wave of greif swept over her.

Rick groaned and thrashed his head. "Alice?" His voice broke her heart.

"No, I can't do this." She raced out into the night and headed toward the church.

Lights were on at the parsonage. Janice must still be in labor. Why hadn't she heard anything earlier? Like a gunshot? Still unnerved and feeling vulnerable after years of blackouts, Alice slid her hands into her skirt pockets, and listened.

Friday nights...

When Joe was at Marshall University in Huntington majoring in languages and political science, he would only make it home for the weekends. Friday nights meant stopping at Daria's for a sandwich, then roller skating and sometimes, when they could afford it, a movie in Montgomery, or even something silly, like a black cow, root beer and chocolate ice cream, at the Montgomery druggist's counter. Then they'd park on the bank of the Kanawha River and watch the barges.

After they'd married and moved to New York City, they continued the tradition and went to a restaurant and the movies. It was one of those Friday nights, when Joe told her he'd enlisted.

They were having dinner after watching Mrs. Miniver starring Greer Garson. Just as war changed Mrs. Miniver's life in the movie, Alice couldn't help wondering if their lives would be forever altered by his decision.

She thumbed a stray tear off her cheek.

After Joe had gone off to fight, she never missed a movie release. When Lois couldn't go with her, she would go alone. She always made sure she got there early to watch the newsreels about the progress of the war. Somehow it made her feel closer to her husband.

The light in the upstairs bedroom of the parsonage turned off. The stars were so bright, so majestic. She set out briskly toward the river. She needed to take a walk to sort out her feelings.

The day after Western Union delivered the telegram about her great loss, Alice found an all-day movie theater and watched one movie after another, somehow trying to recapture those moments with Joe. The last one, a new John Wayne movie, *They Were Expendable*. Like her husband.

At midnight when the theater closed, she walked in the snow to her apartment three blocks away.

In Burning Bush, during snowfalls, the ground looked so white and clean. On the Manhattan sidewalks, it turned to dirty slush as the sounds of the city rushed by. A taxicab horn, a milk truck making its rounds, a group of rowdy sailors standing outside a club, they all took on an ominous tone. Danger lurked beyond every skyscraper.

A sailor staggered toward Alice and put his arm around her. She wriggled free and ran the last block, trying to get away. When she had finally arrived at the apartment, she had fallen in a sobbing heap in Lois' compassionate arms.

Alice came within sight of the sheriff's office. Doc's old '38 Buick was parked out front beside Pete's truck. She hurried toward the jail.

A shadow detached from the side of the roller skating rink. She should have smelled the tobacco and moonshine as a warning, but she'd been so intent on forgetting about Rick and wondering why Pete and Doc were at the sheriff's office, she hadn't noticed.

"Al-Alice Morgan. What're you doing out so late?"

She crossed her arms and glared at Frank Summers. "You're drunk. Move along, now, before I get Sheriff Jenner."

"They're all busy." Frank lurched toward her, cigarette waving dangerously close to her hair.

Alice sidestepped him and backed away. "Frank, go on home before you get hurt. Sleep it off."

"I'd rather go home with you." He stumbled. "You know I alwa-always carried a torch fer you, but noooo, high and mi-mighty, only had eyes for Joe Brighton. Even in high school, you never gave another guy a chance."

Alice was in the middle of the street now. She looked over her shoulder toward the jailhouse. "Don't be a fat head. You know I'm married." Even as she said it, she realized her mistake. She wasn't married any more.

"The war... the war did sumpin to all of us, but it's not over. Oh, no, siree. We haft-hafta keep fighting. To protect our freedoms from the commies."

"Frank, be quiet. You don't know what you're saying. Take a powder."

She wasn't quite quick enough when he rushed her again. He grabbed her shoulder, and pulled her down. She shrieked.

"What's going on out there?" A screen door slammed and the porch lights at three of the neighbors came on. "Aw, Summers, not again!"

"Help!" Alice struggled.

"Miss, this ain't no public house, if you get my--"

"Help me, get him off me!" Frank's unconscious weight was squeezing the breath from her.

"What's going on?" A woman came from the house across the way.

"Rosemary!"

"Good heavens! Alice. Winston, do something!"

Soon, Frank's heavy body was tugged away, and Alice gasped with relief. Rosemary knelt nearby. "What's going on? Are you all right?"

Alice held her hand at her throat and sat up. Rosemary's husband Winston kept a firm grasp on Summers' arm. Summers groaned and shook his head.

"Here, here. What's all this?" Sheriff Jenner came out of his office. "Summers. Should have figured."

"Sheriff, he assaulted Alice Brighton," Rosemary said, wrapping her arm around Alice's shoulders.

"He did, eh? Summers, you're under arrest. The rest of you, go home now. Show's over."

The few neighbors who had ventured out dispersed.

"Busy night." Jenners grabbed Summers arm and turned toward Alice. "You're all right, then? The doc's over at the jail attending to a prisoner. Maybe you ought to have him have a look at you."

Alice, with the help of Rosemary, got to her feet. "I thought he was at the parsonage with Janice."

"Show's been over a while now." He looked Alice up and down then nodded at her friend. "I'll take care of Mrs. Brighton, Mrs. Lance. Thank you for your help, Winston." The Lances took the hint.

"It's a boy," Rosemary said before she disappeared into her house.

"You might as well come tell me what happened." Sheriff Jenner led her and the groggy Frank Summers to the jail.

"I'll give you my statement, Sheriff."

He nodded. The big square sheriff's office was ringed with barred jail cells. Two of the cells were already occupied. Frank was dumped in a cell to the right. "Doc! Got another one for you."

Doc Brenner was just putting on his hat and closing his bag when he backed out of the center cell.

The door opened again behind Alice.

"What is this, Grand Central Station?" the sheriff said to whoever entered.

"What's the matter, Mrs. Brighton?" Doc headed toward her.

The occupant of the center cell lifted his head and looked in her direction. Her knees buckled.

"Oh, say, what a nasty bruise," Doc said, his clucking fading from Alice's consciousness.

"I got you, Sis."

*****

Alice gagged and pushed away the bottle of ammonia spirits from under her nostrils. She twitched and opened her eyes. "Where am I? Oh!" On her own bed back in the upstairs apartment. "How did I..."

"There, there, now, lie still." Lois held a white cool cloth over her right temple. "Frank Summers must have clocked you one as you fell."

"How do you know--"

"Never mind. You're going to be just fine."

"But, but--"

"Oh, he's fine too." Lois sent a glance at the open door. "Doc checked him out and gave him a couple of stitches. Told him to rest a couple of days."

"But, but--"

"Janice is fine, too. Healthy baby boy named Eugene James."

Alice struggled against her sister-in-law's ministrations and sat up. "Lois, stop it. Glad to hear about Janice, but where is Rick?"

"Greta gave up her room for now, though Rick insists on going back to his own place. I helped Greta clean up the -- you know -- in the shop."

"Lois, what was he doing in jail?"

Lois gave her a blank stare. "I don't know what you mean."

Pete stretched himself in her doorway, and gave them both a grin. "There you are. Say, I gotta help unload the cargo." He jerked his head in the direction of the other room. "Then I'll be back to take you home."

"Pete!" Alice lifted her knees and swung them over the edge of the bed.

"Lucky timing, me getting there before you swooned."

"I did not swoon. I want answers. Now."

Rick, still white-faced, appeared behind Pete. He wore his black suit jacket across his shoulders and already had on his fedora. "Tomorrow."

"Ready, old man?" Pete made a motion to swipe Rick's shoulder, but backed off. Rick put up his left duke and winced.

Alice glowered at them both. Rick gave his maddening wink and followed

Pete downstairs.

"Oh, Lois. What am I going to do?" Alice slid back prone.

Greta came into the room next, wafting in the aroma of mercurochrome instead of the cinnamon sugar scent usually seeming to accompany her.

"You rest, now," Greta told her. "Herr Morrison will heal in no time."

"I won't," Alice said. "All this mess over a barn quilt tour. It's not worth it. Mrs. Toliver tried to warn me and I wouldn't listen. Now, look what happened."

"You didn't do anything wrong." Lois stood and put her hands on her narrow hips. "You heard Greta. This will all work out."

Alice sank into her pillow as a drowsiness overwhelmed her desire to stay awake long enough to get answers to her questions. "It will as long as Herr Morrison stays as far away from me as he can get."

Chapter Thirty-Three

Alice woke with a throbbing headache. She sat on the edge of her bed and squinted at the clock -- ten thirty. Greta should have called her. After getting dressed, she zipped into the kitchen for a quick cup of coffee, and then downstairs to help mind the shop.

Greta was busy showing Mrs. Collins yarn but glanced up at Alice and nodded.

"I want something other than blue," Mrs. Collins said. "Everyone will be making something blue for the Felton boy."

Alice stepped over to them. "What about green or red? Both colors would go with blue."

Mrs. Collins smiled. "Glad to see you up and about after the attack last night." She picked up two skeins of apple green yarn. "This will do nicely. I'm going to knit him a sweater set."

"I will take care of the sale," Greta said as she and Mrs. Collins moved to the counter. After she finished the transaction and Mrs. Collins left, Greta turned to Alice. "Are you feeling A-Okay?"

Alice tried to keep from grinning. It had become Greta's favorite American expression. "Yes, I'm fine. A bit of a headache, but no worse for wear."

"Good. I did not want to wake you. After last night, you needed rest. Too much excitement."

"Sure was." Alice bit her bottom lip. "Greta, do you know what happened to Rick last night? Why is Deputy Eddie in jail? Did he shoot Rick?"

"Tsssk, no, of course not. Did not Sheriff Jenner tell you?"

Alice rubbed her temples. "Tell me what?"

"When Sheriff Jenner and Deputy Eddie helped Herr Morrison look for Herr Holmes and Herr Toliver, they found them meeting with a man at a cave outside of town. After Herr Holmes and Herr Toliver left, the man saw them and pointed a gun at Herr Morrison. Shots were fired, and Eddie pushed Herr Morrison out of the way, but he got a nasty bump on the head and a bruised jaw fighting to subdue the man."

Alice gasped. "Then if the deputy saved Rick's life, why is he in jail?"

"No, the other man is in jail. They took Eddie there to lay him on a cot. He was sick in his stomach, and the doctor worried he was hurt bad."

"Why did Rick come here?"

"He say doctor too busy. It was not a bad wound, only creased. He asked us to wrap his arm."

Alice grabbed a bolt of fabric and placed it on the shelf. "Is Deputy Eddie going to be all right?"

"Yes, he will be." Greta sorted the threads, but Alice suspected they didn't need to be organized. "He will be sore and bruised a few days, but no concussion or broken bones."

"Greta, who shot Rick?"

The bell over the door rang, and Violet Spencer came in. "Mrs. Brighton, congratulations on your quilt tour being allowed to continue unabated."

Alice plastered a smile on her face. "What can I do for you, Miss Spencer?"

"Two things." The teacher held two fingers up as she counted them off. "Number one. I wanted to let you know we've changed the date for the wedding. Our nuptials will take place one week later so we won't interfere with all of the events of the day." She grunted. "Besides, Pastor Round advised us he'd be too busy to perform the ceremony that day."

"Oh." Alice resisted the temptation to gloat. "You mentioned two things."

"Your shop advertises a seamstress service. I was wondering if you could make my wedding dress. I have the pattern and material, you know, but I've never had the patience to be any good at sewing. I usually buy my clothes readymade at Woolworths in Montgomery, but of course, they don't sell wedding dresses."

Alice rubbed her hand across her mouth. She hated to give up business. "I'm so sorry. I couldn't possibly. With the quilt tour less than two weeks away, I won't have the time."

Greta stepped forward. "I can sew the dress."

"Oh, could you?" Miss Spenser practically squealed.

Alice placed her hands on her hips. "Greta, I'll need more help with the shop as the tour gets closer."

"It will be A-Okay," Greta said. "I will only need a week to finish the dress. I can work on it at night."

Alice twisted her mouth, wondering if Greta was using this as a reason to avoid her for the next seven days. "All right, but the money goes toward bringing your mother to America."

"Agreed." Greta pulled her tape measure out of her pocket. "Come with me to the back room, Miss Spencer, and we will get measurements. You brought pattern and fabric? Good."

As Greta showed Miss Spencer to the fitting room, Alice decided one thing. She was going to get answers, if not from Greta, then tonight from Rick.

*****

Alice paced as she waited for Rick to arrive. Greta had insisted she didn't need help fixing dinner, so Alice decided to meet him in the shop. She'd never been this nervous around him before, but tonight was different. Not only was she determined to find out Rick's secrets, she planned to tell him whatever was going on between them was over.

She shouldn't have let it go this far, but when Rick came along, her resolve to protect her heart crumbled.

Not anymore. The image of Rick, lying in his own blood on the linoleum floor gripped her with the fear of losing someone else she loved. She had to end it.

Seated at the quilt frame, she decided to keep her mind off Rick's arrival by stitching on the sampler quilt for the raffle. Each block matched one of the painted designs on the barns of the tour. She hummed, letting her mind drift as she pushed her needle up and down through the taut fabric and batting of Janice's nine-patch, making sure she got at least eight stitches to the inch.

Mamie's Aunt Eulah had taken pride in making twelve stitches to the inch, but once curious little Alice had taken a ruler and measured from the bottom when they thought she'd been playing. After Alice had called up from underneath, "Aunt Eulah counted wrong," her aunt had gone home with a choking fit.

Alice had yet to see little Eugene James. What a blessing Doc had been ready for a surprise visit from the stork. She let up a prayer the stork would visit Pete and Lois soon.

She realized she was humming *I'll Be Seeing You* and stopped short. She wouldn't be seeing Joe again on this side of heaven. *Think of something else, girl!*

There had been dozens of women coming in today to buy yarn to knit something for Eugene, each worried everyone would be knitting something in blue. It looked like Janice's baby wasn't going to have anything blue. The apple green yarn Mrs. Collins had chosen would make a handsome outfit. Maybe after all this quilt tour business was over, Alice would knit him a blue sweater and booties.

A knock on the door caused her heart to skip a beat. Reminding herself to stay strong, she squared her shoulders and opened the door to find Rick wearing his usual nonchalance and black suit.

"Hi, doll." He held out a bouquet of daisies. Feeling her face warm, she glanced up. Of course, Joe must have told him they were her favorites.

She motioned him in and took the flowers. When he leaned forward to kiss her, she scooted away with the skill of an army scout doing recognizance. "I'm sure dinner's ready. We should go upstairs."

Rick raised an eyebrow. "Okay. Do you like the daisies? Joe told me once they were your favorites."

"Yes, they're beautiful." Alice turned away and headed up the stairs. "It's just Greta's been cooking, and she wouldn't let me in the kitchen, and... well... we should go up and eat."

Rick didn't say any more as he followed her with firm and constant footfalls. Alice blew out a sigh of relief. First, she needed to find out what was going on in Burning Bush and who shot Rick. Then she would explain they could never be more than friends.

As they entered the kitchen, her mouth watered at the aroma of Greta's sauerbraten and potato dumplings. Even though Alice considered herself a good cook, Greta was a culinary master. The girl could open a restaurant in New York City and make a fortune.

Alice put the flowers in a milk bottle and set them in the center of the table.

"Greta, I always look forward to your cooking," Rick said as he placed his napkin on his lap.

"You are too kind, Herr Morrison."

"Rick, remember?"

Greta nodded. "Rick."

They prayed over the meal and made small talk while they ate. Alice decided not to press while they were enjoying the meal, but as soon as she poured coffee after supper, she started her interrogation. "All right, Rick. You said you would explain everything. I think it's time you start."

He took a sip of coffee. "I'm not sure where to begin."

"I shall take my leave," Greta said and rose. "Please excuse me."

"No, please, Greta, stay. There are no secrets here." Alice looked at Rick. "Right?"

He saluted. "As you say."

Greta looked from her to him and back. She set her napkin next to her plate and lowered back to her chair. "Is so. I will listen."

Alice placed her hands on the table and interlaced her fingers. "How about you begin with who you work for?"

"I'm not FBI."

"I thought..." A knot lodged in Alice's stomach. "Was I wrong about you?"

"No, you weren't wrong." Rick pulled a leather wallet out of his jacket pocket and handed it to her. "I'm part of the CIG, the Central Intelligence Group."

Alice studied the identification card inside. Central Intelligence Group was printed across a black banner on top. Below was Rick's name and employee number with his picture on one side and a seal with an eagle on the other. Under that, his status read Active CIG Field Agent. "I've never heard of it."

"After the war, President Truman disbanded the OSS, but there was a need for an agency to gather international intelligence and to investigate communist agents infiltrating American interests. The president enacted the group in January. If all works well, he'll make it an agency next year."

"Now I know who you are." Alice handed the badge to him. "How about you tell me how you and my husband are involved with this whole rotten business in Burning Bush?"

If Rick noticed she'd referred to Joe as her husband, he didn't blink. For the next half hour, he laid out everything, how Joe worked for a government intelligence agency called CIO in New York City before the war, how he and Joe were in the OSS military intelligence during the war, and how Joe found information on traitors working for communist spies throughout the United States including one in Burning Bush, his home town.

"Joe and I were captured while meeting his informant." Rick studied his hands folded on the table in front of him. He glanced up at Alice. "He wasn't killed by the Germans during the Battle of the Bulge."

Alice took in a gasp of air as she reminded herself to breathe.

He kneaded the back of his neck. "He died a hero saving my life."

"How did it happen?" An empty sinking feeling rested in Alice's stomach. "I need to know."

The muscle in his jaw twitched. "We were meeting Joe's informant to find out more about Burning Bush. Somehow the Russians found out, executed the informant, and captured us. They planned to torture us until they got the info they wanted and then kill us. I had to do something."

He pulled at his collar. "I made my move, and Joe pushed me out of the way. He died instantly. In the confusion, I took off. One of their bullets got me, but I managed to get away. I'm sorry." He placed his face in his hands.

Alice reached out to touch him, to comfort him, but drew her hand back. She couldn't risk being close to a spy.

A chill went through her. Joe had been a spy. In her heart, she knew the job in New York City was more than just an interpreter, but she pretended she believed Joe for his sake. "Are you Bear?"

Rick head jerked up. "How did you know I was called that during the war?"

"Joe said if something happened to him, I could trust Bear."

Rick's Adam's apple bulged "You can trust me."

A dull empty feeling gripped her chest. She could trust him with everything but her heart. "Go on."

He finished telling Alice everything she wanted to know. After the war, he was assigned to the CIG and sent to West Virginia to find out what he could and thwart their plans.

Alice took a sip of coffee. "What about the Tolivers?"

Rick placed his hand on hers. "Henry Toliver is a traitor, a card-carrying Soviet agent, and his wife and nephew are in on it."

"It's so hard to believe." Alice thought back at the dinner parties her parents used to have with the Tolivers. After they were sent to bed for the evening, she and Pete would watch them play board games and listen to their conversations about politics. Pappy and Mr. Toliver rarely agreed. Pieces of the conversations began to fit into place now. Worker's Rights. Unions. Spews about President Roosevelt and the fall of capitalism. Pappy would get angry sometimes and ask the Tolivers to leave. "I've known them most of my life. Looking back, I should have suspected."

"From what we've learned, Henry and his brother-in-law, Stan Holmes, were arrested during the Red Scare in 1919 when Communists were infiltrating different organizations. We believe the Russians contacted them after they were released from jail. Lucien was raised to be a Communist agent. He was trained at a private military school run by Soviet infiltrators. The Tolivers moved to Burning Bush and awaited instructions for when they were needed."

Rick gazed into her eyes. "Alice, your parents were on to them. Dewey and Goldie Morgan reported to the FBI the Tolivers weren't on the up and up, but before an agent could get out here to interview them, the accident happened."

Alice drew her fingers to her lips. "You don't think they had something to do with..."

Rick nodded. "We believe they caused the accident killing your parents, but we can't prove anything."

Alice stood, walked over to the sink, and placed a wet towel on her face. Her knees weakened, and she swayed.

Greta placed an arm around her and helped her back to the table. "Your mutter and fadder were very brave. You can be proud of them."

Rick waited until Alice composed herself. "Do you want to hear the rest?"

"There's more?" Her voice barely rasped out. "Yes, I need to hear it all."

"I didn't know who all was involved, but I came here knowing the Tolivers were a part of it. They needed to find a way to get their information to their fellow conspirators. Then all of a sudden, Mrs. Toliver is in on this quilt tour." One side of Rick's mouth turned up. "I'm sorry I gave you such a hard time about it."

"It does explain a lot," Alice said. "Greta, how are you involved?"

Greta smiled. "When Herr Morrison found the feather at HQ, he thought I might be, how you say? In with the Tolivers."

"Greta? Ridiculous. After all she's been through, it would be more likely I was a spy."

Rick chuckled. "I considered it. There is somebody in town calling the shots, and it isn't Henry Toliver. We just haven't figured out who yet. When I checked out Greta with my superiors, they told me all she'd done for our troops and suggested I let her," he winked at Greta, "in on this."

"I knew something was going on between you two." Alice flustered. "So you told Greta everything, but you couldn't trust me with any of it?"

"I wanted to, but I had to get an okay from my boss. Besides, after you got all chummy there with Lucien, I didn't know how much he'd charmed you with his lies."

She got to her feet, her legs no longer wobbly. With her hands on the table, she leaned toward him and stared him in the eyes. "Let me tell you something, Rick Morrison. I've given more than most for this country. Joe was killed, and so were my folks, not to mention what my brother went through. For you to think anyone, even pretty boy Lucien, could turn my head..." She poked her finger into his shoulder to emphasize what she was saying.

Rick cringed.

A stab of guilt went through her. She'd forgotten his wound. "Oh, Rick, I'm sorry."

He nodded, though his face turned ashen.

Greta stood. "Would you like some ice for your shoulder, Herr Morri... Rick."

"Yes, Greta." His voice grew thick. "Thank you."

Greta went about filling the bag with ice.

Alice suppressed a grin, remembering how good Greta was at keeping her ankle iced. "So what about the quilt tour, and what do you want me to do? Should I cancel everything?"

Rick wiped his forehead with his handkerchief. "We're not sure what their plans are yet, or if anyone else in town is involved, but we want the quilt tour to go on as scheduled. The town will be filled with CIG agents. We hope to arrest everyone involved. It's very important you don't say anything to anyone, not even Pete. The fewer people who know, the better."

Alice placed her hand on her heart. "I promise."

Greta copied Alice. "I, too." Then she settled the ice cubes wrapped in a dishtowel over his shoulder.

"I need those quilt patterns Gwendolyn originally wanted for the tour. The men at headquarters will be able to crack the code."

Alice had almost forgotten he'd asked for them. She rushed into the bedroom, pulled the plans out of her underwear drawer where she'd hidden them, and turned them over to Rick.

"Thanks, these will help." He leaned back in his chair and took a swig of coffee. "So, have I answered all your questions?"

"Not all of them," Alice said. "What about Sheriff Jenner and you getting chummy, and who shot you?"

"Sheriff Jenner is easy. When I was arrested, I showed him my ID card and gave him a number to call to check me out. He's been cooperative ever since."

"What about the shooting?"

"Some low-level operative from outside Burning Bush. An agent with the FBI took him into custody today. If Deputy Tyler hadn't pushed me out of the way... let's just say I'm grateful to him."

"Well, then," Alice said, "there's just one more thing. Why don't I walk you to the door, and we can talk about us."

"Okay." Rick turned to Greta and handed her the towel filled with ice.

"Greta, thank you again for feeding this bachelor and the great patch job." He followed Alice down the stairs and wrapped his healthy arm around her.

His arm felt warm, comforting, but Alice forced herself to step away. "I need to say something, and I don't want you distracting me."

"All right." Rick leaned against the wall. "Shoot."

"That's not funny. When I saw you there, lying on the floor, maybe dying..." She blinked to keep from shedding any tears. She needed to be strong. "I'll help you all I can, and I want to be friends, but it can't ever be more. I can't fall in love again, especially not with another spy. I can't risk it."

A myriad of emotions passed across his face: confusion, anger, hurt. "Alice, please." He reached for her.

She backed away. "It's better this way before we get too involved."

"It's too late." He stroked her cheek with his hand. "I'm in love with you."

"I'm sorry. I can't do this." Alice ran up the stairs to get away from him. She would never allow herself to give in to those feelings again, and she couldn't bear to see the hurt in his eyes.

Chapter Thirty-Four

On Monday afternoon, Alice stitched on Janice's block at the store while she listened to the muted voices of Greta and Miss Spencer talking over alterations to the pattern. Janice was still resting at the parsonage after the birth of baby Eugene, though Pastor Round had teared up when he made the announcement yesterday during the church service. Of course he was spilling old news, but nobody minded.

Although the sermon about God instructing us to fear not because the Lord is with us had touched a chord in Alice's heart, she was more concerned with who hadn't attended church. She knew Janice wouldn't be there so soon after the birth although she was surprised to see Jeff Felton there for the first time in years. Rick, of course, was out with Sheriff Jenner looking for Luke.

The Tolivers had also been absent from their usual pew. How could Mr. and Mrs. Toliver, close friends of her parents, be communist spies? Or, worse yet, Mamie and Pappy's killers. Joe must have been just as bewildered when he'd learned the truth.

She adjusted her seat in front of the quilting frame. Rick had said the quilting tour should go on as planned, but how could she act nonchalant when there might be a communist traitor under every rock?

There was no place safe. Nowhere in the world... nowhere. The idiocy of two World Wars had settled nothing. Things were even crazier than ever. Even here in Burning Bush where she thought she'd be sheltered.

Alice made a few more stitches, catching the needle underneath the quilt with her free hand, and popping it back up. Janice's block would be finished soon.

Gwendolyn's block was nearly untouched. Lulu had worked on it for about twenty minutes one day. The Dresden fan had long lines and Lulu's stitches had to be at least half an inch long and crooked as a streak of lightning. Alice debated removing them and starting over.

Starting over... could she? Despite being so sure she would refuse to lose her heart again after Rick was shot, the light of day made everything foggier.

Greta ushered Miss Spencer to the door. "Your dress will be *wonderbar*, beautiful, with the lace."

"I want just a short little veil. Thank you. I'm so happy," Miss Spencer said, waving and sailing through the door.

Greta stood there, looking bemused.

"I've never seen her act giddy," Alice said. "Like one of her students."

When Greta didn't reply, Alice furrowed her brow. "You're not making promises you can't keep, are you? You can't let her believe--"

"*Nein*," Greta said, turning to her and taking her hands. "She found love. This is what I am thinking on so diligently. At her age, she never gave up on finding someone she could spend her life with. You should not be so afraid of such a gift as love."

"I don't know what you mean." Alice blinked to keep her eyes from watering. "I had love once."

Greta held her gaze steady. "You have it again. With Herr -- Rick."

"No! We were just caught up in the moment. It's not love." Alice tried to pull away, but Greta kept a firm hold.

"There was a boy in our village, Rolf. I always thought there was plenty of time."

"There wasn't." Alice finished for her tearful friend.

"Mein mutter always say to us, in Latin, when we had complaints. *Carpe diem.* It means--"

"Seize the day, Oh, Joe." She let go of Greta's hands and slumped on the stool by the worktable. "He'd tell me, 'Life's too short, kid. You gotta seize the day. Take each moment captive.'" She drew a circle on the tabletop with her fingertip.

"Right. Just like the verse Pastor Round used in Deuteronomy 31:6. 'Be strong and of a good courage, fear not, nor be afraid of them: for the LORD thy God, he it is that doth go with thee; he will not fail thee, nor forsake thee.' Is it not God's way of saying seize the day?"

"I used to get so mad when Joe wouldn't let me feel sorry for myself." Alice looked up. "It's like hearing his voice again."

"*Ja.* What would he tell you now?"

"To get off my duff and get going."

Greta laughed. "I do not know 'duff,' but I guess is good advice?"

"Is good advice." When Alice heard the echo of her morose tone, she laughed too. She stood and rubbed her hands together. "Well, putting all matters of the heart aside, we do need to help Herr Morrison save the country from the other members of the spy ring."

"Such a thing." Greta tsked.

Alice picked up a soft cloth to polish the glass display cases. "Where do you think Luke and the Tolivers are?" With a quick glance toward the door, she lowered her voice. "Oops, I suppose we better not talk espionage down here."

"True." Greta followed Alice's look and whispered, "However, I do not think they went far. Their mind training would compel them to complete their duty."

"Mind training?" Alice couldn't stop her voice from squeaking. She looked at the clock, then at the door. Four thirty. They could close early. She went to the door, locked it, and turned the sign to "Closed." "Come on, sister, I want to hear all about this."

Chapter Thirty-Five

"Ladies!" Alice knocked on the anvil with Mrs. Toliver's gavel. The committee members had all agreed to meet early since last week's regular meeting had been called off. Sheriff Jenner agreed the area was safe during daylight hours as long as they met in groups and no one went there alone.

Both the sheriff and Rick recommended it would be better to tell the town the shooting was done by some tramp who came in on the train. Tramps came through town often, so nobody questioned it or the fact the shooter had been escorted out so quickly and quietly.

"Thank you for coming today. We've had a lot of excitement since our last meeting. As you know, last Friday the mayor agreed to keep the tour as planned, including the four stops on Mockingbird Road."

Lois jumped up and started applauding which made the others follow suit.

Alice rapped the gavel. "Yes, we're all happy, but we have lots to do. We'll have reports later. Right now we need to confirm the quilt blocks and the final colors. I know some of you have been assigned blocks not on your list of choices."

A murmur confirmed Mrs. Toliver's meddling ways. Alice held up a paper. "Let me go through the stops and the blocks in order. I'm reading from earlier notes, now, so raise your hand if you note any discrepancies." She looked over the assembled women. "First stop is at the river. So, the sheriff's office will start the tour. Did you decide yet, Mrs. Jenner?"

"Red is my favorite color, and I've already bought the red paint," the sheriff's wife said. "Anything with red hexagons would be good."

"I'm afraid only the pattern with hexagons is Grandmother's Flower Garden."

"I have that one." Andrea Collins stood up. "I have all kinds of colors." She ticked them off on her hands. "Greens, yellows, pinks, blues, whites." She looked at Mrs. Jenner and raised her brows. "No red."

"It's not fair," Mrs. Jenner said. "You cancelled those meetings so I didn't have a chance to say what pattern I wanted."

Alice counted to ten as she remembered all the times she tried to get Mrs. Jenner to decide. "Let's come back to the Jenners." She cleared her throat. "As we continue through town toward the holler, Mrs. Lance, you have the crazy patch?" At Rosemary's nod, she went on. "Then, Mrs. Garrett, you have the pinwheel, correct? Red, white, and blue?"

"Right," Mrs. Garrett said.

"She has a pattern with red in it." Mrs. Jenner sounded like a pouting child.

"Mrs. Jenner," Alice said. "We'll get to you. Let me get through the other assignments already decided first."

The sheriff's wife leaned back in her chair and crossed her arms. She blinked several times to hold back tears forming in her eyes.

Alice bit her tongue determining to be patient. "Next is the parsonage. Mrs. Round, you have Steps to the Altar? Correct? We wanted shades of lavender -- a dark and a light? Good." Alice checked it off.

"Then we proceed to the holler. Mrs. Toliver," she rushed through hoping no one would say anything, "chose the Dresden fan. The Montgomerys can have the Butterfly patch."

"Now before we go on to Mockingbird Road." She blew a loose hair out of her face. "Mrs. Jenner, since you never chosen a pattern, I thought we could use Miss Spencer's honorary Double Wedding Ring for your barn." She'd paint the block herself if she had to.

"The Double Wedding Ring doesn't have any red hexagons, does it?"

"No, Mrs. Jenner," Alice said, moving quickly from puzzled to annoyed. "The pieced rings are made of small tapered squares, although I suppose we could use some red in it."

"I still want hexagons." Mrs. Jenner stood and crossed her arms. "There can be two Grandmother's Flower Gardens. After all, mine will have different colors."

What was with Mrs. Jenner and red hexagons? "Mrs. Collins, would you mind if she did the same pattern?"

Mrs. Collins bit her lip for a moment before answering. "I suppose if it had different colors, it would be all right. Anything to keep the peace."

"Thank you. We appreciate your understanding."

Miss Spencer's honorary Double Wedding Ring would have to go somewhere else. Of course, it would mean one more stop to add, and the programs would have to be changed. Pete and Lois had planned to take the finalized copy to the printers in Montgomery tomorrow. Unless... "Mrs. Jenner, would you mind having a double stop? We could paint the Double Wedding Ring and the hexagon pattern on both sliding doors of your barn. One on each side."

Mrs. Jenner paused as if world peace depended on her answer. Maybe it did. "I suppose it will be all right. If my husband will allow it."

Alice would talk to Sheriff Jenner about it herself. No way was she going to let Mrs. Jenner's stubbornness and the sheriff's attitude toward his wife ruin the tour at this point.

"I have to go now. The sheriff insisted I be home in an hour." Mrs. Jenner ran out of the shop.

"What's with her?" Bernice asked.

Alice shook her head. "I don't know. Let's move on to the patterns on Mockingbird Road and then the committee reports."

After the reports had been read, the women enjoyed Bernice's lemonade and brownies while chatting and catching up on news. Alice reminded them of the unfinished quilt on the wooden frame at the shop. They agreed to try to finish it in time and to sell fifty raffle tickets each. The mayor had gotten the church men's group to sponsor the printing when they learned Henry Toliver hadn't signed the contract.

"The tickets will be ready for pick up on Friday," Mrs. Wilson said.

"Good. The shop is open for anyone who wants to help with the quilt. We're almost ready for the border," Alice said.

"I'll be there," Bernice said.

"Count on me," Lois said.

Alice quirked a brow at her sister-in-law's cheerful disposition. Something was different about her. Not off, but glowing? Alice shook it off, smiling. Trust Pete to do something to make his wife happy after all their early struggles.

The talk turned to Janice and the baby. A few volunteered to bring meals to the Feltons after Janice went home. Everyone was elated to see Jeff Felton at church Sunday. He'd told Pastor Round seeing his new baby convinced him he needed to get right with God.

Even though Alice was excited for the Feltons, she only half-listened to the conversation. She couldn't stop her mind from thinking about how Joe and her parents really died.

"All those poor people. Burned to death, you know."

Alice tuned in to the conversation. "What deaths?"

"Why, those people in the hotels," Henrietta Montgomery said. "Haven't you read the news?"

Alice shook her head, abashed. She'd been busy with other things. "Where was it? Was it big?"

"They were in Chicago just two weeks ago," Henrietta said, looking over her eyeglasses at Alice. "LaSalle Hotel. Killed over sixty souls." The older woman shuddered, then encouraged by her audience's rapt attention. "Just four days later, there was a terrible fire in Dubuque, where Junior's cousin lives. He's on the fire department, says it was just awful." She shook her greying head dramatically.

Alice took a breath and prayed for wisdom as she turned the talk to politics, studying each person around the loose circle they'd made while partaking of refreshments. "I was listening to the train last night, and it made me think about President Truman's decision last month to take over the railroads. Ahem... you know, so the men wouldn't go on strike."

"Oh! Those dreadful unions," Henrietta said right away. "Day laborers thinking they're better than the bread and butter farmers. Honest wages. Forty-hour weeks. Who can work only eight hours a day? My Buford works from sunup to sundown. So should all honest workers."

"Now, wait a minute," Alice said. "Safety on the railroads, safety for the men in the mines, those aren't frivolous issues. Your husband doesn't work much in the winter. Or even every day all year round."

Henrietta sniffed and finished her brownie in one bite. "Very good, Mrs. Gorman. I'll be going now."

Alice groaned inside. "You can stay. I didn't mean to upset you."

Henrietta patted her shoulder. "I need to go anyway. Buford will be wanting his lunch soon." She walked out the door.

"My Donald is on the labor relations board, you know," Jennifer Garrett said.

"I think it's a good idea to limit the age of children who work," Lois said.

"Well, the president knows what he's doing." Mrs. Round folded her napkin. "The Reverend and I have absolute faith in him."

"Did you read his schedule?" Andrea Collins said. "I heard he was coming to White Sulphur Springs to take in the waters, you know, like President Roosevelt."

"When?" Bernice asked.

"On the Fourth of July," Mrs. Collins said.

"I heard he was going to the baseball game. He's a fan, you know." Mrs. Garrett smiled. "The Senators play at Griffiths Stadium."

"Oh, we heard he'll spend the holiday in Florida," Mrs. Round said, coloring rosy when the group turned their eyes on her. "We don't pay attention to gossip, of course." She waved her napkin. "They do have the Little White House down there, you know, at Key West. Why, the Reverend's parents live there."

"Wherever President Truman decides to holiday, I'm sure it'll be historic with it being the first Independence Day since the war ended," Alice said. "Ladies, I must return to the shop. It's been an honor working with you."

As she walked back to the shop from HQ, Alice couldn't help but jump at every dog or child rustling in the woods nearby or shouting in the distance. What if it was Luke? She'd left Greta alone in the shop. She picked up her pace.

Chapter Thirty-Six

Alice rushed into the shop, but the only intruder there was Rick, sitting at the counter deep in conversation with Greta. When they saw her, they stopped talking, the classic sign of guilt.

A pensive look had replaced Rick's good humor. Dark circles under his eyes showed how much sleep he'd lost looking for Luke. He started toward her. "Alice, I..." He stopped and adjusted his black tie. "I have news."

Her stomach flopped. She'd had about all the news she could handle in the last few days. It wouldn't surprise her if the Communists were invading Burning Bush. Then again, it appeared they already had. "What happened?"

"How 'bout I buy you a root beer float at Daria's and clue you in?"

"Rick, look." Alice twisted her wedding band. What Greta said before about seizing the day made sense, but she couldn't risk it. Her shattered soul hadn't mended from the last time. "I meant what I said about us just being friends."

Rick wiped a hand over his mouth. "There's nothing friendlier than a root beer float."

"I don't know."

"You go," Greta said as she pushed Alice toward the door. "I will man the shop."

Alice could have sworn Greta winked at him. Rick offered his arm.

"It doesn't look like I have a choice in the matter." Alice placed her arm through his. "Let's get this straight. This isn't a date. I just want to find out what the news is. We're friends, and it'll never be anything more."

"Deal. For now." Rick opened the door for her and walked a little too close as they made their way along the railroad tracks toward the diner. A whiff of his Old Spice aftershave almost caused her resolve to weaken.

When they got to Daria's, he asked for the booth in the back corner, the one Joe and she always sat at when they had a date. The one used by couples who were in love. She almost objected, but they needed a quiet place to talk. They ordered floats, and waited for Daria to deliver them.

Alice took a sip when their order arrived. "All right, friend. You had some news for me. Spill."

"The Tolivers are back in town." Rick studied her. "I thought I should warn you in case you ran into them."

She didn't look forward to seeing them again, but this was a small town, and Mrs. Toliver was still on the quilt tour committee, at least, officially. It was sure to happen. "I don't know if I can pretend to be cordial now since I know who they really are."

"I know you have it in you, doll. You'll do fine."

"I'm not your doll."

He winced.

She softened her tone. "Did they say where they were hiding after the meeting Friday night?"

He leaned back into the booth and gazed at her with those hazel eyes of his.

"Sheriff Jenner asked. They claim they went to Beckley to take the nieces back to their mother. They didn't understand why anyone would be looking for them."

"Are they suspicious you're on to them?"

"They suspect I'm here investigating something." Rick didn't even blink, but kept staring at her. "No, they don't suspect I know they're involved. Remember, you and I are the only ones who know Lucien doesn't work for DuPont."

She looked away. His puppy dog eyes were getting to her since she'd stopped focusing on his aftershave. "Thinking back, he never actually said he worked at DuPont. He was mighty slippery when he talked about it, and I jumped to conclusions. Any sign of him?"

"Not yet." He took a sip of root beer float.

The ice cream gave him a mustache. She repressed a chuckle as he wiped it on his napkin.

"The Tolivers claim he had to go back to the plant to do some security work," Rick said. "He might just be laying low until the quilt tour, but he might worry you know something after the last conversation you had with him. If they decide it's not worth the risk, they might call the whole thing quits. We have enough to arrest them, but I sure would like to snag their fellow conspirators."

"They won't call it off. Greta says their mind training won't let them stop until they've carried out their mission."

His eyes widened. "Mind training?"

She blushed, realizing how foolish she sounded. "You know, brainwashing. I guess Greta's been watching too many American spy movies."

He pressed his lips together. "No, Alice, she hasn't. Hitler was able to brainwash an entire country. If these traitors already are dedicated to their cause, this mind training might be a way of making sure they don't have second thoughts."

They finished their floats in silence. Alice never understood why anyone would follow somebody as evil as Hitler, but history was full of cases where it had happened before. It was a scary thought one man could mesmerize a whole nation. At least in America, something like that could never happen. Americans would never allow the government to take away their rights.

On the other hand, Luke and the Tolivers were Americans, and they were turning their back on the freedoms and principles it stood for. Maybe, under the right circumstances, it could even happen here.

Alice slid her empty glass away. "I do have a new development with the stops for the tour. Mrs. Jenner insists on a pattern with red hexagons. She's even willing to do a double stop to make sure she gets her hexagons."

"Thanks, I'll pass it on to my superiors. It might be nothing, but then again, Mrs. Toliver might have duped her into taking part in the scheme." Rick took her hand. "Alice, I know what you said about us just being friends, but I'm giving you fair warning, I'm not giving up on you."

She pulled her hand away. "Rick, please. I can't go through the heartache again."

"Just hear me out." His Adam's apple bulged. "When my ex-fiancée wrote me a Dear John letter, I had a rough go of it. I thought I'd never meet a dame who could hold a candle to her, but God knew, even if I didn't, because I didn't know about you."

A sinking feeling caused the float to unsettle her stomach. "Rick, please--"

"I fell in love with you before I ever met you, seeing you through Joe's eyes. I always told him he was one lucky guy. I never thought I'd have a chance with anyone like you, but then I got to know you for myself, and well, there's no going back. I'm crazy about you, and I plan to marry you as soon as this spy business is taken care of."

Her breath caught. "Don't I have any say in the matter?"

"Sure." The Cary Grant smirk reappeared in full force. "You can plan the wedding and set the date, and you could finish that log cabin quilt for us."

Heat traveled up her back. She stood. "How did you know about the quilt?"

He pulled out a dollar and placed it on the table. "Joe told me your mother helped you piece together a log cabin quilt for your wedding, but you never got it done. I figured, you marry me, you can finish it off proper."

"How dare you?" Tears filled her eyes. "You could never take Joe's place in my heart. I won't let you." She stormed out of there as fast as her Mary Jane heels could take her.

"Alice!" His voice called out behind her.

She turned and delivered a glare she hoped would show him how angry she was. "I'll find my own way home."

"Don't be silly." He reached for her. "With the Tolivers back and Luke still missing, it's not safe for you to be on your own."

"I am on my own! Leave me be." She ran toward the river. She had to get away from all of it, her memories of Joe, the love they shared, and Rick. She didn't want a home, or children, or any log cabin quilt. Not if it ended with her heart being ripped apart.

When she got to the river, she stopped and looked back. He hadn't come after her. Why did it leave her empty inside? She sat on a felled tree facing the Kanawha River. A barge filled with coal passed by as a doe and her fawn darted into the woods.

"Alice?"

Her heart raced. She stood and turned to find the male voice behind her wasn't who she thought it would be. Her knees weakened and she backed up, tripping over a rock and landing on her bottom.

Mr. Toliver smiled with oily charm. "Careful there, Alice. You wouldn't want to end up in the river."

His normal affable manner didn't show anything sinister lurking beneath. It unnerved her even more when he seemed harmless, like the man she'd known most of her life.

No matter how determined she was to act normal, she couldn't stop shaking. "I... I didn't see you there. I mean... you startled me."

Mr. Toliver offered his hand. "Are you all right? You didn't reinjure your ankle, did you? I could take you to the doctor."

Her mouth felt like it had sand in it. "No! I... I need to get back to the shop." She swallowed hard.

He reached for her hand and pulled her to her feet.

Rick appeared from nowhere. He must have been following her after all, maybe at a distance, making sure she was safe. She rushed to his side and buried her face in his chest. A whimper she tried to tamp down escaped her lips.

"Are you all right?" Rick put his arms around her and stroked her hair.

"She had a bit of a fall." Mr. Toliver's tone stayed calm. "Alice, you need to be more watchful."

"Thank you, Henry, old man." Rick grasped her around the waist and led her away. "I'll make sure she gets back to her shop, safe and sound."

Mr. Toliver nodded and didn't say any more as Rick led her back to the road.

She didn't know how she managed to walk with her wobbly knees, the pain searing at her lungs and throat. As they reached the shop, her legs gave out, and she started to fall. Rick swooped her into his arms.

"No," she said faintly. "Your stitches."

He ignored her and pushed the door open.

Greta ran to them. "What happened?"

"She's had a start." He set Alice in the chair beside the quilting frame. "She ran into Mr. Toliver down by the river."

"Alice," Greta said, the fright clinging to the tone of her voice. "Did he hurt you?"

She shook her head, unable to speak.

"Get a wet cloth."

As Greta ran up the stairs, Rick grabbed another chair and propped up her feet. Greta clomped back down the stairs, and he placed the cold cloth behind Alice's neck.

The lump in her throat loosened.

"Doing better?" He dabbed her forehead while Greta offered a glass of water.

She nodded and took a sip. "I don't know what got into me. When I saw him, I... I couldn't move, or breathe, or anything."

"I've seen it before," Rick said. "Even with the best soldiers. It even happened to me once. Sometimes it just gets to you."

Alice took another sip of water. "I can't believe you ever froze. Not someone like you."

He lowered his eyes. "When Joe was killed, I lost it for a moment. It almost got me killed too before I gained my wits about me. I promised myself it would never happen again."

"I don't know if I can do this."

He knelt beside her and patted her hand. "Alice, after what you've been through, I'm surprised you didn't fall apart earlier. If it's too much, I can see you get away, somewhere safe."

"No, please. I can do this, for the United States and for Joe's memory. Those people have to be stopped."

"That-a-girl," he said.

Alice stood. "I'll be fine. I promise I won't let it happen again."

"I know." He touched her cheek with the back of his hand. "I won't let anything happen to you. You know that, don't you?"

"Thank you for helping me." She blinked at the hot tears forming in her eyes. "I haven't changed my mind about us."

Sadness flashed across his features. "Neither have I. You can overcome the fear of falling in love just like you'll overcome the terror of Toliver startling you. I'll wait until you do." He ambled to the door and placed his hand on the handle. "I'm going to marry you, Alice Brighton. I'm not giving up on us. Or on my promise to Joe."

Chapter Thirty-Seven

Alice hoped she wouldn't see Mrs. Toliver before the quilt tour committee meeting on Friday. She wanted to remain strong. If she had all of the other ladies around, she was sure she could manage it, but if she had to see the woman alone...

The way she'd acted yesterday with Mr. Toliver disturbed her. She needed to keep it together. Joe had given his life for this country and their freedom, and she would do the same if she had to.

She straightened the counter and checked the yarn supply. Lois had bought some blue yarn, the only one who hadn't gotten red, green, or yellow. Bernice had agreed to teach her how to crochet since the knitting didn't work out. Lois had giggled. "I only need one needle with crocheting."

"Greta, could you get some more yarn from the storeroom?"

"A-Okay," Greta said as she strode to the back.

The door chime rang. Alice turned and came face-to-face with Mrs. Toliver, only she wasn't the woman Alice knew. She always dressed impeccably with her make-up just so, but today she looked frazzled with very little make-up, puffy eyes, and a rumpled dress. Maybe she'd slept in it. Today, Mrs. Toliver didn't look so intimidating.

Alice swallowed and forced a smile on her face. "I heard you were back. How can I help you?"

"Oh, dear, I don't know." She looked so unsure of herself.

"Perhaps some yarn for Janice's baby." Alice walked toward the display.

"No, I don't need any yarn." Mrs. Toliver grasped hold of the counter while she stared at the display of candy bars. "I can't be in this quilt tour scheme of yours, Alice. I just can't be involved." Her shrill voice cracked. "My nieces won't be a part of the parade either. I've taken them back to Beckley to be with their mother."

Heat rose to the back of Alice's neck. She pressed her lips together to keep from blurting out good riddance. "My tour? It's for the whole community. We've worked together for nearly a month." At least she wouldn't have to deal with Mrs. Toliver at the committee meetings any more. "I'm sorry you feel so strongly about it. I know we've had some disagreements about the tour stops, but you don't have to quit."

"You don't understand. I can't be a part of this operation any longer. I can't." The former chairlady gaze pleaded with Alice as she grabbed her hand. Alice had to grit her teeth to keep from pulling it back.

"You be careful, you and Mr. Morrison," Mrs. Toliver whispered frantically. "Do you understand?"

"No, I don't." Alice pulled her hand away and stepped back.

"They won't let you get in the way. Either of you."

Before she could say another word, Mr. Toliver came into the shop and Mrs. Toliver immediately transformed into her old self.

Fear gripped Alice's stomach. *Lord, please help me.*

"There you are, Gwynnie," Mr. Toliver said. "You disappeared on me."

"Oh, Henry, you say the funniest things. I needed some yarn to knit Baby Eugene a sweater."

An inexplicable calm came over Alice. "What color would you like, Mrs. Toliver?"

She startled as if she forgot Alice was standing there. "Oh, I suppose red. Everyone will make something blue."

"Red it is." Alice grabbed two skeins of red yarn.

"I hope you're feeling better after the nasty spill yesterday," Mr. Toliver said to Alice. He was back to his easy going self as if nothing had changed between them. "You should be more careful." A flash of maliciousness crossed his eyes. There was a double meaning in his warning.

Alice ignored the comment as she rang up the order. "Mrs. Toliver, I'll miss you at the quilt tour meeting tomorrow."

Mr. Toliver's head jerked toward his wife.

Mrs. Toliver blushed and took a step back. "I don't know what you're talking about, dear. Of course I'll be at the meeting. The quilt tour is only a week away."

"You said--"

Mrs. Toliver grabbed Alice's hand and implored her with her eyes. "I'll be there, Alice."

"All right then," Mr. Toliver said. "I'll have her there bright and early."

Alice handed Mrs. Toliver her bag of yarn and receipt. "Oh, are you attending, Mr. Toliver?"

Mr. Toliver smiled but didn't quite manage the affable grin. "With Lucien away on business, I'll take his place for security. We all must do our part."

"Yes, of course," Mrs. Toliver said as she made her way to the door. "Tootleoo."

Mr. Toliver followed her out.

Alice sank to a nearby chair.

*****

July 2, 1946

Alice's alarm clock jangled. She groaned, reached out to smack the off button, and shook her hair back off her sweaty face. If only it would rain or something to dispel the oppressive humidity already built up at six forty-five. Her Emerson silver swan fan circulated the hot air, but in this heat, it didn't do enough to cool things off.

Acknowledging her grumpy mood was due in large part to her strange dreams and lack of sleep, she swung her legs from under her sheet and stood up. Another Friday had come since the last Burning Bush Quilt Tour Committee meeting last week. Ten a.m. was too soon for another one. She had a full day ahead of her. The whole tour and Fourth of July celebration was only two days away.

She trudged toward the window hoping to catch a cool breeze. A smudge on the curtain made her pause. One step closer... "Ouch! What in the world..."

A stone large enough to break her window skittered in front of her bare toe where she'd accidentally kicked it. So, she hadn't imaged the scuffling noise last night, a pattering she dreamed was rain. Good thing the window was open, or she's be cleaning up broken glass.

In the kitchen, Greta ran water and clanked pots.

Alice pulled on a light robe and went out. "Good morning, Greta. How did you sleep?"

"*Guten morgen*," Alice's roommate responded. "Ach, not so good again. Hooligans out there, now with school out, have nothing better to do than cause mischief all night. Where is sheriff?"

"They threw rocks at my bedroom window. I found one on my floor."

"We should report, *ja*?"

"*Ja*." Alice poured some coffee for them. "So you think it's hooligans?"

Greta shrugged. She cracked four eggs into her heavy skillet. "Same as home. Young ones with little supervision."

"Maybe it was kids who dragged those heavy pasture gates onto Mockingbird Road the other night to stop cars? Bernice Gorman almost had an accident. Good thing it wasn't dark yet and she stopped in time."

"What else could it be?" Greta dished up their eggs and toast on to plates and handed one to Alice. "I don't buy the bacon. I forgot."

"I forgot too. I should get dressed, I guess. Is okay to eat first?" She grinned.

"*Ja*. Is A-Okay. Sit. I pray."

Alice did as she was told.

Several bites later, Greta brought up the final meeting they'd planned for today. "There is some *krumkaka*. You want me to bring it for treat later? I can lock up the store."

"I've lost all my excitement about the quilt tour. It's not fair."

"Tsk. Nothing is fair." Greta placed her cool hand on Alice's arm. "I have faith you and Herr Rick will succeed."

"I guess I'd better get on with it, then." Alice got to her feet. "Maybe you'd better stay at the shop this morning. I hate to close up when we've had so much out of town business. We can have a meeting without cake just this once."

At ten a.m. on the dot, Alice rapped the gavel to call the meeting to order. The knot of cooing women surrounding Janice and baby James slowly unwound. Alice gave them time. Excitement and anticipation mixed with a little disappointment at not having refreshments this time.

Gwendolyn Toliver didn't join in, not even to acknowledge the baby. She sat by herself in the back row, hat on head, feet planted, pocketbook on her lap. She acted as though she had a train to catch.

Alice took a deep breath and let it out slowly. "Ladies! I call this meeting to order. Let's rise for the Pledge of Allegiance."

After they'd regained their seats, Lois read the minutes of the last meeting. Lois had become a new person the past few weeks. She'd always had a certain measure of confidence in herself, but now it wasn't because of the latest fashion or hairstyle or some newfangled gadget she thought would make her life easier. She'd produced several edible meals in a row according to Pete. Her cheeks were glowing as she opened her notebook and poised to read.

Alice was so proud of her sister-in-law for settling down and learning some country ways, as well as her brother who'd secretly ordered a new gas stove and the necessary pipes and fittings to begin the process to outfit their homestead with indoor plumbing.

"Mrs. Round reported she has secured the marching bands from Oak Hill and Montgomery High Schools for the parade," Lois read. "A total of fourteen units of bands, floats, bicycles, and dignitaries in their automobiles have signed up so far to participate. An open category will be included for the purposes of judging. The prize divisions have yet to be determined."

Mrs. Round stood. "We'll have it worked out later today, Madam Chairwoman."

"Thank you," Alice replied. "Please continue, Madam Secretary."

"The Burning Bush Barbershop Quartet under the direction of Deputy Eddie Tyler will provide entertainment during the barbecue dinner provided by Daria's Diner. Mrs. Felton reported nine hundred raffle tickets have been sold so far..."

At the gasp, Janice's face went pink. "A lot of people stopped in to see James. Jeff made sure they left with raffle tickets."

Alice laughed. "Very good."

Lois wrapped up. "Pete and I rode over to Charleston to make sure the ad campaign went as planned." She turned and frowned at Mrs. Toliver, who stared blankly at her gloved hands. "We stopped in Montgomery to pick up the revised map of the quilt tour stops."

"Thank you," Alice said. "I need a motion to accept the secretary's report."

Bernice moved and Mrs. Collins seconded. Alice moved right through the rest of the business before her nerves got the better of her. As annoying as Gwendolyn Toliver's difficult mannerisms were when the tour first got underway, seeing her silent and preoccupied like today felt more ominous.

At least Mr. Toliver hadn't come along. All bluster and brag at Friday's meeting, he'd reported he put together a security team of off-duty police officers in three nearby communities to guard the entrances to Burning Bush and make sure no trouble ensued. All travelers who dared to brave the dangers of Mockingbird Road would be safe.

Alice thought they'd be more likely to frighten visitors, but with Rick urging her to keep quiet, she didn't say anything.

"Are there any reports from those of you who have tour stops?" Alice asked. "All the blocks are painted?"

Andrea Collins raised her hand and stood. "I have something to report." She looked at Gwendolyn Toliver before facing front. "The sheriff came out already, but we had some vandalism last night."

"Ooh!"

"What?"

"Oh, no!"

Alice tapped the gavel to quiet the ladies. "Go on, Mrs. Collins."

"Someone or ones unknown tried to damage our quilt block." Andrea Collins had the Grandmother's Flower Garden block, the one with all the little hexagons.

Everyone but Mrs. Toliver showed alarm. Alice and Lois exchanged nods.

"My husband was able to chase the person away. Our block had been finished and was all dry, so we were able to wipe off the splotches of black paint the miscreant tossed at the barn."

"Did you catch him?" Mrs. Round asked.

"No, but Sheriff Jenner has some ideas," Mrs. Collins said.

"Thank you, Mrs. Collins," Alice said. "The difficulty of your block is well noted, and I, for one, am glad you were able to save it."

Mrs. Jenner was not in attendance today, not a surprise. The poor woman hadn't been seen since she demanded red hexagons and ran out of the meeting a couple of weeks ago. She hadn't even made it to church Sunday. Alice walked by the Jenners on her way to the meeting to make sure the two quilt blocks were painted on the sliding doors of their barn. They were. After this tour business was over, she would reach out to the sheriff's wife and help her any way she could.

With all the hooligans, as Greta called them, causing havoc, the sheriff couldn't be causing too much grief with his wife. On Saturday, before Rick left town again, Alice had wondered if the sheriff might have something to do with the spy ring, but Rick laughed off her concerns. "Don't sweat it, doll, the evidence is mounting for the real culprits."

Alice had shaken off the ire of Rick calling her doll. He'd gotten her to agree to another dinner date in Montgomery when he returned tonight despite her best instincts. He said he needed a quiet place away from Burning Bush to discuss the quilt tour.

"All right, ladies," Alice said, "only two days to go. I feel confident matters are well in hand. We have the display quilt finished and could use some help with the raffle quilt. Until the tour, the shop will be open in the evenings as well as regular hours for those who might have time to come and help us out." She nodded as a few hands went up.

"Good, thank you. We won't meet again until the big day, but if you have any problems, please stop in the shop and talk to me about it." She hated to ask, but it was customary, and necessary according to Mr. Roberts Rules of Order. "Is there any other business to discuss before I call for a motion to adjourn?"

Mrs. Toliver stood. "I move we abandon the tour." She tightened the grip on her pocketbook.

Before the murmurs got out of control, Alice rapped. "Ladies, ladies, we have a motion on the floor. We need a second in order to open discussion. If there is no second, the motion will die. Do I hear a second? No," she rapped, "hearing no second, the motion dies. Is there a motion to adjourn?" Several of the committee members so moved, and with heart-pounding relief, Alice closed the meeting.

Mrs. Toliver slipped from the room before anyone could talk to her. Alice hesitated briefly, brushing off concerns and questions as kindly as she could, then hustled after her nemesis.

Once outside, she scanned the path toward town but Mrs. Toliver was nowhere in sight. She rotated, gazing the landscape. Ah! A little dust in the distance showed where Mrs. Toliver was headed. Away from Burning Bush toward the woods by the river. *Hmm.*

She picked up her pace and jogged. Looking over her shoulder, she hoped someone from the committee saw her heading this way. Maybe this wasn't a good idea.

Mrs. Toliver glanced back, and quickened her pace.

"Wait!" Alice called. "I just want to talk!"

Mrs. Toliver left the road and ducked onto the path some of the boys took to get to a large flat rock they often used for fishing.

Alice slowed down and almost headed back toward town. A muffled scream changed her mind. She almost called out again but stopped herself. She approached the path. No reason to worry. Probably some kids playing near the water.

There was no sound now. Nothing. Not even a breeze rustling leaves of the red maples, hemlocks, and sweet gums. Majestic oaks with their huge trunks were easy to hide behind.

With one last look back, she straightened her shoulders and stepped off the road. All this spy business had her spooked for no reason. She might be at odds with Mrs. Toliver, but she wanted to help her if she could.

She caught a glimpse of Mrs. Toliver occupying the fishing rock, and darted behind an oak tree. She dared a peek.

Mrs. Toliver stood awkwardly with her hands tied in front of her and a gag tied around her mouth. She was tugged along the rock by the rope around her wrists. A splash confirmed her entry into the river.

Every nerve in Alice's body urged her to flee. She turned and tripped headlong, scraping her palms on roots and pebbles. She glanced back, worried someone had heard her.

A male figure faced the river where Mrs. Toliver had landed. "You shouldn't have double-crossed us, poor, late Gwynnie," Mr. Toliver intoned low and deep.

Alice twisted away and sat up, gasping, shaking in fright and trying to hold in her tears.

Someone grabbed her arms, but before she could see a face, someone else thrust a dusty, dirty sack over her head. "No!" She screamed, "Help!" She gagged as she sucked dust down her throat into her lungs.

"Shut her up!"

The blow to her temple was almost welcome.

Chapter Thirty-Eight

Alice groaned and tried to swallow. Her throat swelled with a bitter metallic taste. Her head hurt. She raised her hand to the bump on her brow. What had she run into? She opened her eyes and touched her eyelids. She could see nothing "He-hello? Anyone there?"

Cold! She shivered and tried to sit up. It hurt too much and made her stomach churn, so she curled up in a ball. Vague memories began to swirl. Mrs. Toliver tied up and... "No!"

A man's laughter echoed.

"Who's there! Where am I?" Alice struggled at the ropes binding her hands and feet."

"No! Lay still!"

She halted, a new chill replacing the angry shivers. "Rick?"

"It's me, doll. Do me a favor. Just lay real still now."

"What? Where are we?"

The sinister laugh bounced around the walls.

"Rick?"

"Shh. Don't pay attention to that punk. We'll be all right."

"Who, Rick? What's happening?"

"Near as I can tell, we're--"

"Shut up in there!" The voice no longer laughed. Alice recognized the sound now. She swallowed again and coughed.

"You okay?" Rick whispered.

She nodded but realized he couldn't see her in the inkiness of their surroundings. "Yes." She might have heard him whisper, but she didn't think he was that near to her. "Where are you?"

"I said, shut up!"

Alice cringed at the booming voice of Lucien Wendell Holmes ricocheting off the walls. They must be in some large empty chamber. Cold and damp. Underground. A cave? No, the floor felt hard and cold, like rock. Maybe a mine.

"Luke, please," she said in her gentlest voice. "What's going on?"

"You want to know what's going on?"

The maniacal tone seeped through her body.

"Alice, don't make things worse," Rick said. "Just lie still and let me handle him."

Knowing Rick was here kept her from melting away, but his condescending attitude was beginning to wear. "Don't tell me what to do." She wiggled, testing her bonds.

"Don't move!" Rick's voice contained a hint of fear.

"Why do you keep saying that?"

"Oh?" Lucien said. "You want to see? Let me help you."

The sound of a heavy switch accompanied the glow from a lightbulb hanging from a beam overhead. The large room was surrounded by wood supports. Openings branched out in different directions but were hidden in the shadows.

In the middle of the room, the single bulb illuminated a man slouched in a chair wearing only trousers and an undershirt. His feet were tied to the chair legs and his hands were bound behind him, with a rope snaked out of the circle of light. The man raised his head.

Even from the fifteen-foot distance between them and the feeble glimmer, she could see the blood and bruises and swollen eye on the right side of his face. "Rick!"

"Don't move. Whatever else, just... don't... move."

"But..."

Rick winced. "Your boyfriend has us tied up pretty good, doll."

Alice ignored Lucien's laugh and Rick's "doll" comment. "How do we get out of this?"

"I'm afraid, my dear," Lucien said as he stepped out of the dark behind Rick, "the only way you'll get out of this is to stop being so obstinate and hear me out."

"What do you mean?" Alice wiggled her fingers to keep her circulation going. It was freezing in here, and she didn't want to lose the use of her hands. She tugged at the ropes.

"I'll give you some time to think about the predicament you're in before I explain. I'll be back in a bit, my dear." Lucien walked away, his footsteps echoing.

"Rick? Talk to me!"

"He showed me..." Rick's voice grew fainter.

"Don't you pass out!" Her wrists were being rubbed raw from wriggling against the knots, but she didn't care. "Tell me... tell me what happened to you."

"Huh." Rick shook his head a little.

"What happened?"

"Ha-happened? I came back early. Surprise you."

"Early when?"

"About dawn. Stopped by your place. Window was open."

"I knew it! You threw a stone at my window."

"Thought we could talk... you know, quiet-like." Rick cleared his throat. His head bent forward again.

"Rick! I'm so sorry. I found the stone this morning. I never heard you."

"Should have just rung the bell."

"Yes. Then what happened?"

"Wasn't expecting them. Not like me. Four of 'em jumped me."

Her heart stilled. Nuisance tears gathered, ones she couldn't wipe away with her hands tied up. "I'm so sorry. I should have been there for you."

"No. Might have been killed."

"So, look where I ended up?" she pointed out.

"How?"

"I was following Mrs. Toliver after the meeting. Down by the river. Rick, I think they killed her."

"She came to me. Said she'd changed her mind. I should have taken her into protective custody. My fault." Rick raised his head. "We have to get you out of here."

"You too!" She resumed struggling.

"Don't move. Please, Alice."

"Why?"

She followed his stare along the rope until it disappeared into the murky darkness of one of the tunnels. Or did it? She squinted at the bulky shape hidden in the shadows. "What is that?"

"It's Fat Boy's little brother, and we're both tied to the safe-ready switch." Alice's heart did a drum solo.

Luke strode into the room, or cave, or whatever it was. More like a room in a cave, like one of those abandoned coal mines Pete worked in before the war. Her brother hated those mines and swore he'd never work in one again. The thought of ending up buried in one caused her shivers to return.

Luke walked toward her and knelt on the ground. His dark eyes bored holes in her skin, but she tried to keep eye contact. She wouldn't give him the satisfaction of knowing how scared she was.

"It's like this, dear heart." Luke shrugged and tilted his head toward Rick. "He's not going anywhere. The only reason the traitor is still alive is I need to know if he's on to us."

Alice pressed her lips together but didn't say anything.

"You're different. I care deeply for you." Luke touched her cheek, and it took all her willpower not to shrink back. "If you hadn't seen us taking care of my Aunt Gwynnie, I would have never brought you here."

"You killed her. Why?"

"Not me. Uncle Henry had no choice. She betrayed the cause. He needed to stop her from telling the CIG what we were up to." Luke shrugged. "He would have taken care of you too, but I convinced him to let me bring you here."

He stroked the side of her face with the back of his hand. Her heartbeat throbbed in her ears.

"If you'll let me explain to you how the United States government is responsible for the predicament the world's in, well, I'm crazy about you. I don't want you to end up like your landlord over there. I could help you out of this."

Alice wanted to spit in his face, but her throat was so dry, she doubted she could produce enough saliva.

"I understand." Luke stood. "You need time to think about it, but consider this. It's not the Nazis or the Communists who killed thousands with atomic bombs, is it?" He started pacing. "The Nazis were a part of it, I'll give you that, but think about why they put Hitler in power. The Jewish bankers and Wall Street tycoons plunged this whole world into a Depression. People were starving in the streets while American Imperialism made the rich richer. It was worse in Europe and Germany. Desperate people do desperate things. Even elect an imbecile like Hitler."

Luke strode to Rick and punched him in the jaw then straightened his tie and adjusted his suit jacket. "Blokes like him want to help Truman make it worse."

Alice turned away. She couldn't help it. Seeing Rick being hurt when he couldn't defend himself made her heart bleed. She was a fool thinking she could protect herself by sending Rick away. It was too late for that.

Luke directed those dark empty eyes of his toward her like rockets. "Don't you see? We want to make things better for the common people. Believe me, the farmers and coal miners in this area would thank us if they knew how much better life would be under Communism. They wouldn't have to risk their lives for poor wages so some rich mine owner could get richer. Everyone would get their fair share."

Alice managed to swallow despite her dry throat. "You want to take away our freedom and our rights just like Hitler tried to do."

"You don't appreciate what we're trying to accomplish, my dear? The end of capitalism means the life you've always wanted but never thought you could have. The end of capitalism means freedom."

Luke squatted beside her. "I'll tell you what. I know you don't understand it all but if you'll agree to let me mentor you--"

"You mean brainwash me. I've heard about your mind control techniques."

Luke laughed. "You've been watching too many Boogie movies. It's the good old US of A brainwashing you. Think of it, the schools, the news media, the government. None of them tell the truth about the repression of the common man. All I want is a chance to help you see the light. Do you want to suffer the same fate as your landlord over there?"

He leaned toward her. For a moment, she thought he might try to kiss her, and her stomach churned. "I'll give you some time to reflect on what I'm saying. If you don't decide soon, it will be out of my hands. No matter how much I adore you, I won't be able to protect you."

He turned and walked away as the shuffle of his footsteps faded into the darkness.

"Alice, you should do as he says." Rick's voice sounded weak, too weak.

"You want me to become a Communist?"

"No. If you make him think you're at least open to it, he might let you go. You could get help."

She squinted to try to make out his features. "Sure, and he'll believe I saw the light just like that. It's not going to happen."

Rick shook his head. "Maybe not right away, but you're as smart as you are pretty. You'll find a way."

"You'd be dead by then." She rose as much as she dared without moving the rope tied to her ankle. "Rick, I'm sorry about what I said about us just being friends. It's more than friendship, and it has been for a long time. I can't protect my heart from breaking if something happens to you by pretending I don't care. I'm not leaving you no matter what you say."

A hint of his smirk returned. "I love you too, doll. We'll both get out of here, and when we do, I'm going to marry you."

She grunted. "It would be nice if you asked instead of issuing an order."

"I can't exactly get down on one knee, now can I? Please play nice with him. It's our only chance."

She struggled to think of some way at least one of them could get loose. Maybe the cavalry or the CIG would swoop in and save the day. It didn't look like she had a choice. Their only hope was for her to schmooze Luke and look for a way out. "I'll do it. As soon as he unties me, I'm going for help, but you better stay alive until I get back."

The shadows must have been playing tricks on her eyes because she could swear Rick winked at her.

Footsteps sounded, and she prepared herself for the greatest acting job of her life. Maybe watching all those movies would pay off.

She had no way of acting her way through what happened next. Sheriff Jenner, Deputy Eddie Tyler, and Pete appeared at one of the openings and marched into the chamber.

"What are you doing here?"

Pete grinned and tucked his thumbs in his overalls. "We came to rescue you."

Rick's eyes popped wide open. "How did you know where we were?"

"Greta." Deputy Eddie shrugged as if that explained everything.

"Never mind," Rick said. "Don't bother with Alice. Get me untied first."

Pete's charming farmer grin turned into a scowl. "Now look here. That's my sister you're talking about. Whatever happened to women and children first?"

Rick glanced at her with his *trust me* look, but he could have saved the trouble.

"There's a rope attached to my ankle," she said. "It could set off a bomb. Untie Rick first. He'll know what to do."

Pete uttered a sheepish "sorry" as he freed Rick.

All four men encircled Alice and stared like she had turned into a munchkin from *The Wizard of Oz*.

"What should we do first?" Sheriff Jenner asked. He was clearly letting Rick have the lead on this.

"I'll follow the rope," Deputy Eddie offered. "Before I was a fighter pilot, I had some bomb defusing training. I'll see if I can cut the rope without blowing us up."

Rick nodded and took hold of Alice's hand. It comforted her having him so near, but... "Rick, Pete, all of you need to get away. There's no reason for you to be here if this thing goes off."

Rick squeezed her hand tighter. "Deputy, you got anything?"

Eddie appeared out of the shadows with a pair of wire cutters in his hand. "Piece of cake. There is a bomb, but the rope was more for show than anything."

Rick let out an audible sigh. "Let's get out of here."

"Not so fast." At the sound of Luke's voice, Alice's heart skipped a beat. Luke stepped out of the shadows holding a pistol. "You're not going anywhere."

"Luke," Rick said. "You have a lot to learn about being a spy."

Alice raised an eyebrow. What was he up to?

"For instance, when you're holding a gun on a group of people, you should make sure there's nobody hiding in the shadows. Do you think these men would come in here without the Calvary backing them up?"

Luke glanced behind him for just a second, but it was long enough for Rick to kick the gun out of his hand. Sheriff Jenner and Deputy Eddie tackled him to the ground. After the sheriff slapped handcuffs on his wrists, they pulled Luke to his feet.

Pete's hand fisted. He uncurled his fingers, lifted his hand in a gesture to slap Rick on the back, then groaned and rubbed his hand through his hair. "Would somebody tell me what's going on around here?"

Rick wiped blood from his lip. "Luke and the Tolivers are part of a Communist spy ring. They're planning to pass information about planting a bomb at DuPont using Alice's quilt tour."

All three men stared at him with their mouths dropped open.

"The bomb is a distraction for their real plan to steal the blueprints for the atomic bomb and assassinate President Truman," Rick said, "but this needs to be kept on the QT. The Central Intelligence Group has agents in place to arrest the conspirators tomorrow when they show up in Burning Bush."

The muscle in Pete's jaw twitched.

Rick placed a hand on Pete's shoulder. "Your folks knew about their group. We think the car crash wasn't an accident."

Before anyone could react, Pete punched Luke in the face with a force knocking him to the ground. Blood trickled out of Luke's nose.

Alice couldn't help but chuckle. Luke's face now looked worse than his handiwork on Rick. He wasn't the sheik of Burning Bush any more. Her chuckle died in her throat as another gun pointed at Rick.

This time, Mrs. Jenner had her finger on the trigger.

Chapter Thirty-Nine

"It's a good thing the Soviet way of thinking doesn't leave all the action to idiot *myooshcheeni*," Mrs. Jenner said. She no longer looked daft, or acted meek. She exuded the self-assurance and danger Barbara Stanwick showed in *Double Indemnity*, and her slight accent become more pronounced.

Alice's heart just about stopped. "What did she say?"

"Men," Rick replied, sounding disgusted. "It's Russian for men."

"Remove all your weapons, slowly. On the ground. Kick them toward me," Mrs. Jenner said.

Deciding to ignore the fact Rick understood Russian, Alice turned toward the sheriff who unbuckled his gun belt, eyes never leaving his wife's face. Stunned was too mild of a word for the expression he bore.

He took a step toward her with his hand out. "Mara, what's all this about?"

"*Pateteecheskooye*," she spit out and waved the gun. "Get away from me, you stupid man. Get back with the others."

"Pathetic," Rick muttered. "Mara Jenner called her husband pathetic."

"Quiet," Mrs. Jenner said in a no-nonsense voice. "You too. Give me your gun."

Rick held up his hands. "Not on me." He touched his purpling jaw. "You people just don't have a clue, do you?"

"Don't believe him," Luke shouted. "There's no one else--"

A deafening explosion from Mrs. Jenner's pistol echoed in the cavern. Luke clutched his chest and fell backward. Alice swallowed a scream and locked anguished eyes with Rick.

"Idiot," Mrs. Jenner repeated. "He was always so gullible, always letting a woman turn his head. *Svoyekoristooye*--"

"Selfish," Rick supplied, earning himself a target from the muzzle of her gun.

"I don't understand," Alice said. "Who are you?"

"I'm the woman holding the gun. Mrs. George Jenner, American citizen and wife of the sheriff of Burning Bush, West Virginia. American men are so stupid." She tilted her head toward Luke's dead body. "He's the worst. So easily fooled by a woman."

"She point the barrel of her gun toward Sheriff Jenner. "It was easy to get the sheriff of this backward town to marry me. Everyone feels sorry for me after the way he treats me. Hillbillies. Americans."

She cursed. "They even believe I was from Estonia. The Immigration Department didn't even bother to check visas and paperwork from such a small, insignificant country not even when I applied for citizenship. Nobody comes from Estonia. All so trusting. So *toopoy*."

"She means stupid." Rick offered with a smirk as Mrs. Jenner glared at him.

"He," she tilted her head toward her husband, "never even knew why he was about to lose the next election. It was so easy to convince the women voters you were a bully. They were so willing to believe you were a bad man."

"Mara, please..." Sheriff Jenner took a step toward her but changed his mind when she pointed the revolver at him. "I never hurt you."

"You couldn't have if you wanted to. Didn't you notice how I would always start an argument before we would be seen in public? I'd stick my fingers in my eyes to make them puffy and let nature take its course. You'd belittle me in front of others, and I'd act timid and scared. All I had to do was let out a few innuendos, and those gossiping hillbilly housewives filled in the rest."

"Mara, you're not feeling well," the sheriff said with a shaky, soft voice. "Whatever's happened, I can help you. We'll take you to a doctor in Charleston."

The gun went off again, the flash and ricocheting bullet making Jenner dance into the shadow.

"It was so easy to hide here waiting for our moment of triumph." Mrs. Jenner frowned at Luke's body.

"I don't understand," Alice said.

"She's a commie spy from the Soviet Union, the mastermind," Rick said. "Had almost everyone duped."

"Almost?" Mrs. Jenner stalked toward them. "Almost? Babysitting those mindless pigs like the Tolivers and Holmes." She motioned toward Luke's body. "Having to deal with pretty boy there. Always thinking with his glands. Pretty faces, sweet voices, dances..."

The gun's muzzle pressed warm against Alice's cheek.

"Lucian let himself be taken prisoner because he was too busy looking at you. You should dance for me, Mrs. Brighton. Lucian couldn't kill you when he was ordered to, but I'll have no trouble at all."

"Wait!" Pete surged forward ignoring the glint off the blade appearing in Mrs. Jenner's other hand. "You'll kill all of us. My sister is still attached to the bomb."

"I heard you," Mrs. Jenner growled. "There is no threat. We hadn't even armed the bomb, yet."

"Do you know for sure?" Pete seemed abnormally calm to Alice. "Luke sounded like he knew what he was talking about, ready-switches, safety pins, and triggering mechanisms."

Rick pressed his lips together and tilted his head toward her. Warning her? Of what? She blinked and shook her head.

"You know nothing!" Mrs. Jenner said and waved the knife while pressing the gun tighter against Alice's cheek. "Quiet!"

The acrid smell of gunpowder from the recently fired weapon stung Alice's nose and eyes.

"Since you murdered Luke," Pete said, eyes piercing Mrs. Jenner, "you can't know he didn't arm the bomb."

Mrs. Jenner narrowed her eyes.

Alice wished the young deputy would have been able to finish cutting her loose. She believed him earlier when he said the ropes were just for show, but she hated the feel of it tied around her ankle. She'd love to distract this crazy woman and crawl away, but what if the deputy suspected Luke or someone had been listening? What did she want?

Where was Eddie, anyway? Alice turned slightly to search for him.

The gun pressed into her cheek. "Do not move," Mrs. Jenner said in a menacing monotone. "The weapon is irrelevant. What I need from you now, Morrison, is information. Tell me now, or this woman gets another hole in her lovely little face. Who. Else. Knows?"

Alice blinked and swallowed again. "Don't, Rick. Don't--"

"Anything!" Rick wiped a hand across his bloody lip. "Whatever you want me to say."

No one breathed.

"I'm waiting!" Mrs. Jenner passed the knife along Alice's ear. "She doesn't need two of these."

"Stop! Who else knows? About me? I can give you the addresses of all my rental properties," Rick said. "My serial number, my records--"

"No! You're not in real estate." She grinned, feral, in the feeble light. Sweat prickled her hairline. "Your employer is Uncle Sam. Are you OSS, FBI, CIG? What did you tell them?"

"Lady, I'm self-emp--"

"I will shoot her." She nodded toward Luke's body. "You've seen how I handle someone who disappoints me when he's on my side. Imagine what I'd do to her. At this range, it will be messy, and I don't like cleaning up messes, do I, George? Tell me, or I'll hurt her."

"It's no use," Pete said. "Rick, the cat's out of the bag. Don't let her hurt my sister, please. Or do anything to set off the bomb."

There he goes with the bomb again. "Pete!" Alice said. "You're not helping. Deputy--"

"Hush, now, angel," Rick whispered.

"What are you up to?" Mrs. Jenner stood and waved the knife at them. "Over there!" She pointed toward the sheriff at the edge of the shadow. "Get out here in the light. There was another one! Where are you? Come out! Now!" Pete slowly backed up.

"*Ja*! I come out!" Greta leaped from the shadow and smashed Mrs. Jenner's gun-wielding hand with a cast iron skillet.

The gun clattered toward the sheriff. He picked it up.

"Greta, look out! She has a knife," Alice called. Ah -- So Pete was distracting the woman so Eddie could go for help, but why Greta?

A red stripe appeared across Greta's cheek where Mrs. Jenner slashed. The deputy crept along the corridor behind the Russian women.

"Rick, do something!" Alice pleaded. "Sheriff! What are you waiting for? Shoot her!"

"I -- I can't! She's my wife!"

"She ain't my wife," Eddie said and took the weapon from the sheriff, aimed, and fired.

*****

An hour later, their small group crowded into the sheriff's office, Jenner plopped into his seat behind his desk, his face gray and anguished. He shook his head when Doc Brenner approached him.

Alice applied pressure to the ice pack she held against Rick's jaw.

Deputy Eddie kept hold of Greta's hand he'd taken when antiseptic and a bandage were applied to her cheek. She started to grin at Alice, but it quickly turned into a grimace. "You told me to bring a skillet next time."

Alice couldn't help but chuckle. She wouldn't want to be on Greta's bad side.

"Hey." Rick turned Alice's face toward him. "You're supposed to be giving your undivided attention to your fiancé."

"I don't know." She glanced once again at the surprising couple. Or not so surprising, thinking back. "She did save us, and he's not too bad on the eyes."

"Him? He's just a kid." Rick frowned. "She did, did she?" He looked miffed.

"It was Herr Morr... Rick's plan all along," Greta said. "He said if he or you went missing, I should bring help to the mine shaft where he was shot. When you never came home from the meeting, I knew what to do."

"You sure did." Alice glanced toward the two black-suited sober-looking men who finished taking Pete's statement. Black suits, white shirts, and narrow black ties must be the required uniform for the job. One by one, they shook hands with Rick like he was their boss or something.

If she'd even wondered before about Rick's real job, she didn't any more. "By the way, you're not my fiancé until you ask me. You can't just order me to marry you."

Rick leaned toward her and kissed her, then winced and held his jaw.

Mayor Wilson stood in a corner, hand on his chin, probably trying to process Communist agents infiltrating Burning Bush. Rick had tried to keep things on the down low, but he felt the mayor needed in on it. Poor Sheriff Jenner was instructed to say his wife's mother became ill, and she had to go out of town to care for her and wouldn't be able to help with the quilt tour after all.

Yes, the tour would go on.

"You can do this." Rick squeezed her hand, the one holding the ice pack.

"I don't know. To think there are more of them... and if we didn't suspect Mrs. Jenner... Mara, I mean, who can we trust?"

"You cannot live in fear of every neighbor," Greta said. "They tried to make us do that in Germany. We must not treat others so."

Eddie put his arm around her shoulders. "Well said."

"What do they want?" Alice shivered.

Rick took the pack. "Enough ice. We should get you home."

She shook her head. "Not yet. Was Mrs. Jenner--" She took a peek at the sheriff who was under interrogation now, and whispered, "the real leader? I thought Henry Toliver--"

"Toliver took his orders from Mrs. Jenner, but we have it all under control. Don't worry about anything but your quilt tour, doll," Rick said, putting his finger across her lips.

She shivered again, but for a different reason. "Another thing. About this doll business." She grinned at the uncomfortable look on his face. "I kind of like you calling me doll."

The smirk she'd grown to love reappeared.

"I'm off," Pete said. "You okay, Sis? I have to get home and check on Lois. She shouldn't worry in her condition."

Alice's head tilted up. "Lois is expecting?"

"Now I've gone and done it." Pete banged his palm on his forehead. "She wanted to tell you herself. You'll act surprised, won't you, Sis?"

Alice chuckled. "Go on home to your wife. I'll keep your secret. I've become pretty good at keeping secrets lately."

"I'll take care of your sister," Rick said.

Pete gave him a pat on the shoulder and left.

As much as she'd tried to portray herself as an independent businesswoman who could handle anything, Alice didn't mind the thought of a strong man taking care of her. As long as she could spend her life taking care of him.

She glanced at the sheriff again. He looked more like a puppy who had been kicked in the gut than a lawman who supposedly bullied his wife. Who would take over if Jenner was arrested? Deputy Eddie did seem young, though handled himself well today.

"Will the sheriff be all right?" Alice asked.

"There's nothing to charge him with," Rick said. "He didn't know what his wife was up to."

"To think he never realized," Alice said, "all these years, living with a Russian spy. How could he have never guessed?"

Greta shrugged. "Most see only what they want to see."

"I didn't have a reason not to believe she was anything but the sheriff's wife." Deputy Eddie took Greta's hand. "I didn't know her well. She brought in food to the prisoners and sometimes, when I was on duty, she'd stop and talk. Never anything serious, though. I always thought she was shy, you know. She had a slight accent, but Sheriff Jenner said she emigrated from Estonia as a young girl." He glanced at his boss. "Never believed much on those rumors. Sheriff Jenner didn't seem the type to beat up on a woman. Of course, now I know she was the one started them."

"You want to believe," Greta said. "To think people are good. Especially those you haf known a long time."

"Or those I'd like to know better." Eddie's gaze roamed her face and lingered on the bandage. "I'm glad you didn't need stitches. You had me plenty worried."

Rick sighed. "Sometimes you never truly know the one you love."

Alice squeezed his hand. *Oh, Joe, we knew each other all our lives, but I never knew this side of your life, but I loved you so.*

She and Rick stared into each other's eyes until throat-clearing made her blink. The black suits stood ramrod straight nearby.

Rick kissed her forehead, pulled away, and stood. "Okay, people, this is the plan."

Chapter Forty

The next evening at Daria's Diner where Rick had taken Alice for a quick supper, she picked at her piece of pie. When she told him she was too busy to eat, he had practically kidnapped her, insisting he was going to make sure she didn't make herself sick.

"I thought apple pie was your favorite." Rick leaned in toward her with his characteristic smirk, a little softened by his swollen jaw.

"Too much on my mind, I guess." She pushed the dessert away. "There's so much to think about, all the details for the quilt tour tomorrow, the CIG setting up base at the Jenners, what happened yesterday. It's all so much to handle."

"I know." Rick grabbed hold of her hand across the table. "You keep telling me how much you love Burning Bush. When my assignment is over next week, you know I'll... we'll be leaving."

Alice hadn't even thought of moving with everything going on. "Where will we live?"

"A small city outside Washington D.C. where CIG headquarters are, McLean, Virginia."

It surprised her how much she didn't mind leaving Burning Bush, though her hometown would always have a special place in her heart. Maybe she could keep a piece of it. "I don't want to sell the shop."

Rick pulled his hand away and rubbed the back of his neck. "I guess we should have talked about this before I asked you to marry me. I don't want to drag you away from Burning Bush kicking and screaming. If you don't want to leave--"

"No, my home is where you are." Alice tilted her head. "By the way, you never did ask me. If you do decide to propose, my home is wherever you are. What I meant was, I'm thinking of having Greta run the shop. Maybe she can bring her family over sooner."

"Good idea. She wouldn't have to pay rent since I own the lease."

"Do you really own it? I thought the government bought it."

Rick's hazel eyes lit up. "I never turned in the receipt to get reimbursed, and now, I don't think I'm going to. It's all mine. Do you want to tell her now?"

"Un uh, Mister. I'm not telling her until I'm actually engaged."

"Kind of bossy, aren't you? Is this what I have to look forward to? Well, all right, then, if you want it all romantic-like. I guess it won't kill me to make you happy, doll, but I'll decide the time and place."

As Alice got ready for bed, she had one last conversation with her dead husband. "Joe, I'll always love you, but it's time to move on. Thank you for sending Rick to take care of me. I love him too."

She took off her wedding ring.

*****

Thursday, July 4

Only Rick's reassuring look kept Alice's knees from buckling in front of the microphone where she had been forced into emcee duty during the hour-long parade. Thank heavens the weather had been blue skies all the way. Jeff Felton and Ralph Gorman had built the perfect dais for them and some borrowed speakers from Eddie's singing group broadcast her voice, just like Eleanor Roosevelt. A very nervous Mrs. Roosevelt who was about to send her man on a very dangerous mission.

Mayor Wilson, who led the parade, promised to take her place as soon as his much beloved 1927 Erskine Six Studebaker convertible coupe with the red, white, and blue bunting reached the end of the route.

Rick and his agents would be ready and waiting to round up the rest of Mara Jenner's gang on Mockingbird Road. Some men had been placed at the Collins farm last night. One of Rick's agents had come up with the plan of covering the painted blocks on the barns with canvas until the tour got under way after the parade was over.

Tickets for the guided tours sold briskly all morning, at a dollar per family for the wagon rides. Even the sales of the printed brochures Lois had designed for those who chose to go on their own had done well. They had a map and history of each block and went for a nickel a piece.

The clang of the bell from the fire engine forced Alice's attention back at her script. She'd missed a float from the Boy Scout troop, and hurried to catch up in a light-hearted voice.

"Excuse me, folks. I was just so stunned by the sight of those wonderful boys, weren't you? Troop number 17."

"Next we have the pumper truck from Fayette County's Volunteer Fire Department. Isn't she a beaut? I don't know about you, but I feel safer just knowing I'm so well protected." Ah! There was the mayor headed this way. "Now I'd like to turn the microphone over to our own Mayor Wilson, who will be your host for the rest of the parade. I know you'll all join me later for the Burning Bush Barn Quilt Tour!"

To a round of applause, Alice bowed to the mayor and scurried off the dais, but she didn't see Rick anywhere. With her heart in her throat, she motioned at Deputy -- no, Acting Sheriff Tyler -- who delivered a curt nod. "Mrs. Round has your group scheduled to sing later on, I believe," she said, grasping at any bit of normality. She took a deep breath and prepared to lead the first wagonload of tourists to the first stops in town. The Jenners' barn had been struck from the tour.

Greta took over handling the shop for the day, which had been filled with shoppers and browsers. Rosemary Lance and Jennifer Garrett had been recruited to help, and Rosemary had already been hired to stay on a few hours a week to teach basket making. Alice shook her head when she recalled how she felt about Greta at first. How could she have been so foolish? Just like the Tolivers... so foolish, and so wrong.

People were starting to leave the sidewalks where the parade had passed and were gathering at the Quilt Tour starting point.

Janice Felton, with Baby Eugene's carriage right by her side, took tickets. "This way, those of you in the first group, come this way."

Ralph had cleaned up his hay wagon, painted the rails, and built wooden benches along the sides. With a lurch, they were off. The passengers didn't need to disembark during the three stops in town, the Steps to the Altar at Round carriage house, the Pinwheel at the Garrett's barn, and the Crazy Patch at the Lance's garage.

With a flourish, Ralph and Pastor Round tugged the first canvas away.

"Folks, our first quilt block stop," Alice intoned, "is called Steps to the Altar. As many of you know, the tradition surrounding the origins of the names of the blocks is shrouded in mystery. Steps to the Altar certainly sounds romantic, doesn't it? Every girl's dream..."

She couldn't help but think of Rick and his promised romantic proposal. If they survived today. *Keep him safe, Lord. Please, keep them all safe.*

"This is one of the building block quilts made by stitching different size squares together." Noting the glazed look on some of the accompanying men's faces, Alice hurried through the next stops, making sure she engaged everyone who was willing to shout back ideas and comments on how the designs were put together, and how a simple design could change dramatically just by changing the color scheme.

The further into the holler they traveled, getting ever closer to Mockingbird Road, the higher her voice rose. Which of these men were members of the Communist spy ring? Would there be any trouble? She hadn't detected any guns on her passengers, but she wasn't an expert. Several women carried purses, and she knew for a fact not all women were trustworthy.

In the distance following them, dust rose as the first of the auto tourists followed behind. They had to get out of the holler and up Mockingbird Road to Grandmother's Flower Garden before too many innocent bystanders showed up.

Alice stayed quiet, studying each passenger without trying to be too obvious about it. Sure enough, as they traveled up the mountain, one man in particular became agitated. She thought initially he'd come with another couple, but when he sat alone near the gate at the back and didn't interact with anyone, her suspicions were hard to keep to herself.

When Ralph made the turn into the drive, she nodded at him and gave a little eye roll in the lone man's direction. Ralph turned all the way around to stare at the man in question, who now stood. Alice's breath hitched. "Sir, for safety's sake--"

He leaped off the wagon and ran headlong for the barn before the wagon could pull up to the side facing the house. He stopped, stared, and then put two fingers to his mouth. Alice jumped at the loud whistle.

She was certain he had not expected four men in black suits with guns pointed in his direction as a response. The man ducked and ran back toward the wagon, but one of the men in black suits, Rick, tackled him in the dirt.

Her heart fluttered for a moment, but Rick had things under control. He was like Joe in so many ways, ready to take the lead in fighting for what was right. Her heart swelled with pride. Even with the danger involved, she wouldn't want it any other way.

Gasps and shrieks accompanied the performance. Alice turned about and put on her game face. "Ladies and gentlemen, we have arrived at the stop of perhaps the most complicated block--"

"Who was that man?"

"Does anyone know what's going on?"

"Why do they have guns?"

"Will they hurt us?"

While men took the terrorist away and Alice let out a breath to calm her nerves, Rick, wiping a trickle of blood from his lip, approached the wagon. More shrieks and a charge to the other side of their transport made him chuckle. "There, now, folks. Nothing to be worried about." He raised his voice, but the upset tourists didn't settle until Alice took his hand and climbed down.

"Hello! Everyone, the situation is over! You're safe." Out of the side of her mouth she whispered, "We are, aren't we? You're okay?"

"Sure, doll, I'm swell. We picked up two of his pals as you pulled in. Say, you looked cute up there conducting the tour. Now since you have an open seat, I'd better come along the rest of the way." His smirk had returned full blast as he picked up her left hand and studied her empty ring finger.

"Oh, you!"

He feigned innocence then grinned at the tourists. "Good afternoon, there, friends. Sorry about all the excitement, but I want to thank each and every one of you on behalf of the US Government and President Truman. You might have just saved his life by helping us capture a known criminal. Now, for the record..."

Alice exhaled a shaky breath and leaned on Ralph for a moment as Rick charmed the tourists into believing they had saved America.

Chapter Forty-One

Alice didn't make it any further than her sofa the next morning. All the excitement of the previous day had made for another sleepless night. She sat, nursing a cup of coffee while she reflected.

The quilt tour was a great success, bringing in people from all over, even Ohio, Kentucky, and Virginia. The townspeople were shocked to learn the Tolivers had been arrested by the FBI for conspiring with Communists, the story Rick and his boss had decided to relay. Pete and Lois, Eddie, Greta, and Mayor Wilson were sworn to secrecy about the rest.

People reacted in different ways. Frank Summers announced he'd just been playing along. He knew all along they were traitors and spies.

Jeff Felton said it wasn't right to arrest someone for his political beliefs. Didn't we defeat the Nazis so we could think like we wanted? He agreed later the plan to assassinate the president wasn't a political belief in the best interest of the country.

Ralph Gorman described the Communists with an uncharacteristic swear word, and Bernice said the government needed to crack down on this or the Commies would take over Europe just like Hitler did.

Rick didn't need to mention Mrs. Jenner since Sheriff Jenner had resigned and announced he was joining his wife in Akron to take care of her mother. He planned to get a job in one of the rubber plants there. Until a special election could be called, Eddie was the new acting sheriff.

Mr. Toliver had been interrogated by the CIG. He finally admitted the whole plan, including the secret of the red hexagon. Several codes had been set up by the Tolivers. A particular shape and color on a certain block meant either blow up the DuPont plant or assassinate the president depending on his schedule. Both were to cause confusion and turmoil while they managed to steal the plans for an atomic bomb. With rumors rampant about President Truman's whereabouts on the Fourth of July, their strategy had been up in the air. Rick said it was probably the reason the Tolivers acted so strange about the location and colors of the blocks.

All the loose ends had been wrapped up except one. Rick still hadn't proposed. At this point, Alice only had a few days left to plan the wedding. Maybe he was having second thoughts. As much as she had tried to avoid loving Rick, she would be crushed if he left town next week without her.

"Who died?" Lois said as she sat beside Alice on her fern green couch. "You should be happy, and you look like you swallowed one of your pins."

Even though Alice was the one who lived there, Rick had invited over Pete, Lois, and Sheriff Eddie, and of course Greta to celebrate the quilt tour success. Amazing, and he called her bossy.

"I am happy, Lois, and not just about the quilt tour. You and Pete are going to make great parents."

Rick stood and cleared his throat. "I have a couple of reasons for inviting you here."

Alice blinked to keep the moisture away. She knew the reasons, to celebrate the tour and to say goodbye.

"First, I wanted to have a chance to celebrate the quilt tour and Pete and Lois's good news. I also wanted to tell you all I'm going to miss you. You've become like family to me."

Alice pinched her nose. So this was goodbye. No matter what, she wouldn't shed a tear.

"There's one more reason, the most important one." Rick knelt on one knee in front of Alice and pulled a ring box out of his pocket. He opened it and showed her a diamond ring. "I never thought I'd find love again, but the love I feel for you is greater than anything I've ever known. You may have been the one who sprained your ankle, but you've swept me off my feet. Alice, will you marry me?"

Alice wiped the tears flowing down her cheeks. Rick had come through with the most romantic speech she'd ever heard. "Yes, yes."

Rick wrapped his arms around her and kissed her.

She was vaguely aware of people clapping.

He let go of her and turned to the others. "We need your help." He put his arm around her. "We have a wedding to plan in two days."

Alice gasped. "We can't get a marriage license in two days. It takes three, and we need a blood test."

Rick smirked. "Haven't you learned by now I've got connections?" He pulled out a government waver negating the waiting period.

The next couple of hours were filled with activity and wedding plans. Alice called Pastor Round to explain the situation, and he agreed to perform the ceremony.

After a while, Pete and Lois announced it was time for them to leave. Lois needed to get her rest.

"I'm going to miss you." Lois hugged Alice. "Especially with the new baby on the way."

"I'm not going to war." Alice blinked to keep the tears at bay. "McLean, Virginia is only six hours away. I checked. We'll be back to visit."

Pete was next to give her a hug. "Sis, thanks for everything." He tilted his head toward Rick. "I think you found a good one there."

"Me too."

After they left, Alice tuned to Greta. "We need to talk."

Greta bit her lip. "I am happy for you, Alice. I just wish there was a way I could stay here."

"Then why don't you stay?"

"With you leaving," Greta's voice thickened, "I will lose my visa."

"Not going to happen. We have it all worked out," Rick said. He let go of Alice. "You'll take over the shop as manager. We'll give you seventy-five percent of the profits."

Greta splayed her hand over her open mouth. "I can bring my mutter and sister here sooner."

"You don't have to worry about that either," Rick said. "I do have some pull with the State Department. To thank you for your service to the United States, they're flying your family over and giving you all permanent visas."

Alice raised an eyebrow. "You can do that?"

Rick winked. "I'm with the CIG. You'd be amazed what I can do."

"I don't know what to say," Greta said. "Thank you, Herr Morr-- Rick. They will be a great help to me, manning Alice's shop."

Eddie wrapped his arm around Greta. "I'll help too."

Greta blushed. "If you will excuse us, Eddie and I want to go outside and... and look at the stars. A-Okay?"

Alice laughed. "You go ahead. I want to show Rick something."

Eddie and Greta left, and Alice led Rick to the chair. "You sit here. I'll be right back." She went to the trunk in her bedroom and pulled out the unfinished log cabin quilt, then returned to the living room.

"What's that?" Rick said.

"It's my log cabin quilt. It's time I finally finish it."

Rick took Alice in his arms, and she leaned into him. Their lives and their love might not be safe, but it was worth taking a risk. Perfect love casts out fear.

The End

About Tamera Lynn Kraft

Award winning author Tamera Lynn Kraft has always loved adventures. She loves to write historical fiction set in the United States because there are so many stories in American history. There are strong elements of faith, romance, suspense and adventure in her stories.

Tamera been married for forty years to the love of her life, Rick, and has two married adult children and three grandchildren. She has been a children's pastor for over twenty years. She is the leader of a ministry called Revival Fire for Kids where she mentors other children's leaders, teaches workshops, and is a children's ministry consultant and children's evangelist and has written children's church curriculum. She is a recipient of the 2007 National Children's Leaders Association Shepherd's Cup for lifetime achievement in children's ministry.

Check out Tamera's other novels and novellas at http://tameralynnkraft.net.

CPSIA information can be obtained
at www.ICGtesting.com
Printed in the USA
LVHW031201220419
615060LV00002B/97